Kawokee

STACY BENDER

&

REID MINNICH

Byrnas Books

This is a work of fiction. All of the characters, places, and events portrayed in this book are either products of the author's imagination or are used fictitiously.

Kawokee

Design by Elizabeth Mackey

ISBN: 1721885978
ISBN-13: 978-1721885978

CHAPTER 1

The bay doors in the back of the shuttle craft opened, and Jasmine's head suddenly felt as if it was pressed in a vice. She forced a yawn hoping to hasten her relief from the pressure. After months in space, the planet's higher gravity made it feel like the shuttle still was moving, making it difficult to walk a straight line.

The voice of the shuttle pilot sounded tinny coming over the speakers. "Optimum angle for shuttle liftoff is in three minutes. Please clear the pad by then."

With a touch to her wrist-com, Jasmine's luggage activated. It hurried to her heels like a well-trained dog. The wheels made a purring sound as it buzzed along the corrugated floor just inside the cargo lane, designated by bright yellow lines on the metal sheeting.

Soldiers shouldering heavy packs rushed ahead of her out the bay doors unmindful of the forklift bot unloading pallets of supplies.

When Jasmine reached the great maw of the shuttle bay opening, the view through the doors looked more like a picture into another time as evenly spaced burning torches lit the tarmac.

The cool outside air carried a hint of smoke from the

surrounding fires. After eight months of sterile ship air, it smelled wonderful. In the light of the twin moons, the buildings appeared to lean.

"Jasmine Char?" A heavyset man hurried along the landing platform, pausing long enough to direct the small group of soldiers to one of the few lighted buildings. As the forklift bot zipped back up the shuttle ramp, the fat man waved for her to hurry. "Miss Char? Quickly now."

Before she was off the ramp, the bay doors closed behind her. Jasmine barely had her feet on the landing platform when the hatch closed and the shuttle prepared for launch. Her luggage almost toppled over as the retracting ramp caught a corner of the case.

The fat man grabbed her wrist and pulled Jasmine away from the shuttle and off the landing platform. "I'm Corbin, mayor of this…" He waved his finger above his head. "Town. I've spread word that you're looking for a guide. There are several new faces in town already. The rest should be here by morning."

"Thank you, Mayor Corbin. Do you know if any of them speak Kawokee?"

Corbin screwed up his face in disgust. "No one speaks Kawokee. And it's just Corbin. The position of mayor isn't an honor. It falls to the one too slow to get out of it. There are only fifty of us left, so we have to take turns."

The ozone smell of the shuttle's liftoff stung Jasmine's nose. A blast of wind almost pushed her to the ground, like a giant hand pressing at her back. The surrounding fires threatened to blow out and cast her into darkness. Her luggage rammed into her leg and would have had her stumbling to her knees if not for Corbin catching her. The luggage did a jig as static electricity played havoc with the internal sensors. She caught the handle and disengaged the automated controls. The deranged thing ceased its fits.

Jasmine waited a moment to catch her breath before reengaging the luggage. The luggage stopped its frantic thrashing, but neither did it move when she stepped away.

She could hear the soft whir of the wheels spinning and the wet spatter of mud.

Her heart jumped as three small figures the size of children with large pointed ears and elongated snouts hurried from the darkness. Their fox like faces seemed to smile. Even standing on the toes of their elongated feet, none of them came to her shoulder. Each wore drab colored shorts and pale sleeveless shirts over thick fur.

The sudden rush of excitement at seeing live Kawokee took Jasmine's breath away.

"We pull fo' you, mam," said one, its head bowed. To her ears, they sounded like children even though textbook knowledge told her that the structure of Kawokee mouths and tongue muscles made it impossible for them to pronounce R or CH.

A sudden kick from Corbin sent the creatures scurrying away back into the darkness. "Don't leave anything unattended with Kaw around. They'll steal anything they can get their paws on."

"But—" Jasmine snapped her mouth shut as Corbin pointed to the same building he had directed the soldiers and gave her luggage a good swift kick, jarring it from the mud. "Bedrooms are upstairs."

She stumbled trying to keep up with Corbin. In the dim light of the twin moons, she could just make out the giant cracks which riddled the pavement as sinister looking weeds threatened to crush the stones between their roots. Many of the surrounding buildings stood dark and ominous.

Inside the tavern, an odd assortment of furniture filled the room. Broken pieces sat near the fire. The soldiers gathered around a table near the far wall. A large, grungy man slept in a chair leaning against a fireplace. The oil lamps barely illuminated the room, making it difficult to see if the floor was wood or resin covered dirt. The smell of wood smoke mixed with a delightful something that made her mouth water.

"Soup is almost ready," said Corbin. "I'll understand if you're taking precautions, but I'm clean."

To find someone not infected, yet living on a planet where the Kaw virus originated, was hard to believe. Jasmine had a box of the standard issue protein bars packed in her luggage. Not that they would last more than a few days. The virus spread by saliva, blood, or sex. Cooked food was safe. Not that it mattered to her, but she still needed to put up a front.

"It sounds heavenly," she said. "I'd love some."

The man's face lit up, and he grinned. "Make yourself comfortable. I'll be right back."

Jasmine settled into one of the empty chairs near the group of soldiers. She strained to listen to their conversations as they talked and pointed to a map in the center of the table.

Corbin carried two steaming bowls to Jasmine's table and sat down across from her. "I'm sorry you didn't get a better welcome. Since the quarantine, people here are angry. The supplies are too expensive and infrequent."

Jasmine stirred the concoction before her. "Why are there only fifty people left? This settlement had thousands at one time."

"Before the quarantine, those who could afford it, got out. Since then, life's been hard." Corbin waved a slice of bread in the air. "A Pox outbreak took a lot of us. Now there aren't enough of us to keep everything going. Attacks by natives are always a threat. We don't have the power cells to defend ourselves. Luckily, the wild ones don't know that, so they stay outside the camp and pick us off if we so much as poke our noses out."

The sound of movement caught Jasmine's attention, and she watched as the soldiers carried their gear up the stairs leaving her alone with the mayor.

"How's everything going among the outside worlds?" asked Corbin.

"Not good. Statistics say the virus has infected

anywhere between five and fifty percent of the population, depending on the planet. No one knows the real number, considering are no symptoms other than miscarriages, and many people refuse testing."

"Why would they refuse?"

Jasmine looked up from her bowl. "Would you like being a leper in society's eyes?"

"I'm already thought of as weird for not having it." He pursed his lips and frowned. "Does this mean there's no cure yet? I thought I heard some bigwig figured everything out. The whole town wants to get off this world."

"There've been several false reports. Whether information is released premature by people wanting their five minutes of fame or political posturing, a decade of research has failed to isolate the genetic vector. The only thing anyone knows for sure is that the virus is manmade. Some believed it's a terrorist plot cooked up by a breakaway planet, or an experiment gone wrong by a corporate world."

Corbin pulled another slice of bread out of his pocket and offered it to her. When she declined, he dropped the bread into his soup. "The other scientists stay in the safety of the ship and send soldiers to collect what they need. What brings you down here?"

"I'm an anthropologist here to study the Kawokee. There might be a clue to the cure in their culture."

He swallowed hard, finishing his bowl. "Anthropology is the study of human beings; isn't it?"

"Yes." Jasmine steeled herself against the irritation she felt and bolstered her patience.

"But they aren't human." Corbin shrugged and sat back. "Yes, they talk, they think. They're not animals, but they're not people either. The ones around here are safe enough, but the wild ones will kill you first chance they get. You don't know how dangerous they are. Since the quarantine three years ago, I've seen several groups come to study the natives. The only ones who make it back are the ones that are well armed. There's not a weapon on you, not even a knife."

"You can't win someone's trust holding a gun to their head."

Corbin reached across the table but stopped halfway and pulled back before he touched her. "It might prevent getting an arrow in the chest. Please. Don't go. Besides, the missionaries burned all their heathen charms and converted the natives. If they had a culture, it's dead now."

Jasmine ground her teeth at the thought of people destroying a culture. The idea that humanity had evolved past such atrocities required blindness to the evidence of history and current events. "Let's hope for our sake that's not true. Kawokee culture may be our last hope."

Corbin stared at Jasmine for some time before he blinked. "There's no talking you out of it?"

"No. But it's nice that you tried." Jasmine slid the empty bowl toward him. "After months of ship-grown, processed plankton disguised as food, the soup was delicious."

A wide grin spread across Corbin's face. "I've got more." He picked up her empty bowl and took a step toward the kitchen.

With a shake of her head, he shrugged and disappeared into the kitchen. The crash of dishes and splashing water startled Jasmine and reminded her too late that modern sanitation did not exist here. Bile filled her throat as he returned, drying his hands with a filthy towel.

"Which room is mine?"

"Take your pick. Makes no difference." He regarded her closely. "Are you feeling all right? Bathroom is through there." He pointed to a curtained doorway beneath the stair.

Jasmine shook her head and forced a smile. "I'm fine." She nodded at the man sleeping in the chair. "What about him?"

Corbin scowled. "No money."

Jasmine nodded. "How much do I owe you?"

"Well," Corbin put his hands in his pockets and looked down at his feet. "The room, the food, let's say two power cells."

Considering what the cells cost her compared to a night in a luxury hotel, it sounded like robbery, but Jasmine scooped a handful of cells from her luggage. The silver, pencil thin tubes were no longer than a person's finger, which included the protective covering around the prongs at one end.

Corbin shoved her hand back into her pack and scrutinized the man sleeping in the chair by the fireplace. He whispered, "That was a joke, miss. The supplies your ship delivered are priceless. I won't ask anything more from you. Please don't show these around. Many a man would kill for just one of those."

She swallowed hard and put the cells back in a side pocket. All luggage had a lock setting, not that anyone ever used it. It took a moment to find it on her wrist-com.

"Thank you, Corbin." She whispered, excused herself, and went toward the curtained room.

The rustic bathroom was not as dirty as she feared, but she still placed toilet paper on the seat as a precaution. The mirror over the sink was cracked, and she tried not to think about why the water that came out of the tap had a reddish tint.

Once back in the main room, she quickly took several coins from her luggage and stepped outside into the empty street. Corbin seemed nice enough, but she needed to talk to the Kawokee. Corbin's presence would be a hinderance.

The wooden buildings looked like the set of an Old Earth horror movie. None of them were lit. Jasmine took a deep breath and let it out slowly before she stepped into the dark alley where she had seen the natives disappear earlier. She continued straight past row after row of empty homes. Torn curtains and crumbling shades hinted at how much time had passed since their abandonment.

Light coming from up ahead caught her attention. When she reached the third row of houses, a series of old fashioned lampposts lined both sides of the street. The fires which lit each glass dome set the entire street aglow. Jasmine spotted a few natives on the porch of a house down the street. Several more watched her progress from a balcony one level up. All eyes turned to her as she approached the house. One of the natives hurried forward followed by others. Jasmine was soon surrounded.

"Mam want yiff?"

She played the words back in her head. "What?"

One of the Kawokee pulled the rope around his pants and let them fall to his ankles exposing his maleness.

"O' me." The voice of the Kawokee next to him was higher pitched. She lifted her shirt showing two small breasts.

Shocked by such blatant propositions, Jasmine froze with the realization she stood outside the local whorehouse. Those natives who had not disrobed pushed her toward the building.

With the sight of the open door in front of her, she jerked back and shouted, "No."

The Kawokee scattered as if kicked. They disappeared from the porch and the balcony. Jasmine saw by the light of the flickering streetlamps the reflection of their eyes in the shadow of the house.

She regretted her reaction the instant she saw their fear. When she first left the tavern, Jasmine had no clear plan on how to find a translator, and she grasped at the first thing that came to mind. She said softly, "I just need some help. Help with my luggage. It's back at the tavern."

"Not mad?"

Jasmine shook her head. "No. I'm not angry." None of the Kawokee moved until she held up the coin. "I need three of you."

At the sight of the coin their fear of her disappeared, and they swarmed her. Each clamored for her attention shouting, "Me. Me. Me."

Afraid they would do more than just shout, she chose three at random. The others shuffled away with shoulders slumped and ears lowered. Their actions made Jasmine's heart ache, and she wanted to reach out and comfort each one. The knowledge she could do little more forced her to turn away while holding back her tears.

She listened to the gravel crunch beneath her feet as the three natives followed her back toward the tavern. With a desire to fill the silence, she asked, "Do any of you speak Kawokee?"

The sound of their footsteps stopped. Unsure of the cause, Jasmine turned to see their wide eyes staring back at her, their shoulders shaking in fear. "What's wrong?"

The smaller of the three wiggled his head from side to side. "We no speak Kawokee. Not allowed, mam."

She stared at them for a moment, shocked at their acceptance of the blatant destruction of their identity. Coming from a place where at least a dozen different languages were spoken within a ten-kilometer radius, language defined the community in which a person belonged. Her own family language was part of her identity. To see the annihilation of a culture in practice and not hidden in the digital archives of text had her longing to strangle the person who dared make such a decree.

"I need a translator, so I can speak to those in the villages."

All three hissed and stepped back. One grabbed his shredded right ear and said, "Not us. No go back."

She wondered if mere association with humans made the natives hate those who lived in the towns. Jasmine intended to learn the language and worried about finding someone to teach her. "Come." Her voice sounded hollow to her own ears as she turned and shuffled toward their destination.

The Kawokee followed her up to the door of the tavern but no farther than the threshold. Each native peeked in from the side as Jasmine held the door. "The luggage is over there."

"Cowbin say no Kaw."

"Corbin says it is ok this one time." The man's voice bellowed through the place, making not only the natives jump, but Jasmine.

The Kawokee slipped through the door but kept an eye on the man's feet.

Corbin barked, "Be quick," and they stumbled over themselves to get the luggage up the steps. More than once, Jasmine thought all three would fall down the stair. As much as she wanted to voice her concern for their welfare, Corbin's watchful glare informed her that her worry would fall on deaf ears. That and the thought she should have asked Corbin's permission before asking the natives for help. Once at the top of the stairs, the Kawokee disappeared down the hall with the luggage. She heard a heavy thump of plastic hitting wood and the rapid patter of small feet. They dashed down the steps and out the door to stand outside in the moonlight with their small hairy hands outstretched.

When Jasmine realized what they wanted, she felt like a fool. She was not used to tipping for services, and the few times she had done so, the person looked at her as if she had beaten their favorite pet. Jasmine dug into her pocket and pulled out what she had. Three one-credit coins. The closest native snatched the coins from her outstretched hand and scampered away, leaving his two cohorts running after him.

"You gave them too much." Corbin shook his head, closed the door, and extinguished the lanterns. "Good night."

She looked away hoping he did not see the embarrassed flush she felt warm her skin. "Good night."

Jasmine's mind wandered back outside in the darkness. She did not turn away from the door until she heard Corbin's steps recede into the back room. The room was still lit by the waning embers of the fireplace where the sleeping man remained in his chair. With a sigh, she shuffled away from the door. The stairs creaked and popped as she climbed. "I'm in over my head, but what choice do I have?"

The second floor of the tavern was lit by a single candle at each end of a short hallway. Both candles were burnt so far down that Jasmine doubted either would last another hour. Shadows crossed one of the four curtained door frames, and the soldier's movements made the thin fabric sway. Their voices were soft and muffled.

A moment of panic stopped Jasmine at the top of the stair. She could not remember how many soldiers there were or if Corbin mentioned the number of rooms in the tavern. Would she have to share?

Laughter preceded a soldier stepping out of a room. He motioned to the far end of the hall. "We left the last one for you."

"Thank you." The soldier disappeared down the stairs and into the gloom before she could say a word.

She headed for the room at the far end of the hall and pulled back the curtain. The light from the hallway just reached inside the threshold. In the moonlight from the single window, she could just make out the narrow, woven mat that lay on a wooden frame which passed as a bed.

Jasmine stepped back out into the hall and removed the candle, along with its mount, from the wall. With slow short steps, and her hand held before the candle to keep the flame from blowing out by any sudden movement, she examined the room.

There were no pictures on the unvarnished plywood surface. Both the walls and floor had discolored patterns and stains giving hints to rough usage and sloppy repairs. Why the wall would need repairing flitted through Jasmine's mind before deciding she did not want to know.

When she moved to the single window, she felt a draft of chilly air around the leaky frame. The flame of the candle she held flickered and went out leaving the tip of the wick to glow before it too disappeared. The tavern sat on a small rise. Jasmine could see past the landing pad across the entire town to the three-meter-high wall of logs that surrounded the place. Lights were placed along its length at intervals, though what good that served she could only guess. Entire neighborhoods were burned out. The houses that remained were a patchwork of repairs. If it looked bad in the light of the moons, Jasmine knew it would look worse in the morning sun.

On a hill beyond the town, were the flickering lights of a Kawokee tribe. She longed to be there despite the harsh conditions. Jasmine set the candle and holder on the floor and grabbed the sheet from the bed. With the cloth wrapped around her shoulders, she lay down.

If she had a future, it would start on that far hill.

CHAPTER 2

The noise downstairs and the sound of boots on the stairs woke her. Jasmine stretched stiff muscles and smoothed her wrinkled clothes. She had to pee, but the thought of the soldiers lined up in a que had her worried. She would have to make a dash for the bathroom and hope there was no waiting. If she had to plead for a few minutes on the toilet, she would.

Jasmine quickstepped out of the room and down the hall. The curtains of the other three rooms were all pulled back revealing empty quarters. Many voices were talking downstairs. Something about the noise seemed odd after the subdued quiet of the night before. Her luggage sat forlorn in the hall where she left it, pushed up against the wall. Someone had written in neat block letters using a red marker on the surface of the case, 'Be careful, Doc'.

Embarrassment over her forgetfulness mingled with the warm thought that at least someone cared, yet both were trumped by the adamant call of nature. Jasmine crept to the stairs and saw a dozen men seated below. Not one was a soldier. Their conversations stopped as she set foot on the first squeaky step. Several left their tables and blocked her way to the bathroom as she raced down the stair.

"Name's Jack, mam."

Another pushed him aside. "Are you looking for a guide?"

Frantic with the pressure building in her bladder, she pushed her way between them and swept the bathroom curtain aside, ducking under the thin folds. A burly man stood full in view before the toilet buttoning his fly. "Morning, mam. Smitty's the name." He abandoned his fly and held out his hand.

Knees locked together, Jasmine stood planted to the floor, unsure how to get him out of the tiny room.

"My rate is just five credits a day. None of them others will give you as good protection for that rate. I've got more firepower than half of them put together."

She gestured toward the curtain and snapped, "Out," then added, "Please."

"I'll be right out here."

The toilet was clean last night. By the light of the morning, the room looked as if a herd of buffalo tramped through. There was no more toilet paper. Desperate to relieve herself, Jasmine held her breath, bent her legs, and hovered over the bowl as she grabbed hold of the sink beside her for balance. Only then did she notice the dead silence outside the curtain. With the knowledge that the entire tavern would hear every drop, it somehow made it harder to start. When she finished, she pushed the handle to flush. It gave easily and a metallic thump came from inside the tank. When she turned the faucet lever to the on position, no water came out.

Confusion over why there was no water this morning when it was fine the night before had her brain working faster than coffee ever could. Jasmine had to remind herself that she was no longer in a thriving city, but in a dying settlement. She had slept in too long, and the main water tank that supplied the tavern had run dry.

Jasmine stood with her back to the wall and let her

frustration dissipate before stepping toward the curtain.

Taking a deep breath, Jasmine let it out and flung open the worn cloth. She marched to the center of the room, pushing people out of her way. They were all talking at her, each voice trying to yell over the next in a clashing crescendo that hurt her ears. She climbed onto a table and yelled, "Quiet."

With all eyes on her, she pointed to the door.

"Everyone go out into the street and form a line with your gear out for me to see."

There was a mad dash for the door. With everyone outside in the street, Jasmine watched the comedy from the tavern entrance. None of them could decide which way the line should go and who should stand where. Each person jostled the other for their space on the street with one pair almost coming to blows. There was pleasure in having the tavern empty.

Corbin came up and stood beside her. "Crazy bastards."

"I'm surprised there are so many people willing to be guides."

"Willing, but not able." Corbin leaned close to her and whispered, "Don't be fooled by big guns. They take more power. Small handguns take less power. I'll bet not one of those big guns has a live cell."

She sighed. "Thanks. I'll remember that."

When the prospective guides quit shoving each other, Jasmine stepped out of the doorway and into the street. A few wore old military fatigues bristling with knives and guns. Others displayed sophisticated camping gear and teams of horses. All of them were healthy and strong and their gear looked new or well cared for.

Except for one. Jasmine returned to him for a second look. He was thin and stood in line without so much as a backpack. With shoes made of animal skins, a torn shirt, and frayed pant legs, he looked like an old chew toy for a small dog.

"Where is your gun?"

The man's voice was barely a whisper. "I don't have one."

The crowd exploded in laughter.

"Not even a knife?"

"This is all I've ever needed." The man produced a tarnished metal object. He flipped through its many spring-loaded attachments before presenting an unintimidating blade as long as her finger, more suited for slicing fruit.

The cackling and coughing laughter from the others assaulted Jasmine's ears.

Jasmine took the man by the shirt sleeve, hauled him toward the tavern, and pushed him through the door to the jeers of the others. Their laughter stopped when she turned and said, "The rest of you, can go. Thank you." Jasmine ducked into the tavern and slammed the door behind her. She fumbled with the hook and eye latch that was a poor excuse for a lock but managed to get it secured. The thick door muffled the footsteps and voices, but not the banging on the door. Jasmine pressed her weight against the door to keep them out. "I said go away."

Corbin joined her to keep the entry barred but eyed the thin man. "Are you serious?"

"Dead serious."

Corbin shook his head. "What am I doing? Half of those guys haven't paid me yet."

A sudden blow wrenched the eye hook from the jamb and almost threw them back. Corbin nodded toward the kitchen, "How about you two slip out the back?"

"My gear." Jasmine raced up the steps two at a time. She yanked her luggage to the edge of the stairs and let it crash down hard on each step with no attempt to guide its fall. Corbin and the thin man held their backs against the door until she was down the stairs. Another heavy blow to the door sent her new guide stumbling forward. Corbin motioned them toward the kitchen, and together they steered the luggage out the backdoor into a narrow alley between buildings. They ducked into the first house with an open door.

Jasmine sniffed the air. At first, she thought the building smelled. It did, but the odor that tickled her nose differed from the dusty dryness of the brick. The scent was coming from her guide. It was not a bad odor, but it was earthy. Jasmine turned to him and asked, "What's your name?"

"Tim, mam."

"And why should I trust you?"

"Because I don't want your money." His eyes never wavered, and his body language remained calm. "Leave it here if you like. All I want is company. I've lived out there since I was a kid."

Jasmine could not believe her good luck. Nor could she resist bouncing on her toes in anticipation. "You live with the Kawokee?"

He laughed sheepishly and bowed his head. "More like around them. Some of them are nice. They don't want me in their villages, but they let me live nearby. It's safer. The big predators don't go near the Kawokee 'less they're starving."

"Do you speak their language?"

"A few words, but most any tribe has a few members that know how to speak human."

"I want to go where none of them speak human. Can you take me there?"

Tim cocked his head to one side and wrinkled his forehead. "Why would you want to go there?"

"That is where their culture will be pure."

"I can't protect you there." Tim shook his head and pointed his finger at the ground. "The tribes around here know me."

"I don't want protection. I want a guide to get me there. Then you can leave me."

His eyes might have popped from their sockets if they

had been able. "It's a long walk. Weeks. Months even. And there's no road. You'd never find your way back."

Jasmine crossed her arms. "Can you do it, or not?"

"Yes, mam." He nodded and closed his eyes. "If that's what you want."

Jasmine opened her luggage and removed the latest, most expensive camping gear. "I've got a tent, a pack, dehydrated food, ultra-light stove and enough energy cells to last a month. How much water do you think we'll need?"

"We don't need any of that stuff. It will slow us down. I've never needed any of those things. There's plenty of water and food out there if you're not too picky. Like I said, this multi-tool is all I've ever needed." Tim patted his pocket where he had replaced the instrument.

With a smile, she patted his shoulder, "You'll do just fine." Jasmine stuffed a black box and the power cells into a backpack she removed from the case along with her coins and shoved the rest back into her luggage. She scarfed down a power bar and chased it with water from a canteen she hooked to the backpack. The tent and cooking gear she tucked into a dark corner of the barren room.

"What's in the box?"

"My way off this planet." She would never want the luggage case back, and much of what she now carried was expendable.

"When do you want to leave?" he asked.

Jasmine pulled on the pack, pushed Tim to the doorway, and looked down the empty alley. "Let's go."

"What about those things?" He pointed to the equipment in the corner.

"Let the others have it. If I don't find what I'm looking for, nothing else matters."

The pair crept between buildings to the town entrance where a heavy wooden door stood latched with several iron bolts. There was no one around. The bolts slid back, and the large door opened without a sound on well-oiled hinges. As they walked out from behind the barrier, Jasmine got a good view of the stripped area between the wall and forest. Tim moved fast along the barren ground. Jasmine followed and felt almost giddy when they reached the tree line. She half expected to see Kawokee behind every tree. "Corbin said the natives sometimes attacked people who leave the town."

Tim made a rude noise. "How would he know? He's never left. None of them have."

"Where are we going?"

He pointed forward and off to the side. "The cliffs of the hill to the east are riddled with caves. It's better than getting wet when it rains. There's clean water there too. The Kawokee up there are used to me. They call me Bishtak."

"What does it mean?" Jasmine was having trouble keeping up. She hoped her laps around the city park using a backpack weighted down with cans of baked beans and various vegetables pulled from the pantry was enough training for the rough terrain she needed to cover. The rock climbing she did at the local gym was limited by her ability to reserve the needed time slots.

Tim's pace did not slow as he led her up a steep trail. "Mean?"

"Bishtak? What does it mean? Didn't you tell them your name?"

"They gave me that name when I got sick. So sick, I crawled into a cave and couldn't go out for a week. If they hadn't brought me food and water, I would have died."

Jasmine's foot slipped on a patch of soft muddy earth, but she stayed upright. "Do you know their names?"

"I have names for most of them. There's Red, he's kind of a leader. So is Broketoe."

"Wait." She stopped more to catch her breath than out of curiosity. "Do they call themselves those names or is that a translation?"

Tim shook his head and shrugged. "I don't know what

they call themselves. Those are my names for them."

Jasmine had the sinking feeling she had made a terrible mistake. "So, you've lived near the Kawokee for a how long?"

"I don't know how long. Many years."

"Why don't you stay in town? It looks like they need people."

"I stay in towns when the winter is hard, but I prefer to be on my own. Too many people make me nervous. I only go there to trade. That's how I learned about you coming."

He stopped and pulled a plant out of the ground. After shaking off the dirt, he snapped off the root and handed her half.

Jasmine eyed the yellow thing. Not knowing what to expect, she bit off the tip. The root dissolved into a honey-like paste.

"Nice, huh?" He turned and continued walking at a breakneck pace.

Jasmine stuffed the entire root in her mouth and adjusted her pack.

By the time they stopped at a stream, the trembling in her legs had her cursing low gravity of space travel. Using her hand as a cup, she brought the water to her mouth. It tasted like heaven after the excruciating hike. The man did not show the slightest hint of being winded.

After a brief rest, she felt stiff, but her muscles soon loosened as they walked.

"So, tell me about your world. How many people do you see on an average day?"

Jasmine was unsure how to answer. "All people or just the ones I know?"

"All of them? How many?"

She thought Tim would be more interested in the buildings or new devices. Other than the Kawokee world, the only other world Jasmine had visited was Earth during a vacation with her family. It was the buildings she remembered more than the people. Her birth planet was about the same size, but nowhere near as built up. "A few hundred. Maybe a few thousand. I never counted them."

Tim's jaw went slack. "How many people do you know?"

Jasmine considered Tim's life before she answered the question. "I work in a building with fifty people. And I know almost all by name and talk to a dozen every day. Then there's my family. I see some of them every week or at least message them. There are another hundred or more when you include friends who share messages, but we've never met."

"Wow. How could you remember so many names?" Tim stared into the sky as he walked.

Her mouth was already drying out. Between Tim's breakneck pace and her attempts to answer questions, she wished she had taken a larger canteen. Angry at her own weakness, Jasmine bit her lip. This was the price she agreed to pay for the help she needed to find untainted natives.

Other than the ones in town, Jasmine had not seen a live Kawokee since she was a little girl when her parents took her to the local zoo's recreated village. Set on the edge of its facilities, people could come and gawk at the aliens in their pseudo natural environment for the price of a second entry fee. Her fingers had itched to touch their soft downy fur while her face and body was pressed to the barrier by the throng of people wanting to see the new animals. The image of an alien face burned itself into her mind that day. The creature looked miserable when it reached out to touch Jasmine, barred from doing so by the clear glass.

That memory was tainted by their mass suicide not long after, along with the intense news coverage which followed. Some claimed the creatures had gone mad. Everyone from the local vets to pet psychics were interviewed for their professional opinion. As a child, Jasmine knew they had it all wrong, but fear of adults scolding her kept her from voicing her opinion.

She knew better now than to make assumptions of alien feelings based on human expressions. The reason they killed themselves remained a mystery. Jasmine guessed it may have been their inability to breed. Zoo records showed there were no Kawokee births but several miscarriages. Autopsies found they all had what was at the time called Acquired Infertility Syndrome. The cause shocked scientists when they identified a virus that had all the telltale markers of being manufactured. For a time, scientists puzzled over how the simple, isolated race came into contact with such a virus. It became known as the Kaw virus. Now that it threatened all inhabited worlds, no one cared how the Kawokee contracted it.

That question still burned in Jasmine's mind. Her doctoral thesis theorized since the virus originated on the Kawokee homeworld and they had not died out, there was a cure somewhere on the planet.

Her legs threatened to give out when they reached the top of the hill. It wasn't any easier as Tim's pace quickened, and he led her down the other side.

Tim found another honey sweet root and shared it with her. "So, what is music like? Can you teach me a song?"

Jasmine did not want her wonderful snack interrupted by more questions, but when she realized she had eaten the last bit, she knew she did not have a choice. She ground her teeth and adjusted her pack, all the while reminding herself of why she was here.

The setting sun dropped behind the far hill, and the air became chilly as the trail descended into a deep valley. She almost crashed into him when he stopped.

"We'll sleep here."

While Jasmine bent near the edge of the stream to refill her canteen, Tim stood about fifteen meters away. He scraped the ground under the pine trees until he had a large pile of needles. To Jasmine's surprise, the long thick spines were soft and spongy. Warm, dry, and protected from rain and wind, she fell asleep within seconds of laying down.

Just before dawn, came the call of nature. Jasmine hoped to sneak off and do her business while Tim was asleep. She peeked at the pile of pine needles under the next tree. Tim was gone, and her backpack lay on its side between the trees. Fear constricted her chest. Jasmine reached for her backpack and stuck her hand inside. The cool smooth side of the black box reassured her that she still had her things. Being drawn out into the wilderness and abandoned was one of her many fears.

She calmed herself and decided to take care of her needs before Tim returned. A nearby clump of bushes provided some privacy. When she stood, she saw movement across the stream.

"Heya."

Jasmine jumped, turned, and saw Tim carrying a green parcel. He stopped in front of her and unwrapped the leaf, careful not to let the berries roll away. "If you don't like these, there are others."

"What are they called?"

"They're just berries." He funneled a handful into his mouth.

The delicious root they ate the day before was encouraging, but the mottled color of the berries looked suspicious. Curious, she took a berry and crushed it between her teeth. The strong citrus flavor stung her dry mouth. Crushed and put over fish or placed in a sweetened drink the berries would have given a dish a wonderful zing. However, eating them as is, was akin to downing tiny lemons. Jasmine did not want to look ungrateful, and she was hungry. She took another handful, popped them one at a time into her mouth, and swallowed them whole. "Aren't you going to eat?"

"I've eaten. Those are for you." Tim stepped back and untied his pants.

Every muscle in Jasmine's body tightened at Tim's

actions but relaxed as he relieved himself in front of her. Uncomfortable with the situation, she looked away and tried to eat the remainder of her berries. Knowledge that primitive societies often had an open and familiar lifestyle was well documented, but book learning had not prepared her for the experience.

Jasmine hoped to appear nonchalant about his actions as he stuffed himself back into his pants before helping himself to a few berries. The thought of him not washing his hands made her cringe, then she realized she had done the same thing. Her biobots could protect her from dysentery, but not the unmapped diseases of this world, which could destroy her mission. The customs of antiquity, like washing-hands and cooking food, were effective if she could convince Tim to use them.

"We should be near the Kawokee camp by night." Tim wandered to the edge of the trail.

"That's great. These aren't the wild ones; are they?" Jasmine downed a good portion of her canteen before sprinting over to the stream to refill it and attach it to her pack.

"There are only two types of Kawokee, the town-dwelling Kaw and the Kawokee villagers who don't speak human. Some Kawokee villages won't let us get near, but this one knows me. They might help us get to the next tribe."

Jasmine wasn't sure if her legs would take another day of hiking as she followed him through the woods. "Do the villages trade with humans?"

"Some Kawokee trade with towns, but they don't allow humans to go into their villages. Not anymore." His pace slowed. "Some of the people from the town I grew up in used to visit the Kawokee villages. I was only a kid, but they let me come along. Then we heard about the virus. Everyone had to be tested. Me and some others were tainted, dirty. Our parents wouldn't let us in the house. We had to live together. Everyone was afraid of us, so I left.

Some towns killed entire villages. Since then humans and Kawokee stay far away from each other. Even after years of living nearby, they won't let me go into their dens." He turned and walked stiffly down the trail.

She could imagine his parents with their own pain, holding the door closed against their son. Tears distorted Jasmine's sight, turning Tim's image into a wavy form that stormed down the trail.

Jasmine also felt rage at the town for killing the Kawokee. How anyone could get away with this on such a grand scale strained belief. History was full of accounts where strong cultures crushed weaker ones. Why would humans treat the Kawokee any better?

"You never went back?"

Tim stopped. "I didn't know how to get back or want to. When I stumbled across it, my parents' house had fallen down. The few people there didn't remember me or my parents. There were no records. I guess they went off world. Or maybe they died. I don't care which."

The similarities between her and Tim made her shiver, but where Tim did not care for the family he left, Jasmine longed to return to hers. Her fingers brushed her short cropped tendrils.

Tears threatened to spill and her throat tightened at the memory of the ceremony in which she lost her braid. Among her people, cutting one's hair was done as an act of mourning or shame. Hair was a physical manifestation of the spirit and all that had brought a person to their place in life. To cut it was to abandon the past. It was a custom which dated farther back than the migrations from Old Earth.

There was no physical pain, but as the blade sliced through her meter-long braid, it may as well have cut through her heart. Her decision was more practical than symbolic, but her family knew she might never return. For them, it was a funeral. They buried her hair in a grave beside her great grandmother. If she could ever go home, her short hair would mark her among her family. Not that she would ever let it grow long again. The comfort of short hair and the ease of care was worth the stares. The absence of weight was easier to get used to, but the entire first day she felt light headed.

Tim stopped occasionally, and both of them drank from the many streams they crossed. When he found nuts, berries, or roots, Tim handed them to her with no explanation.

She jumped when her communication link pinged. Tim watched as she threw off her gear and pulled the box from her pack. In the back of her mind, she knew her frantic motions were unnecessary. The call would not go to voicemail. Jasmine opened the box, hit the accept button, and the screen lighted. A one-fifth scale three-dimensional image of her friend's face materialized above the surface.

"Are you all right?" Arluza's eyes showed his tension. They softened the second she stepped back, and he could see she was fine.

"Sorry I haven't checked in. But things have gone very well so far." She pulled Tim into the view of the black box's camera. "This is my guide, Tim." She could feel the tension in Tim's arm. The shock on his face was comical. A 3D screen was a novelty on less developed worlds. This one was as backward as they came. Clearly, Tim had never seen one.

With eyes wide, Tim crouched down close to the screen and touched the image.

Arluza threw up his hands. "Hey, that tickles."

Tim jumped, lost his balance, and fell on his back.

Jasmine knew she should have been prepared, but when she started laughing, she couldn't stop. Mostly because of Tim's reaction. Tim no doubt believed Arluza felt his touch. That kind of playful banter was what she loved about her best friend. It also showed his genius. He could have been a great impromptu stand-up comic. The theater's loss was science's gain, and she would never have been included on this mission without him.

"Arluza, behave."

"Do I have to?"

Jasmine did her best to scowl at him, which only granted her a bigger smile.

"I'm glad one of us is ahead of schedule. I have to rearrange my lab to be ready for the samples the soldiers are collecting from the locals. They're going to get samples of Kawokee blood as well."

Surprised at the news, Jasmine asked, "Kawokee samples? After Campion publicly ridiculed my ideas, I thought he'd never consider it."

"They don't tell me anything. I'm guessing they want to check Kawokee blood for antigens." Arluza looked over his shoulder. "Got to go. Check in next time." The image disappeared.

"Where is he?" asked Tim. His gaze cemented on the box.

"On a ship in orbit."

"Did he really feel me touch him?"

"No. He was just teasing you." Jasmine stifled another fit of laughter by biting the first knuckle of her finger. Once she had her desire to laugh under control, she secured the comm-vid back in her pack and hoisted the backpack in place.

Tim used the opportunity to unbutton his pants and pee. Instead of becoming irritated, Jasmine realized she needed to do the same. She was not sure how Tim would react, but neither did she want to make a spectacle of herself. A wide tree near the trail offered minimal privacy. Unfortunately, Tim came looking for her before she finished. There was no way she could stop or move when he walked toward her.

Personal space did not seem to exist in Tim's nature, for he acted as if seeing a stranger pee was an everyday occurrence. He came up beside her and pointed. "We have to cross some difficult ground. So, we'll rest for the night soon."

She pulled up her pants too soon and tried to pretend nothing was wrong. "It's only mid-day."

"The village is at the top of a steep hill. Cliff really. The path is dangerous in the dark. We'll get as close as we can and start in the morning."

The trail led them upward. With what little information she gleaned about Tim's life, Jasmine could not help but pity him.

If the Kaw legislation passed, her life and the lives of millions of others would become just as bad if not worse. Debate raged on how to segregate the infected from the general population. Public opinion stopped just short of concentration camps while her planet's government pushed for a closed moon colony. Many people believed humanity faced extinction if the virus went unchecked. Jasmine feared what others would do with her as one of the infected. Her personal need for a cure drove her tired legs onward.

The tree line ended twenty meters from a vertical cliff. Shale covered the span in between.

After walking in the heat of the day, the shadow of the cliff felt like air-conditioning. Jasmine stretched out on a flat rock. Too lazy to remove her pack, she used it to cushion her back and dozed. Tim's questions started up again, but they were few. He seemed preoccupied. She answered them without opening her eyes.

Jasmine heard the crunching of stone under boots but did not think much of it until she remembered Tim wore moccasins. An odd sound between a cough and choking had her opening her eyes and saw a big man ten meters away leaning over Tim who slumped forward on the rocks. At first, her mind refused to recognize the situation. She thought Tim had passed out, and the man was trying to help. The idea fled when the man pulled a large knife from Tim's back. The black metal blade dripped with blood as he stepped over the body.

She recognized Tim's attacker as one of the people who had offered to be her guide. The arrogant stance he had taken in front of his pile of weapons was almost laughable.

Jasmine scrambled to her feet as he raised the knife and pointed it at her.

"Hand over the pack."

Fear and instinct refused to let her process his words. Jasmine stood too quickly and fell backward against the cliff. Regaining her footing, she bolted down the steep hill for the safety of the dense trees far down the trail hoping to lose him in the forest. Her feet slipped on the loose rocks as she ran.

A whistling sound filled her ears as she sprinted for the tree line. The noise rose in volume as if a swarm of angry wasps were descending on her. The whistles were joined with a rain of sharp snapping sounds, and the man bellowed.

She heard him slide on the rocks. The sound of the whistles and snaps tapered off, but the man's screams of pain rose.

Once among the trees, Jasmine dared to look back. She saw him crawling on the ground, his back covered in flighted shafts. While the adrenaline that coursed through her veins urged her to run, shock had her eyes riveted on the man. He stopped moving and lay still with his face in the dirt.

Jasmine looked up through a break in the trees at the cliff to see it lined with fox like faces. Had they avenged a friend, or were they protecting their territory? Suddenly, she did not want to know. She came all this way to be with them, now all she wanted to do was run.

Two ropes sailed over the top of the cliff, their ends landing on the rocks at the base. Kawokee descended in two columns. With renewed fear, Jasmine turned and ran. She stumbled over a root and lost her footing as the tall ferns grasped at her legs as if trying to keep her still. The irrational thought of the forest turning against her had her running wild. Jasmine thought she had a good lead but the rapid pat of feet behind her told her otherwise. The backpack was too important to lose, but it was slowing her down. Before she could form another thought something large hit her legs, taking her off balance and sending her crashing forward. Her hands and knees were on fire as she tried to get her feet back under her. She froze as the sight of an arrow close to her face registered in her conscious mind.

The Kawokee moved the arrow away and pointed it at the ground, making it clear he didn't want to shoot her, only stop her. Even through the fog of her adrenaline-soaked brain, her mind zeroed in on the weapon. The tip of the arrow protruded from a wood and metal device attached to the furry arm by leather straps. The machinery of the thing was intricate. It was some sort of compound bow.

The Kawokee's clothing did little to disguise his gender. Three thin gold rings pierced his right ear. Each ring connected to the other by a thin gold chain. One of his feet drew her attention. The middle toe on one foot rose above the others. Broketoe. Tim had mentioned this one was a leader.

CHAPTER 3

Jasmine ignored the pain she felt and pushed herself to a seated position. Three other natives flanked her. Broketoe pulled at the backpack, and she let it slide off her shoulders. He kept a watchful eye on her as the three other Kawokee with him pulled everything out of the pack and examined each item. One sniffed her ration bars. Satisfied with the contents, they put everything back in the pack. One dragged the backpack toward the cliff. The others prodded her to follow. With two natives on either side and one behind her, there was no way she could escape.

When they arrived at the cliff, a few Kawokee scoured the rocks, gathering the spent arrows scattered on the ground. One Kawokee retrieved the bolts from the big man's body. The gathering of spent arrows made sense to Jasmine. It would take work to replace them, so repairing and reusing items would be easier.

A small group of Kawokee piled rocks onto Tim's body, but no one made any attempt to bury the other man. Sorrow at having his life cut short mixed with panic over not having anyone to guide her through the alien settlement. Jasmine's throat constricted as tears threatened to spill. The burial party stopped to stare at her and spoke with Broketoe in a language with several unique phonemes. She whispered to herself, trying to reproduce the sounds.

Jasmine tried to control her fear by concentrating on studying the Kawokee around her. It was odd that non-humans would bury their dead. From documents she studied, she thought the Kawokee would have left them to the wild animals. Both men were human after all. Lying on these rocks, the bodies would not smell bad for long or contaminate the water. Nature would soon remove all trace of their existence.

The Kawokee scaled the cliff using hand signals for pull, slow, and stop, like the ones humans would use, suggesting the cultural contamination of this group was significant.

Broketoe grabbed her elbow and marched her to a rope still dangling from the cliff. He tied the rope around her arms and under her butt, joining the loops with complex knots. There was no time to consider the strength of the handmade rope before Broketoe called up.

The rope pulled tight. There was a brief sense of alarm as her feet left the ground. Images of her body falling and smashing on the rocks below flitted through her mind. The rope bit into the torn flesh of her palms. Despite the pain it caused her scraped and bleeding hands, she gripped the rope as tight as she could and closed her eyes.

They pulled her up, battering her knees and scraping her shins. By the time they hauled her over the edge, her pant legs were torn. Eight Kawokee dropped the rope allowing one to untie Jasmine and coil the slack. He pushed her out of the way and lowered the rope over the side.

Jasmine sat and examined her injuries which felt worse than they looked. The ground here was sharp stone and sand, which sloped down to a grassy field. Beyond that, short pine trees obscured the source of a few thin columns of smoke.

Her backpack came up undamaged and was left near the cliff edge. A steady stream of Kawokee climbed to the top using the other ropes anchored by stakes driven into the ground. Among them was Broketoe.

"Broketoe?" Jasmine waved her hands at the Kawokee with the golden earrings. She patted her back and asked, "May I have my backpack?"

One of Broketoe's ears moved, as if he were considering her request. It could have been a trick of the light or her imagination, but either way, Broketoe turned his head toward the backpack before facing her and nodding. It would take time before she could read their body language. He called to a soldier who dragged the backpack through the sandy dirt by one shoulder strap and brought it to him. It was not a heavy pack by human standards, but Broketoe showed little effort lifting it to his own shoulder. She revised her estimate of their strength when he pulled her to her feet and shoved her forward.

There were at least a hundred Kawokee atop the cliff, working in small groups, coiling ropes and gathering weapons. The most notable thing that caught Jasmine's eye was a stone watch tower constructed near the edge of the cliff. Three Kawokee stood at the sheltered top. One used a spyglass.

A shove and a hiss from Broketoe hurried her on. They marched down a steep trail and into the woods. Brick steps were set in the steepest areas. Flat, level, and uniform, a primitive culture would not put that much engineering into a simple flight of steps. Their presence had her questioning the validity of the documentation about the Kawokee. The trail continued past a border of trees into a vast grassy clearing in a valley cut by a wide stream. Smoke rose from short stone chimneys that dotted the clearing.

At a break in the trees to her right lay terraced fields and small windowless shelters. There was nothing that looked like a house. Small stone walls marked ramps where more Kawokee appeared and disappeared below ground, making it hard to estimate their number. She guessed at least a thousand.

A crowd formed around her as they entered the village. Jasmine did not mind when they pulled at her clothes and poked at her skin. Each native gave her more information about their culture. If graying fur was an indicator, there were many old ones in the village. Assuming a human growth curve, there were no children in the throng which accosted her.

The females wore more decorative clothing than the males. There were no rules about which parts of their body they covered. Bracelets and necklaces were popular with the females, but some males had them as well. Most clothing was functional. The cloth was not as fine nor the colors as vibrant as synthetic cloth. Neither was it coarse or full of flaws, suggesting it was made in part by a machine. Most female skirts had pockets and pouches, yet were decorated with beads in attractive designs.

A large shelter beside a patio paved with fitted stone caught her attention. Many Kawokee under the shelter stood to get a better look as she passed. Behind them was a brick kiln and rows of pottery. The sheltered area protected the drying clay objects. Most of the objects were unique and decorative. More significant were the ceramic pipes of identical size that looked like they fit into each other.

Farther in toward the heart of the village, they passed a wooden and metal device being used to twist and braid fibers into rope. The workings were too precise and intricate to be made by hand. It reminded her of their weapons. Neither came from humans. Both required advanced engineering knowledge.

A hand grabbed the waist of her pants and yanked her to a stop. "Human." Broketoe ignored Jasmine's questioning look and addressed a large male in the crowd who hurried away. With another command, the crowd disbursed.

The male returned with a rope, tied one end around Jasmine's waist, and the other end around his own. The message was clear. She was free to move, but she was to be watched at all times. It was not a warm welcome, but considering their treatment by humans, it was better than she expected.

She stooped down and touched her face. "Jasmine Char."

Broketoe chewed the words. "Tazama Cow."

"No. Jasmine," she said slowly.

The guard jerked the rope and pulled her away. "Human."

The curl of his lip and the pinch around his eyes screamed hatred. He pulled her to a stop near a small group of Kawokee. As she neared, they looked up. The fur on their snouts and around their mouths was thin and gray. They looked frail compared to most and sat on large straw mats. In the center of several of the mats were piles of wool. Two of the old ones brushed out the wool while the others used foot-powered spinning wheels.

The guard pushed Jasmine to her knees near a mat and showed her how to spin the wool into coarse thread. She tried to copy her guard's actions but ended up with a tangled mass. The cuts on her hands did not help in her attempt, and she soon had blood on the bundle of wool in front of her. Her guard grabbed her wrists and barked something guttural at her.

A wiry female flattened her ears and made a hissing sound. She slapped the guard's shoulder, and he backed away.

The old female sat down beside Jasmine, disposed of the soiled clump, and examined the cuts on her hands. She spoke to a short male who nodded and stood. As the male walked away, his back, crisscrossed by scars through the thinning fur, did not straighten.

The guard made a complaint, but one look from the female silenced him.

The old female beside Jasmine demonstrated how to feed the fibers to the spinning needle. Consistency was the key to produce different sizes and densities of thread.

The scarred male returned with a basin of water and a small bag. He sat beside her and gestured for her to hold out her hands, palm up. She could not read any expression on his face and braced herself as he reached to take her hand. He gently cleaned Jasmine's cuts with a wet towel and patted them with a waxy ointment that smelled of citrus. After a slight sting, the bleeding stopped, and the pain faded. He finished by bandaging her hands and checked her skinned knee.

Relief over the fact that not every Kawokee held a grudge against her mixed with the uncertainty of what the wool workers were discussing.

The old lanky female pointed a crooked finger at a large basket. Jasmine did not understand the words she spoke, but combined with her motions, Jasmine understood she wanted a basket filled with balls of fluff. She felt the mound, trying to learn if it was from animal hair or from plants. No wiser, she handed it to the elder who pulled only a small portion from the clump. The elder placed the wool between a set of paddles she pulled from a basket and showed Jasmine how to comb and straighten the fibers. When she finished, she motioned for Jasmine to try. The bandages hindered her movements. Jasmine had to be careful that none of the ointment seeped out and soiled the wool, but combing the wool was much easier than spinning.

After several hours, a young male carrying two large baskets approached the group, and everyone stopped working. He placed a basket near a mat before moving off somewhere else. The aroma of food reminded Jasmine she had not eaten since that morning. The nearest native pulled three large covered bowls from the basket and placed them on a clear area of a mat. One was filled with bread, another with potatoes, and another with a thick, yellow paste.

The wool workers gathered around, and after a discussion, they made a place for her to join them and motioned to her. Her guard objected, but a quick word from the elderly male who tended Jasmine's wounds sent him sulking away to the length of the rope. There were six buns of bread and six wool workers. Each of them took some of their food and put it on the mat in front of Jasmine.

The bread was coarse but the nutty taste was better than anything she had on this world or the ship. She snapped up every bit as the others talked. There were some furtive glances in her direction as an old male spoke. They were strangely quiet as he placed the bowl of tiny potatoes within easy reach of her, took one and dipped it in the paste. The others did the same.

Jasmine took one potato and dipped it in the bowl. There was little smell although the color of the paste was not appealing. She touched the paste to her tongue. It was a slightly salty hummus. The root that looked like a potato tasted more like a mild pepper. Combined with the paste, the flavors were palatable.

The group stopped eating and watched her every movement. They were waiting for something, testing her. This was a communal society. One didn't need to be an anthropologist to see how much they valued the concept of sharing.

Jasmine did not take more until they all took another potato. She was careful to avoid taking too much of the paste and never took a potato until the others had taken theirs. When there were too few in the bowl for everyone to have another, she took one of the remaining potatoes and broke it in half. She took none of the paste and ate it dry. If this pleased them or not, she could not tell. The next two also broke theirs in half until everyone had eaten an equal share.

Other than the wool workers, not many Kawokee came

near her, although she was a curiosity as they came and went. A pair ran through a field yelling. They disappeared near a short stone wall into a narrow pit carved into the ground. She had no idea how old they were, but they did not act like the adults. *Were there births here within the last few years?* Anxiety poked at her, telling her she was too late, that the Kawokee were dying out.

"Human," the guard yelled, startling Jasmine out of her musings. The wool workers cleaned the empty bowls and placed them back into the basket. Jasmine thought they would go back to work until she noticed the dark clouds in the sky. The first raindrops cooled her face. Several wool workers dragged everything under one of the many bamboo tents. The spinning wheels they took down a ramp that led underground.

Everyone dashed below ground as the rain came down hard. One of the old females from the wool combing group dragged herself toward the ramp. Jasmine had not realized the elder's legs no longer worked. Her first instinct was to pick the female up and help get her down the ramp, but Jasmine's guard had other plans. Before she could reach the elder, the rope around Jasmine's waist pulled taut.

"She needs help." There was no pleading with her guard. He yanked on the cord and pulled Jasmine away. The thought of untying herself and going to the elder flitted through her mind, but so did the possible consequences. Since the only things she knew about their customs was what she had read written by other humans, she was afraid of gaps in understanding. The documentation had come from different sources, and few of them were scientific in origin. She could not be certain of an unbiased perspective or even if what held true of one tribe would hold true for another.

Jasmine's guard pulled her to a small tent and crawled inside. It was barely big enough for him, so he left her in the pelting rain.

Their anger at humans was undoubtedly earned, but she felt tempted to yank the guard out by the rope and drag him through the mud. Indecision and uncertainty kept her rooted to the spot each painful minute as the storm worsened. Once soaked, standing in the rain longer made little difference. Jasmine hoped enduring their harsh treatment would take away some of their anger. Of course, that assumed similarities to human nature.

The lightning blinded her, and the twisting wind threw water in her face wherever she turned. She didn't see the dark shape until it was beside her. He shouted at the guard who scrambled out of his shelter and handed him the rope.

Broketoe looked thinner, and his wet fur looked black. He let the rope fall and took her wrist. Pulling her gently, he ushered her to a ramp that led to a doorway below ground. She had to stoop to enter the doorway and push through the heavy curtain. Darkness engulfed her, and she reached out her hand to touch the stone wall and ceiling. Jasmine used her unbandaged fingers to guide her along the short distance to another thick curtain. When the curtain parted, she stared in amazement at what lay before her. Wooden beams supported the roof of a large circular room illuminated by oil lamps. Tree trunk sized support pillars ringed the center. It reminded her of a huge gazebo decked out for a wedding. A half-dozen Kawokee sitting on thick cushions around a low table turned to look at her. More raised their heads from what they were doing as they sat on thick decorative rugs. Hammocks hung from the back wall barely noticeable because of the intricate paintings covering the wood paneling. Broketoe pushed her toward the center of the room.

Awed by what she saw, Jasmine almost struck her head on a low beam. Several beams had something hanging off them while others supported frames for weaving. She felt warmth radiate from a fire inside a large chiminea style pot. Broketoe pulled her in front of the fire before releasing her and spoke to those nearby. He stripped off his clothing and shook, sending water droplets everywhere. The wet drops that hit the chiminea hissed and evaporated. Two of the Kawokee brought towels. One handed its towel to Jasmine. The cloth was soft and absorbent. "Thank you."

Broketoe untied the rope from her waist and tossed it away. Her clothes steamed in front of her but dripped on the floor behind her. All the natives in the room watched her. A quick count told her there were around fifty to sixty tribe members within the lodge. Jasmine wanted to show them she was harmless and friendly, but was unsure how they would interpret a smile. The warmth melted her tense muscles and made her so sleepy she could barely stand.

When the pure musical tone sounded, she jerked from half-consciousness. Jasmine scanned the room and spotted her backpack beside a table. Those seated around the table scurried back. Broketoe's fur puffed out for a moment. If she read the expression correctly, he was both fearful and angry.

As the tone sounded again, she reached out her hand toward her pack, but didn't take a step.

Broketoe cringed as the noise rang out for a third time. Instead of pushing her toward the table, he brought her the pack before it rang again.

Jasmine unzipped the pack and dumped everything on the floor, spilling ration bars, energy cells, and clothes alike. The black case of the comm-vid landed on the ornate rug beneath her feet and she dropped the pack. She grabbed the box, opened the comm-vid, and angled it toward her and away from the dozens of frightened faces. The screen brightened the room, causing an instant increase in the noise level as the Kawokee huddled on the other side. "Hey, Arluza."

Arluza's eyes widened. "Looks like you've been in a fight."

Before she could speak, Broketoe threw himself at the box, slapping it closed. He put the comm-vid in the backpack and pushed it back under the table. As much as Jasmine wanted to protest his actions, she could not figure out how to make him understand. So, she knelt, head bowed, and silent.

There was an agitated conversation between Broketoe and the others. After several angry shouts, half the Kawokee gathered armloads of possessions and ran out the door into the rain. Broketoe spoke in quiet tones with the ones that remained. Several wore earrings, none as ornate as his. He spoke to them more than they spoke to him, strengthening his image as a leader, but if the grayness of their fur indicated age, he was younger than most.

When the conversation stopped, Broketoe covered himself with a cloak and stood at the entrance. The sound of distant thunder was all Jasmine heard until he parted the doorway curtain. A heavy mist threatened to pour into the room as he pushed through the entrance. The high pitched timbres of rain showed the storm was still raging.

Four males clamored to remove the backpack from under the table and pushed it toward the wall before they sat around the table and talked. The others went back to what they were doing when she entered the lodge but kept their eyes on her.

Jasmine's hair and arms were now dry, but her wet clothes were heavy and cold. Her dry clothes lay in a pile on the floor beside the table. Although there was soft conversations between those who stayed in the lodge, they watched her. Jasmine picked up a dry pair of pants and underwear. Several of the Kawokee of both sexes were naked. She made no quick movements as she changed into dry clothes, and none of them cared. She changed her blouse, gathered her wet clothes from the floor, and hung them from hooks in a beam over the fireplace beside some items of wet Kawokee clothing. She then sat down near the chimenea.

After a while, everyone in the room stopped watching her. They whispered among themselves. At least Arluza knew she was alive. She replayed the memories of that morning. It was less than a day, but it felt as if it had been years since Tim's murder. The Kawokee had every chance to kill her. If they let her run into the woods, she might starve trying to find her way back. The survival articles she studied now seemed silly. No book could prepare her for this. Broketoe must have known that. Why else would he stop her from running off into the woods?

An old, bent female threw aside the entrance blanket with Broketoe behind her. "I am Miwi. I speak for our leadow, Fawsha. What is you name?"

"Jasmine Char." Jasmine rehearsed Fawsha's real name and tried to remove the label Broketoe from her memory.

"G-g-z-ma." Miwi struggled with her first name before abandoning it. "Cow."

As much as it galled her, Jasmine knew she would have to live with the name. Their mouths could not produce the right sounds. Perhaps their ears heard sounds differently as well. The different dialects of the original settlers could also be at fault. Cow wasn't an insult. For the Kawokee, the word did not have negative connotations. Judging by Miwi's strong accent, she had not spoken Standard in many years.

Fawsha repeated the name and followed it with a statement.

Miwi nodded and turned to her. "Fo' a long time, no mo' humans come. Thwee days ago, you came fom the sky. Why?"

"Many humans are sick."

There was a brief exchange between the two Kawokee before Miwi said, "We know. Humans in the town have no young."

"Humans in the sky are sick, too." Jasmine wasn't sure how many of her words they could understand, but she was not about to assume they were ignorant. She could not get very far if they thought she was insulting them. "The ones who left your world took the sickness with them.

Now many in the sky have no children."

"The Kawokee awe not sick." Fawsha dried himself with a towel as Miwi interpreted. "We cannot help. Those who came with you went back to the sky. You stayed. Why?"

Jasmine remembered standing at the tavern room window staring at the lights of fires in the distance. It made sense that the Kawokee watched the town. "I want to learn about you."

"Humans do not wish to know us. All the humans wanted to help Kawokee by making us like human. New talk, new gods; all of it bad for us. We do not want humans with us."

"I don't want to change you. I'll only watch and learn who you are. This…" she pointed to the comm-vid in her backpack, "lets others see and learn without coming down."

Fawsha was quiet for a time before he said anything for Miwi to translate. "You cannot stay. Tomowow, you must go back to the town. Go back to you sky home."

"I can't go back. I am sick."

There was a long exchange between Miwi and Fawsha. If the movements of their ears were any indication, the discussion was intense. Fawsha stormed over to the table, pulled the comm-vid from the backpack, and set it in front of Jasmine.

"You can stay." Miwi glanced at Fawsha before placing a hand to her breast. "When you talk, I must listen. Fawsha wishes to speak to the human on the box."

Fawsha opened the comm-vid and pushed buttons at random. Elated by the news she could stay in the village, Jasmine leaned over it and showed him which buttons to press. When Arluza answered, Fawsha glared at him. The interpreter's tone reflected Fawsha's rigid stance. "You will speak only to Cow. And, I, Miwi, must listen."

Arluza looked puzzled and Jasmine watched as he formed the word on his lips. She could feel her ears burn as she explained. "They call me Cow."

She could tell he was trying hard not to laugh. His lips pressed together in a frown, but his eyes twinkled with merriment.

"Will you obey these wooles?" Fawsha may have been short, but he had an air of command even Arluza could not ignore.

"Yes, sir."

Fawsha closed the comm-vid while Arluza's voice still hung in the air. He turned to Jasmine, pointed, and spoke. Miwi translated. "If you stay, you wok."

Fawsha handed her the backpack before gathering several cushions and placed them near the fire. "You will sleep here."

CHAPTER 4

Chris Arluza arrived at the auditorium early, but dozens of scientists already waited. Jasmine was the only scientist not on the ship. Part of him wished she would be at the meeting. Most people on the ship did not consider her a true scientist. All the others were vitrogrammers, geneticists, immunologists and such. Too busy trying to understand the lost knowledge that created the virus, none of them knew or cared about Jasmine's theory. Arluza listened but did not understand the theory himself. She was the only scientist who dared be on the ground, but learning to make thread from animal hair wasn't getting Jasmine any closer to the cure. It took her three weeks to get this far. At her present rate, she would have to spend years to prove her theory. Hopefully, she would give up when others found the cure.

While he waited for the meeting to start, Arluza read the news from the home-worlds. Some governments were giving tax breaks to clean couples who donated their eggs and sperm for the government baby factories. Some artificial womb manufacturers were getting government subsidies while others were taken over by their governments. And that was the positive news.

Child kidnapping was on the rise. The articles blamed desperate people willing to pay and not be picky about how legal the adoptions were. It was strange to see pictures of the orphanages on the poorer planets void of children. Foster care workers were being laid off in droves. Cryopreservation businesses were booming. In-home artificial wombs were back ordered by years, and those that were available were not always up to industry standards. Con artists were making more money on the promise of children than stealing identities.

Public opinion on what to do with the infected varied widely, but the pressure to do something was causing riots on every world. The articles Arluza read were months old. He knew things had gotten worse. The legislation requiring testing and registration of the infected passed the first hurtle just after their ship left orbit.

Arluza couldn't blame the other scientists for not going dirtside. The entire crew was required to be tested before they could return. It was in their contract. Anyone infected would be permanently assigned to the taskforce or left on the planet until cured.

Everyone was obligated to spend at least a two-year work shift to find a cure, but he hoped it would take half the time. If for no other reason, than to keep his sanity. He never dreamed of being so low on the food chain that his PhD would only merit a technician's position.

Dr. Campion, known more for hopping on the right political bandwagon than for any meaningful study, strode out onto the stage and stepped up to the podium as if expecting applause. "Initial observations confirm that the Kaw have the same symptoms as humans, the inability to carry a child past the first trimester. We have sampled dozens of the towns to verify the initial studies from sixty years ago. While not enough to keep the standard deviation below five percent, the Kawokee population seems stable."

A bar graph showing the town-dwelling Kawokee

population statistics by known numbers and estimated ages appeared on the wall of the stage. The percentage of natives within certain height ranges also appeared on the huge graph. No infants or children were recorded.

Although everyone assumed this was true, Arluza had the unenviable task of compiling the data from the soldiers on the ground. Unless there was other data he never saw, Campion was making unsupportable conclusions. How could they know if a Kawokee was a child based on height without knowing growth rates? He also couldn't see how anyone could say if their population was stable without knowing their lifespan. Not to mention how anyone could trust town records from sixty years ago to be accurate or get reliable data using soldiers as lab assistants.

"Blood samples from random Kaw show one hundred percent infection rate."

Arluza had run those tests himself and agreed with the statement within a five percent margin of error.

"We will soon take blood samples from the savages to see what percentage are uninfected. Kawokee hormones are nearly identical to humans. From hormone levels, the age of children and female fertility cycle times can be estimated."

Campion's words rang in Arluza's ears. He could not concentrate on anything else the man said and held his breath until Campion asked if there were questions.

Arluza's hand shot up. Several people already headed for the door. "How are blood samples to be taken?"

"Villages will be selected to give an even distribution across the continents."

"No. That is not what I meant." Arluza tried to maintain eye contact as someone walked in front of him forcing him to stand up. "How are you going to get volunteers to give blood?"

Campion chuckled and folded his notes. "Obviously, we won't get volunteers. How the soldiers get the samples is up to them."

Arluza pushed his way against the crowd to get to the front. This was more than sloppy science. It bordered on criminal. "This will anger the Kawokee."

Campion turned off his mic. "What else can we do? Are you seriously suggesting we plead for volunteers? There won't be any. The savages hate us already. We don't have years to spend on this while our civilization hangs by a thread. Let's continue this discussion offline." He walked off stage and out a side door.

"Who suggested this approach?" Arluza shouted at the man's back.

CHAPTER 5

"Now you count."

"Yes, father." Jasmine touched each of the spindles and counted in Kawokee. Learning the words was one thing, but understanding them quickly or forming a sentence was difficult. The old male wheezed, which was the Kawokee version of laughter. Small holes in his right ear, void of any rings, was a sign he had given up his name many years ago. The elder male touched the last two spindles and said their numbers showing she had reversed the names of the last two. Jasmine's vocabulary was growing faster than she could have hoped because their words were often combinations of other words. A spindle was a thread-round. A rope was a many-thread. She could usually guess the words. Even if she guessed wrong, they knew what she was trying to say.

Another help was the similarities in nonverbal communications. Even their number system was base ten. How much was due to cultural contamination was still foremost on her mind. Yet, many things were not human. The taking and leaving of a name made perfect sense though she never considered it before. In a small communal society, names were irrelevant unless you held a position. If you gave up your position, you were 'father' or 'mother'.

Someone's shrill whistle called for attention. Several Kawokee near her stopped what they were doing and headed toward the caller. The old male beckoned her to go but did not follow.

Two Kawokee stood as a crowd gathered around them. Jasmine watched from the back edge of the crowd as each yelled and pointed to the other. It sounded like an argument, but there were no back-and-forth accusations.

She couldn't understand enough of the words to make sense of it because they talked too fast for her to comprehend the words. When they finished, the crowd filed past them. Jasmine crept closer to see the audience take a bean from a bowl and place it at the feet of one. The male had far more beans than the female. It appeared the crowd was voting.

The crowd had thinned when the male groaned with his hand to his earring. His groan rose to a scream, and his hand came away from his ear. Blood dripped on the grass as he handed the female his earring. His ear torn and blood covering his neck and shoulder, he staggered away. The female shuffled in the opposite direction, looking at the earring in her hand.

Jasmine felt ill. Was this a Kawokee trial? What passed for law here? Whatever had happened, the scene was barbaric in her eyes. She summoned her professional detachment and hoped the cameras placed around the village caught the event. It was not for her to judge but record and learn.

The female did not go far. She watched over her shoulder after the male, turned, called out, and jogged after him.

Jasmine compared the elements of this to every Old Earth culture she could think of. Nothing fit well. It frustrated her to not be able to ask questions or understand the answers. She did not want to bother Miwi despite her general helpfulness. Jasmine no longer noticed the missing Rs and CHs in her words.

The old male smiled at her return. "Father, have you seen many humans?"

"No. Only Smellrot."

It took a minute for Jasmine to translate the words before remembering Smellrot was the name given to Tim. So much of Kawokee life in this village was unlike what she expected. The first colonist's reports were unscientific and exaggerated, but events like the one she just witnessed could easily give rise to wild stories.

Aside from counting, today she learned how to make plain cloth. The machine did all the work. She only had to keep it turning by pumping the pedals, leaving her in a perfect position to watch the movements of the villagers.

To the shortest villagers, she paid special attention. They worked like the grey haired adults, but had to be taught a task. Why there were no infants or pregnant females in the village was a mystery. The settler's notes never mentioned infants or pregnant females or their absence.

As for the settler's tales of Kawokee orgies, she had seen no evidence. The Kawokee slept with whom they wanted, when they wanted. Some were quite playful or rough, but it was always consensual and sometimes in public. None of them had approached her.

A cook came with the noon basket. He placed the meal on a mat and hurried to the next group. The hot bread was her favorite, the fruit and cooked roots less so. Jasmine longed for meat, but Earth animals did not fare well on the planet, and the Kawokee in the village did not eat meat. On the plus side, she was losing the muffin top she battled with for so long.

Jasmine eyed the bundle of leaves, fearful of uncooked food.

Father touched her hand. "Do not fear." He tore his bread in half and offered it to her in exchange for her bundle of leaves.

Touched by his kindness, Jasmine smiled and tried not to tear up. Her words came out in a jumble of Kawokee and Standard. "Thank you. But I need to get over my fear." The colonists preferred the crops from their homeworlds, which did not thrive here. They avoided native plants and animals, fearful of diseases, especially the Pox. But Tim lived out in the woods for years and stayed healthy.

The old male nodded and took back his bread as she nibbled at the leaves.

"Cow." Miwi waved and walked toward her. "Alooza calls."

Jasmine stuffed the leaf in her mouth and picked up the rest of her meal.

Miwi turned and looked over her shoulder to make sure Jasmine was following. Her actions heightened Jasmine's growing anxiety. Arluza never called but waited for the scheduled time and spoke only in Miwi's presence. Jasmine's nervousness continued as she entered the empty den and placed the ringing comm-vid on the table. She didn't feel any better when Arluza's pinched eyes and knotted forehead appeared on screen.

His eyes darted between her and Miwi. "How fast can you get to a town? Your welcome is about to wear thin."

Jasmine could not imagine why he would say such a thing. He knew she would never leave the planet even if she could. Arluza never spoke in idioms, but it was obvious he was trying to hide something from Miwi.

Miwi glanced from Arluza to Jasmine and asked, "What's wrong?"

"Arluza, you can't lie to save your shorts, so don't even try."

He blew out a long breath. "The soldiers are coming."

Miwi's ears stood straight up and turned forward before flattening to her skull.

He glanced behind him as if startled by a noise. Arluza

leaned forward and whispered. "Get the leader. It's urgent. Call me back."

The screen went black.

Miwi scurried for the doorway. She paused only long enough to see if Jasmine was following. Once outside, Jasmine's long legs made it easy to keep up as Miwi ran through the village calling Fawsha's name. A villager pointed to the top of the cliff.

Arluza's few words chilled Jasmine. He must have struggled before deciding to not only tell her but warn a Kawokee leader. Climbing the hill used to wind her. Today, she hardly noticed.

Fawsha was talking with two males. One carried a leather scroll case on his back. Jasmine had not yet learned to read any of the Kawokee writing. There wasn't much available. Fawsha looked up from the scroll he had spread on the ground. He rolled up the scroll as Miwi spoke.

She talked too quickly for Jasmine to catch but a few words. "… come… Alooza."

Fawsha snapped a command, and the two males followed him down the hill. The descent was much easier, but Jasmine resisted the urge to jump steps to keep up with the males. A broken leg would hinder her work. A broken neck would end it.

The speed in which Fawsha reached the entrance to the den did not matter. They still needed to wait for Miwi. When everyone was inside, Jasmine pressed the call button, and Arluza answered within seconds. He spoke quickly but paused long enough for Miwi to translate.

"The soldiers need blood samples from children and pregnant females in Kawokee villages. They don't want to harm anyone, but it may cause panic. Please don't be angry with Jasmine. She had nothing to do with this decision."

Fawsha answered, and Miwi translated. "Cow is safe. I want to speak to your mayor."

Arluza massaged his temples. "Talk to Campion? That's a laugh. He considers most humans beneath him,

I'm sure he thinks of the Kawokee as lab rats. Campion won't speak to you. He won't speak to me either. If he finds out I told you about the soldiers, I won't be able to warn you again."

"I understand." Fawsha turned and talked to one of the other males in the room as Arluza closed the connection. He took several scrolls from the messenger.

Not knowing what he intended, Jasmine asked Miwi, "What will we do? What can Fawsha do?"

The tension Miwi revealed by her lowered ears magnified as she grasped Jasmine's hand. "He's called for four runners and two message boats. Let us hope we can warn the other villages in time."

CHAPTER 6

"I've got targets." The soldier picked up the med kit.

"Finally." Macalister looked over his teammate's shoulder at the mircro-intel screen strapped to his arm. Three red dots moved from the village heading in their direction. "The first few days were easier. Do you think they've been warned?"

"It seems that way. They must have a communication system between villages." Macalister took the med kit from his partner and handed him the short rifle. "Let me take this one. You made a mess with the last one. Probably injured it."

His teammate shouldered the rifle. "I was trained to make holes, not fix them."

"If I ever get injured, remind me not to ask you for any medical help."

The two ducked under the flap of the camouflage blind and climbed the rise overlooking the village. Three natives walked along a path leading into the woods. Macalister and his partner followed at a distance until the small group stopped to collect berries.

Macalister stared down at his own intel screen. "No one coming." He concentrated on the instrument and listened for three pops. After a minute, he looked up. "What are you waiting for? Take the shots."

His teammate was holding his leg where a quill poked through his pants.

Macalister pulled it out and sniffed at the tip. The other man tried to speak, but made no sound. Macalister dropped the dart and squeezed the man's arm. "We're getting out of here." He looked around to get his bearings on the fastest way to the shuttle.

A small sting to his side distracted Macalister from his teammate. A quill stuck out through his shirt. He felt a moment of panic as a coldness spread through his chest and down his left arm. When he attempted to stand, his legs gave out beneath him. Somehow, he ended up staring at the sky. A furry face filled his vision. The creature spoke in clipped words and rapid gestures. He couldn't move any part of his body or feel anything. He could only watch and listen as numerous natives scurried about.

The idea of dying some horrible excruciating death teased the edges of his conscious mind, but the thought did not mesh with the relaxed posture of a Kawokee nearby. One of the creatures hunched over a scroll scratching marks onto a cream colored sheet. A clear bottle filled with a dark substance sat on the ground near its feet, and the native dipped the writing implement into the bottle multiple times.

The memory of a painting he saw in a museum flitted through Macalister's mind before he was jerked upright. The first thing he registered was being stripped bare and his hands and ankles bound. All his clothes were piled next to him. The thought of how much time had passed was interrupted by the warm tingling sensation that spread through his body as every one of his nerves awoke. The sensation turned into a fire of needles.

Reflex action tightened every muscle in Macalister's body. His scream of pain was answered by several small hands that rubbed and massaged his limbs until the agony receded.

Macalister heard the scream from his teammate a few meters away. The Kawokee covered the man. Macalister could do nothing. The screaming stopped, and the Kawokee stepped away. His teammate was sitting up.

All around in a circle were a dozen Kawokee with spears. One of them said something to the Kawokee that attended Macalister. It grabbed Macalister's head and examined his eyes and mouth. It also pressed its ear to Macalister's chest. When the native was satisfied, it spoke to the note-taker. One of the natives made a high pitched yapping noise and more Kawokee appeared.

They stood before Macalister and his partner in a single line. The first was a tall female who held the med kit they brought to take samples. She opened the kit and loaded a vial into the syringe. Making sure Macalister could see what she was doing, she pressed around on her arm, placed the syringe, and drew blood.

Macalister never thought about feeling for a pulse under the fur but relied on trial and error of many pokes until the needle found its mark.

When she finished, she showed him the vial before placing it in the container. She then drew blood from each of those in line, placing the samples in the kit. When all the vials were filled, she closed the case and shoved it into his chest. The force of her actions was not much, but in Macalister's weakened state it almost pushed him over.

The Kawokee dispersed after that. One guard remained to cut their bonds, but even he did not stay long.

Macalister staggered to his feet. As he put on his clothes, he asked his teammate, "Are you all right?"

"I think so. What happened?"

"We got a taste of our own medicine. Come on. Let's get back to the ship."

They found all their supplies minus the rifles stacked beside their ship. Atop the pile lay a long string of beads.

CHAPTER 7

Arluza took the sample case. It was another heavy one. He opened the box and saw every vial filled. "Another easy one?"

The soldier growled in response. "We show up, they line up. It's like they know when and where we're coming. At least I haven't been ambushed again."

Arluza pursed his lips and shrugged. His eyes focused on the small scar that broke the man's eyebrow in two and traveled up into his hairline. Hintz, was the name the Kawokee gave this one. Miwi said it meant Scar. Arluza looked away fearful that he might be staring. He put the case on the table. "I needed a few samples from each village. This looks like everyone gave blood."

"I only had fifty vials. I selected the young looking ones and as many females as I could and still get a few males."

"Perfect." It was too perfect. The data was better than he hoped. It wasn't his place to tell the soldiers to stop, but the data already collected proved some females had given birth, yet every sample had the virus. There were no infant samples, and every soldier reported seeing no children. Perhaps the Kawokee really did eat their young. Arluza still wanted to know their lifespan, but none of the scientists he spoke with were as concerned that the data was suspect or the conclusions hasty.

"I know a military operation when I see one. They have a mole on this ship."

Arluza's heart jumped at the soldier's words. He was glad he was not holding a vial because he was sure he would have dropped it.

The soldier did not seem to have noticed Arluza's discomfort and kept on talking. "But it's been beneficial to the mission. It's been the same for three weeks now. We walk into a village, and the volunteers line up, or the village turns us away. Most of us take the hint. Any team that uses force is ambushed and beaten to a pulp on their next run. I wonder who is feeding them our schedule."

Arluza knew few of the soldier's names. They did not chat with the scientists, so he was surprised when the soldier was still watching him. His first thought was that the soldier knew he had given the Kawokee information.

The soldier stepped closer. "They know who is going where even if the previous village was a hundred clicks away."

Arluza applied the ID labels and logged them. "They must have a fast communication system between villages."

"Across two continents? I know they aren't savages, doctor, and I'm glad they aren't getting hurt. But if it came to saving our species or hurting a few primitives, I'll save human lives."

Arluza thought about an appropriate response, but when he looked up, the soldier was gone.

CHAPTER 8

Fawsha wiped alcohol across the scroll to erase the previous message and waited for the smell to dissipate. As he wrote the new message, he spoke aloud to the runners so they could memorize the words. "The spring children will leave the nest soon. The humans can see fires from the sky, even the heat from our bodies at night. Do not light fires as you move them and wear cloaks even within the shelter of the trees. No children are to come to this village. Cow has been helpful and intends no harm, but she is intent of finding the children."

A runner asked, "May I see the human?"

Fawsha looked up from his writing at the young runners. "You've never seen a human?"

The runner shook his head. "Are the stories true? They say they're tall and hairless.

The wide eyed look of the young male made Fawsha laugh. "Almost hairless. Any who wishes to see, come, but do not speak to her." The runners dogged his heels. He led them to the weavers where he had seen Cow the previous day.

"Why can't we talk to her?"

Fawsha's ears dipped in aggravation. How could they

memorize his message to the other villages but not understand? Were they not listening? Fawsha's irritation with the young showed his age. He would leave behind his name and the frustration that went with it if he could find one who could do the job. "What did I just say about Cow?"

They recited his words as they were trained to do.

"How does my warning affect those who speak to her?"

"She might ask about the children," said the tallest one.

Fawsha stopped short and turned, committing to memory the face of the speaker. "Would it be enough to not speak?"

"No. To lie or fail to answer would reveal we are hiding the truth. It would tell her something."

"Exactly. I would like you to return with the next season." He continued toward the weavers, and the runners followed.

"Does she look like the drawings?" ask one.

"I heard the humans were sent by the Vaw to trick us," said another.

Fawsha remembered his own teachings. His thoughts differed from what he was taught. Many of his age still clung to the teachings of the priestesses. "How do you distinguish between the sisters and the Vaw?"

They all recited the words. "You will know them by what they do."

"Cow warned us the soldiers were coming and tells us what is happening in the sky-canoe. Is she Vaw?"

At this, there was much discussion. Fawsha knew there could be no answer and did not let them waste his time. "She came here looking for the same answer as the soldiers. If she finds it, she will give it to the other humans. The first humans on this world came to our villages intending no harm, yet we were harmed. The Vaw is in us all to one degree or another. No one is perfect. We do not intend it, but we hurt each other."

His own words caused a pang of guilt. The urge to ask them the question that plagued him was overpowering. "Children and priestesses believe the difference is merely intention. For them, it is easy. Those who intend harm are Vaw. Anyone who means well can bring hurt. I have a question for you. Can you intend harm to bring good?"

Fawsha expected their blank stares. "Perhaps we are Vaw, not her."

He led them to the place where the weavers worked, but Cow was not there. A pile of new cloth burned nearby. The weavers stood away from the smoke, but when they saw Fawsha they ran toward him. They all talked at once.

"Cow is ill. It's the Pox. She is with the healer."

The runners did not follow Fawsha as he ran for the healer's den. The bad smells within the burrow hurt his eyes and nose, but he did not fear them. It was a small den, but filled with the containers and tools of her trade. The room beyond the second doorway was where everyone feared to go.

The healer was not in her den, but Fawsha heard a sound in the next room.

"Healer? Is Cow with you?"

"I am here." Cow's voice was low, but her words were slow and clear. "Don't come in."

Fawsha shifted from one foot to the other. He couldn't think of what to say. He could not imagine how she caught the Pox and wondered what the repercussions would be if she died. Humans could be so unpredictable. "How do you feel?"

"Hot. Itch."

"Don't scratch."

The healer came into the den followed by her assistant. They carried several bowls between them. The small feather which hung from the single ring in the healer's ear swayed with the movement of her head. "You must not be here. It is the Pox."

Fawsha remembered the first time he had seen

62

someone contract the disease. Time had smoothed the edges of his memory but not their scars. "We need to make certain she doesn't die."

The healer glared at him as the hair on her back rose and her ears twitched. "Fine. You can help, but stay back. We must get her to the cave."

"Wait. She's human. There is something we need to do first." Fawsha ran from the den and found Miwi working around the cook pots.

"Miwi, come. You're needed. Cow has the Pox."

Miwi pulled back from him. "Pox? I can't."

"It is important." Fawsha grabbed her arm and pulled her along.

She dragged her feet and whimpered before entering the healer's den.

The healer watched as he sat Miwi near the doorway and told her, "You're safe here. Now tell Cow this. You will be very sick. Kawokee rarely die from this, but some humans do."

Miwi flattened her ears and cringed. "All humans die."

"She doesn't need to hear that. Cow needs hope. Tell her there is little the healer can do but make her more comfortable. Tell her she must not stay within the confines of the village or many will get sick. There is a place prepared to help her and keep us safe. Tell her not to be afraid of what we must do."

Miwi nodded and translated Fawsha's words.

Cow responded in Kawokee. "What must you do?"

The healer interrupted Fawsha. "Tell her she must go to the cave. Her clothes and anything she touches must be burned. Soon the itching will start, but I can help her with that. The salves smell. The fever will make it hard to think. She must be restrained. If she was Kawokee, I would tell her it should only last a few days. But she is human." The healer shrugged and turned away.

After Miwi translated, Cow said something in human. Miwi repeated her words in Kawokee. "She asked, is that all?"

"Yes. Tell her she must trust us. We will do all we can for her."

Miwi again translated and Cow did her best to respond in Kawokee. "I trust you."

Fawsha thanked Miwi who was out the doorway while the words were still on his tongue.

He looked at the healer who nodded. Fawsha pushed the heavy blanket covering the doorway aside. "Come with me."

Cow stood with her clothes in her arms. Small red dots covered her arms and legs.

Fawsha held the blankets aside as she left the den. The healer laid down straw in a path and called out a warning for all to stay clear. As Cow walked the path, the healer's assistant burned the straw path behind her. It was unnecessary to make a path from the tree line to the cave. No one ever stepped past the yellow warning markers. The healer set down several bowls at the cave entrance and told them to wait. She returned with oil lanterns and led them into the cave. Charred wood and ash crunched underfoot. The healer placed the lanterns around the cavern. Four thick stakes with a hole near the top protruded from the ash.

The healer pointed. "Lay down here."

Cow lowered herself to the ground.

The healer motioned that she should put her hands over her head.

She did as instructed.

"She is too big. We must move the posts to here." The healer cleared the places indicated on the charred ground.

Fawsha could not ask anyone else to do it. Even the healer's assistant was keeping his distance. Fawsha went back to the village and gathered a shovel and a heavy mallet.

When he returned to the cave, the healer was preparing supplies at the entrance as her assistant fussed and took notes. "You must hurry. She has already started to itch."

Cow huddled in the far corner and said nothing as Fawsha worked. The stakes were deeper than he thought. His back ached as he pulled the last one free. Cow was making sounds he could not interpret, and it pushed him to move faster. His arms grew numb as he pounded the last stake into the clay.

The healer brought leather straps and motioned for her to lie down.

"I must talk with Arluza." Cow looked as if she were in excruciating pain as she pulled on her outer clothes.

For a moment, Fawsha thought of objecting, but he realized that if the human of the box did not see Cow, he may not believe the Kawokee. Fawsha ran to his den and lifted the box to his chest. Cow had not used it in days, so he suspected it would be clean. Fawsha's legs and arms ached, but he carried it to the cave. Both he and Miwi had learned what buttons to push to make the thing work. He pressed the controls for her. "Say whatever you wish."

Fawsha could not understand a word of what she said, but her message was short. She nodded, and he turned the box off and placed it at the mouth of the cave. Cow removed her clothes again and lay in the ash.

Fawsha called for the healer who wore long leather gloves on her hands and boots for her feet. She tied cords to Cow's arms and legs and attached them to the posts so Cow could move, but not far enough to harm or free herself.

The healer looked over her shoulder as she tested the cords. "You have done all you can do. I will watch over her."

Fawsha knew there was no reason to stay but found it hard to leave. Both he and the healer walked out of the cave. The healer pulled off her gloves and broke roots into a bowl while the assistant built a fire. "Her cries may disturb you. These roots will reduce the stinging."

"Don't burn her clothes."

The healer stopped what she was doing and stared, ears down, at Fawsha. "Have you gone mad?"

Even the assistant stopped what he was doing and gaped in horror.

"No." Fawsha fought hard to find the words he could use to convince the healer of the motives behind his actions. "We may need them. As a precaution."

"Our ancestors warned us about the Pox and many other things. Will you undo all the work they have done?"

"Who's to say it's not already falling apart? The high places are torn down, and few priestesses are left. Those who live hide in fear along with our young. The humans refuse to listen. Perhaps we should make them listen."

"The Vaw will find you if you do this."

"The Vaw does as it wishes. Sometimes the end is bad, but sometimes the Vaw's actions are a benefit."

The healer snorted. "Not until after much pain. Do as you wish, KapFawsha. But know this. I will not help you."

"Would a sealed covered bowl be sufficient? I could bury it far from the cave and place a warning marker in the earth."

His words fell on deaf ears as the healer continued making her concoctions. Not even the assistant dared look at him. Fawsha understood their feigning deafness. He had placed them both in a difficult position. They could neither deny his direct order, nor compromise the healer's oath without inviting the anger of the gods.

CHAPTER 9

The healer's shadow blocked the light. She carried a bowl and a long stick with a cloth wrapped around it. After dipping the cloth in the bowl, she reached out with the stick and applied the oil. The numbing effect was slight. There was a memory, or perhaps a dream, where that stick took away incredible pain.

"How much longer?" The words stuck in Jasmine's throat, and it took a second attempt to force them passed dry lips.

The healer's ears turned toward her. "How do you feel?"

It took a moment to remember the right Kawokee words. "Thirsty, hungry."

The healer disappeared and came back with an oil lamp. She examined Jasmine from head to toe then sat back. "I'll be back."

She left for some time before returning with both Miwi and Fawsha. The whites of Miwi's eyes were easy to see in the dim light. Jasmine caught some words Fawsha spoke, but Miwi repeated them. "Only humans with Kaw live through Pox. You have Kaw?"

Jasmine would never admit to another human she had

the virus. She already told Fawsha. Perhaps he thought her confession a ploy to convince him to let her stay. "Yes."

"I will release you, but you must stay in the cave until I say."

Jasmine nodded.

The healer stepped forward and cut the straps that held her hands. Jasmine's arms ached, and her muscles protested their movement. She rubbed and scratched the surface of her skin. It felt wonderful.

The healer slid a bowl over to her that reeked of turpentine. Miwi translated. "Cover yourself in this."

The substance did not burn as she patted it on her raw skin, but the odor made her head spin. At the healer's gesture, she brushed the thick goo into her hair and scalp.

"Now come out and bathe."

The gentle breeze smelled wonderful. Jasmine stood at the entrance of the cave and let the warm sunlight seep into her bones. As she made her way to the sandy pool where the Kawokee bathed, some of those she met came near. She didn't understand most of their words, but they were happy to see her well. They kept their distance as Jasmine submerged her body into the water.

She cupped her hands and poured the water into her mouth, then over her head. The water felt cool and wonderful, but her throat burned. The moment she swallowed, her stomach twisted in a knot. Dizziness overtook her, forcing her to move to a flat stone in the water and sit for some time to wait for her insides to calm. It gave her time to think. The first thing she needed to do was call Arluza. Jasmine also needed something to eat, but would her stomach allow her? She brought more water to her lips. The thought of gagging again kept her from dunking her head into the water and drinking her fill. This time, there was no negative reaction. She finished bathing and climbed out of the water.

Still weak and trembling, she walked up the hill toward the burrow where warm clothes awaited.

Clouds obscured the sun making it hard to know what time it was. One of the Kawokee must have anticipated her hunger and came running with two buns. She sank to her knees and devoured them. As if on cue, other Kawokee gathered around and hugged her before going about their duties. None of them called her Cow. Instead, they called her Sister. The term caused tears to well up in her eyes. Not only had they accepted her as a friend, but as family.

Smoke rose over the trees that hid the cave. Jasmine sniffed her arms to make sure none of the stench of the cave or the scent of disinfectant still clung to her.

She staggered halfway to her den when she noticed the line of carts and riders on what this world called horses. Unsure when they arrived, she made a mental note to review the cameras placed around the village. Some carts were covered, hiding their contents. Others held fruits. Three carts carried Kawokee. There were so many moving carts and horses she didn't see the man right away.

Aware she was naked, she hunkered down, covered herself with her hands, and scurried close to the ground until she could dive into the den entrance. When she peeked up from the hole, Jasmine was glad he was not looking in her direction. Her first thought was to find something to cover herself with, but she had a hard time taking her eyes off him. The man was bare chested and had a dark tan. She couldn't tell if he was wearing anything from the waist down. He dismounted and disappeared into a sea of moving carts.

Jasmine ducked into the den where Fawsha and a few others were talking around the single table. She dug through her pack and threw on some clothes. The next thing on her list was to get Miwi, so she could use the comm-vid to tell Arluza she was fine. She pushed back through the doorway and looked around but did not see the man who came with the caravan.

Miwi, she knew, was often assigned cooking duties.

Jasmine waited to enter the kitchen den as two Kawokee struggled with a heavy burlap bag. Miwi was busy directing the placement of large and small bags as a continuous line of new faces brought them in. Several looked at her but said nothing. Jasmine shifted around to avoid being run over, but only managed to bump into someone else.

Miwi waved her toward the door. "I will come soon, Cow."

As Jasmine's adrenaline rush wore thin, she became drowsy. Worried she had done too much too soon, she rallied her strength and hurried back to the den. She did not so much as lower herself to the pillows as collapse and gave in to sleep.

Somewhere between sleep and consciousness, the sound of Kawokee talking drew her attention. One of the voices sounded human. Jasmine cracked open an eye and looked toward the table. The man from the caravan was drinking and talking with Fawsha and three other Kawokee. His voice was lower than the others, but he spoke their language like it was his own.

Fawsha looked in her direction. "Cow. Are you awake?" Fawsha spoke slowly and pointed at the man. "This is LutPaul."

The man, wearing only shorts and moccasins, was seated cross legged on an overstuffed pillow. In his right ear were two rings. "Hello, Cow." He turned, gave her a twisted smile, and spoke in Standard, "Please call me Paul."

"My name is actually Jasmine Char," she corrected.

The man stared at her for a moment before he burst out laughing. "Jasmine." He nodded to the others that surrounded the table and they left the den. The man patted an empty pillow next to him. "It's obvious how that happened. They were just telling me you're here to learn about the Kawokee. You've earned a fair amount of trust. They've asked me to tell you anything you want to know and take you to Gehnica, one of their largest hidden cities."

"Hidden cities?"

Paul waved his hand in the air. "This is just an outpost to watch the nearby human settlement and discourage them from exploring. Cities like Gehnica, are where everyone goes to learn a trade and meet with leaders."

"I've learned how to weave here."

"Weaving a plain blanket is easy, engineering takes schooling."

"Engineering?" Jasmine thoughts raced. "There was no documentation of this in the files I read."

"The Kawokee build dens, bridges, wells, dams, and aqueducts if it's an arid region. They try and work with the land as best they can to minimize their ecological footprint." Paul scoffed. "There was probably a lot missing from reports sent to the other worlds. Most humans are used to pressing a button and having their machines do the work. They don't build or design anything, so they don't recognize those who do."

Jasmine moved to the pillow next to Paul. "I don't understand. How is that possible?"

"Easy. You were told the Kawokee were savages. Has anything changed your mind?"

"Too many things to count. Just being in this village, I've learned so much."

"And that's very little." Paul's eyes grew cold. "Most humans refused to step foot in a village. They saw what they wished to see and believed what their leaders told them was true. Even now, some townspeople refuse to acknowledge the intelligence of the Kawokee."

Jasmine opened her mouth to object and quickly closed it. Before she stepped foot on the planet, she thought she was prepared. What she saw in the village made her realize she was lied to. "It's hard to adjust a preconceived notion."

"Very true." Paul nodded. "Each village has at least one skill or product they trade with. This village exists to watch the nearby human settlement, but it also makes pottery and cloth."

"Those here are so different than the Kawokee I heard about."

Paul nodded. "The ones in the settlements idolize humans and became what the humans wanted them to be."

So many questions needed asking, but one was more important than all others. "Where are all the Kawokee children?"

Paul shook his head and drank from the cup that sat before him. "There are still children being born, but how many and where is a closely guarded secret, even from me. The Kawokee population has taken a big hit since the humans came."

Surprised by his answer, Jasmine asked, "Really? How?"

"When humans first came here, the Kawokee swarmed them wanting to meet the sky sisters." Paul held up a hand to stop her question. "It's a story from their religion. We humans immediately began to civilize them. Tens of thousands left their old ways to become human. But humans had no use for them except as servants and prostitutes. Then the missionaries came. To please them, some villages killed the priestesses of the old religion. It caused a lot of strife. Those who clung to the old ways moved their homes far from humans. Most of the ones that wanted to be near the humans have died out. Some believe it is a curse from an angry mother god. The Kawokee religion has very strict rules. Failure to follow those rules results in very nasty consequences."

"Can you tell me about their religion?"

"Me? No. Sorry." Paul shook his head. "They also tell me you survived the Pox. No humans survive the Pox unless infected with the infertility virus. So, you're here to save yourself. You really can't go back."

His words stung almost as much as if he had hit her.

Even she did not want to admit her original motives were far from pure. Jasmine looked at the fading red dots on her arms and wished she had a long sleeve shirt. "I told them as much. Is that why they didn't turn me back."

"You were the first woman who ever came to a village, and you had no gun. There was a fierce debate about what to do with you. That ship in orbit terrifies them. They've come up with a plan to give you answers to all your questions. But only if you're patient and careful to not share what you've learned until given permission. Above all, you must protect them from harm. They want you to go to Gehnica to attend the celebration to the Mother God."

Jasmine's heart skipped a beat. She wasn't sure the Kawokee knew what she wanted, but the mention of a Mother God had the sound of a possible fertility rite. "When do we start?"

"As soon as you tell your friend you'll be out of touch for a while." Paul got up from his pillow and crossed the room. He returned with the comm-vid and set it on the table in front of Jasmine.

She asked, "How long will it take?"

"About a year."

"A year?" Jasmine did not want to wait that long, but what was a year compared to a lifetime?

"And I want to warn you, you might not like what you learn."

In a way, she was glad he didn't know how desperate she was. How could he? Jasmine hesitated to turn the comm-link on. "I should get Miwi."

Paul smiled. "No need. KapFawsha has authorized me to watch over you. You can talk now."

Jasmine turned on the comm-vid and made the call. Arluza's head and shoulders materialized in front of the screen. "Thank goodness. I was so worried. You look great. Though you do look like you're having a really bad hair day."

She quickly used her fingers to smooth down the mess. "I have to make this short. The Kawokee trust me enough to visit other villages, and I've got a new guide who is fluent in their language. The bad news is they won't let me contact you for a year. This is Paul, my guide."

Paul cleared his throat. "Let me clarify. We will be traveling and will not be allowed to take the comm-vid. But we should be able to send messages from time to time."

His words calmed Jasmine's nerves. She did not like the idea of being out of contact for so long.

"So, you're Alooza. Fawsha speaks highly of you."

"Actually, it's pronounced Arluza. Nice to meet you."

As Arluza and Paul chatted, Jasmine felt dizzy and put her head down on the table. At one point, she heard Paul tell Arluza. "I think Jasmine needs rest. We'll contact you when we get back." Jasmine raised her head to see Paul put his finger on the disconnect button and look to her for permission.

Jasmine nodded, and he shut it off. The next thing she knew, Paul picked her up, walked back over to her sleeping pillow, and laid her down on it.

"It's going to take a few days to get back to normal. We can delay while you recover."

She tried to push herself upright but was too dizzy to sit up. "No. No delays."

"Stop being ornery. Lay down and rest. You won't do anyone any good if you push yourself too hard too fast. You need to eat." He turned to leave. "I'll be right back with some food."

Jasmine told herself that she would only close her eyes for a minute. When she opened her eyes not only was she feeling better, but Paul was back. He was reading a scroll at the table. A cup along with a pitcher of water and a small basket of food sat on the floor next to her. Jasmine tried pushing herself up and winced. Her muscles were still sore even after a second nap.

Her movements must have alerted him because he was at her side rubbing her shoulders within seconds. "You need water, food, and rest. Your limbs are still stiff and will need to be worked to get the kinks out."

His hands moved up and down her arms and along her back. The urge to fall face down on the pillow and let him massage her entire body was great, but her thirst had her reaching for the pitcher of water. She drank half the container as he massaged her legs.

"Thirsty?" he asked. The smile that teased the corners of his lips told her he was trying not to laugh.

Jasmine felt her ears burn with embarrassment.

He took the pitcher from her hands and replaced it with a small cooked potato. "Eat, but not too fast."

A covered bowl sat inside the basket. Paul undid the lid and stirred the contents. With the bowl in one hand, he held a spoonful of soup out in front of her. The soup smelled wonderful, but his actions had a feeling of intimacy which disturbed Jasmine. Her immediate response was to ask questions.

"How did you learn to speak their language?"

Paul dropped the spoon in the bowl and set the soup on the floor in front of her. His expression darkened as he looked away. "My biological mother was the judge for the settlement. She was always too busy to be a real mother, so I was raised by a Kawokee nursemaid. Her name was Abaca, and she was a true mother. I learned her language and thought of her son as my brother."

Paul scratched at the back of his hand, and his gaze drifted toward the floor. "When I was a teenager, my father got the Pox. My mother blamed Abaca. The day he died, she killed Abaca right in front of us. She would have killed Antsy too if I hadn't stopped her. We fled the settlement, and the local tribes took us in. The first time I went back to the settlement was about two years ago. Don't ask me what happened to my biological mother. I don't know if she died or left the planet, but the town's been deserted for years." He folded his hands and looked up. "But I like the Kawokee, and they don't care that I don't have any fur. I've forgotten how to be human."

Jasmine picked up the bowl of soup to avoid another awkward moment. "So, you've lived among the Kawokee all this time? Isn't it lonely for you?"

"Not really." Paul's smile looked forced. "Sometimes. But enough about me." He shook his head as if to chase away the clouds of a bad memory. "I'm sorry, it's difficult to talk about."

Paul looked straight at Jasmine. "Everyone worried you'd die and they'd be blamed. Even the Kawokee who still aren't sure of you were glad you survived." He paused a moment before saying, "KapFawsha said your ship came to find a cure. Do they know you're infected?"

Jasmine choked on the spoonful of soup she had in her mouth and set the bowl aside. The question had her guard up. It took her a minute to remind herself that her closely guarded secret had little power over her on this world. "Arluza is the only one who knows. He's the one who tested me when I first suspected. I won't be able to leave this world without a cure."

"And you think the cure is in the culture, not the biology?"

"It must be." Her instinct to fight and argue her reasoning was instantaneous. With back straight and muscles tensed, Jasmine prepared to give him her dissertation, but stopped just shy of giving him a lecture. Instead she asked, "Will there be pregnant females or children at Gehnica?"

"There will be some young. No children, as you think of them. Kawokee mature faster than humans. They reach their full height at about seven years old. By then, they have a standard education. You may see some pregnant females." He stood and reached out a hand. "Are you up for a short walk?"

Jasmine took his hand and pulled herself up. "I think

so."

He picked up the empty food basket. "I'm sorry, but it's my job to learn about what's happening and report back to the Kawokee. They have some questions."

"I understand. Ask anything you like. I have nothing to hide. Everyone already knows my darkest secret." She felt strong and refreshed as they left the burrow.

He turned toward the kitchen burrow. "You're a scientist from the ship. Why are you the only one who came down?"

Miwi had asked that question several times. "The others are trying to engineer a cure in the safety of their labs by experimenting with samples. Unfortunately, they must relearn a technology abandoned hundreds of years ago. Advances in bioelectronics simplified medicine until this virus hit. It's more complex than anything we've seen. I think the Kawokee already have a way to fight the virus, so I've come here to find it. It's not a cure like the other scientists are looking for, but something in their lifestyle allows the Kawokee to give birth."

"So, you think it is not in their biology?" He ducked into the quiet kitchen burrow, and she followed.

Jasmine bit her lip, fighting her first instinct to argue. He was not a scientist scoffing at her ideas. "It must be. Hundreds of Kawokee left this planet before the virus was known. All had the virus. If the Kawokee population has even a twenty-five percent infection rate, they would have died out by now without a cure."

He nodded and set the basket on the floor near the wash basins. "Have you ever ridden a horse?"

She followed him out of the burrow toward the corral. "No. Is it difficult?" Jasmine knew what Paul called a horse was not the same as the Old-Earth animals. What passed for a horse on the Kawokee world looked more like a long-haired llama.

"Not if you're used to them. Those who aren't complain about sore leg muscles. Don't worry. You can ride in a cart most of the time. There may be times when you have to ride. It would be better to show you now rather than teach you while we're on the trail. Ready?"

"Ready."

Carts lined the split rail fence keeping the horses penned. Most of the carts were empty, but one was filled with various human-made objects. "What is this for?" she asked.

Paul lifted a saddle off the fence and onto his shoulder. "Some settlements trade scrap metal with Kawokee villages in return for food and medicine. Kawokee do some mining, but prefer to recycle various metals from towns friendly toward them or scavenge from abandoned towns. I was on my way in from a circuit. I'll be making another trade run on our way to the villages after Gehnica."

Before Jasmine could ask another question, Paul ducked into the pen and was immediately engulfed by a swarm of hairy horses searching him for food. The creatures were not very big. The shoulders of the beasts only came up to Paul's chest. They reminded Jasmine of a flock of birds. Paul singled out a horse and directed it to the edge of the pen. He patted its side before putting the saddle on its back. "Most of these animals are used for pulling carts but they're all saddle trained."

Jasmine watched in fascination as he explained how to put the saddle on, how to mount, and how to steer. It looked easy enough. She put her foot in the stirrup and tried pulling herself up. Her attempt almost ended with her on the ground when the animal moved sideways. Paul let go of the animal and caught her as she stumbled.

Pressed against the hard muscle of his wiry frame, Jasmine temporarily forgot which animal she was supposed to be mounting.

"Sorry about that. I should have warned you. They can be skittish if you mount too fast or too slow." The next thing Jasmine knew, Paul set her down. "Throw your chest on its back and swing your leg over in one smooth motion. Don't kick them in the side while doing it."

When Jasmine swung her leg over the horse's back she realized it was not as easy as it looked. The animal kept shifting its position. Once up, the big surprise was how hot the animal was. The thought of having an infrared radiator between her legs on a warm day did not appeal to her. Jasmine kicked her heels into the side of the animal and made it walk forward. The long, soft, oily hair slid through her clutching fingers. Combined with the animal's side-to-side movement and slow gait, she thought she would slide off the beast at any moment. Jasmine attempted to counterbalance the beast's movements and experimented steering with her legs.

"Very good. Ready for a real ride?"

Paul's words triggered a moment of panic within Jasmine. Her legs tensed causing her mount to toss its head and back up.

"Relax," said Paul. "They can sense your fear. If a horse thinks it can scare its rider off its back, or take advantage in any way, it will."

Paul led her out of the pen along with another horse. He let her plod along in circles as he saddled and mounted the second beast. "Ready?"

"I think so." She steered her horse to follow his and watched as Paul kicked his legs to get it to speed up and lean back to slow down. They went up and down a small hill at various speeds. Each of the horses' gaits required a different set of muscles.

Jasmine was happy when Paul turned back to the pen. She was uncertain how much more her body could take of the animal's jarring movements. "How long did you say you ride in a day?"

"Don't worry. You'll do fine."

At first, Jasmine had trouble swinging her leg over the horse's back, but slid the rest of the way down. Standing was another issue. When her feet hit the ground, her legs refused to hold her. She grasped the edges of the saddle in a panic as visions of being trampled by the beast's hooves raced through her mind.

"I've got you."

She felt her body slam back into Paul's chest as he kept her from falling.

"I'm sorry. I didn't think of how hard your first time would be."

Jasmine bit her lip to keep from laughing in hysteria. His turn of phrase combined with where his hands ended up did not help the rag-doll feeling of her lower half. Her body felt far too warm, and the effort to bring her knees together had her wondering if she would forever remain bowlegged.

"Do you want to use the fence to steady yourself, or would you rather sit down?"

Jasmine could not force the words passed her lips. With one hand, she reached out toward the closest post, thankful that Paul repositioned his hands, but did not let go as he guided her toward the pen.

Once she felt the rough wooden post beneath her fingers, she gasped, "I'm okay."

"Are you sure?"

"Yes."

"I'm going to take care of the horses. Keep moving your legs so your muscles don't stiffen. If you want to, I'll take you back to the den."

"I'll be fine."

With the removal of Paul's hands from her body, Jasmine let out the breath she did not realize she was holding. She watched as he unsaddled the horses, checked their heads and hooves, and guided them back into the pen.

She closed her eyes and chided herself for acting like a teenage fool. The aroma of the evening meal drifted on the breeze making her salivate.

"How are you feeling?"

"Fine." Jasmine's eyes flew open. Her voice was too high pitch with the realization of how close he was to her. She brushed a lock of hair from her face and spotted the remnants of the burning red bumps that peppered her skin. Unlike the marks, the memory of the burning pain was already fading. "I'm just being an idiot," she said.

"How so?"

She shook her head and refused to answer.

"I'd like you to meet my brother, Antsy."

"Antsy?" Jasmine remembered the name from earlier and gave Paul a questioning glance.

He snorted. "No. It does not mean the same, Cow."

"Sorry, but I had to ask."

Paul smiled in answer.

Jasmine liked his easy-going manner. He had a job to do. The Kawokee still had their doubts about her, she was certain, and Paul was the one they chose to ask the hard questions. A good choice really. He was thoughtful and kind, not to mention easy on the eyes.

He grabbed her hand and placed it on his bicep. "Lean on me. If you need me to carry you, I will."

"Thanks." Jasmine avoided eye contact and told herself he was just being nice. He led her into a den she had never been in before. It was twice the size of the one she slept in. This time of day, there was no one inside but for a single male lying atop a mound of sleeping pillows. His suggestive pose had Jasmine wondering if sleep was the real reason he was there.

"Sorry." Paul took a small pillow and attempted to place it over the male's groin.

"No. Don't." Jasmine grabbed the pillow in Paul's hand. "I'm an anthropologist. The last thing I want is for anyone to change because I'm around. I want to study the Kawokee just as they are."

He blinked and cocked his head. An odd expression crossed his face before disappearing. "Does that include me? Most times I have to watch myself around humans to avoid offending them. I haven't offended you yet; have I?"

"Yes, that includes you. And no, you haven't offended me." She tried to sound confident, but was a little nervous as he pulled the pillow from her grasp.

The quick flash of mischievousness was the only warning she had before he slapped it down on the sleeping male's groin. Jasmine jumped back in shock and worried how hurt the Kawokee was.

The male thrashed sending pillows flying. He bared his teeth, and his ears flattened as he looked up from his position on the floor. Even in the dim light, Jasmine could see the whites of his eyes showing. She didn't understand the words he spoke, but the loud, guttural tone needed no translation. When he saw her, his tone softened, and an ear rotated forward.

"Jasmine, this is my brother Antsy." Paul's voice trailed off when he pointed at her.

Jasmine patted Paul's arm and shook her head. "It's okay, Cow is fine." She turned to Antsy and said, "Hello, Antsy. I'm Cow."

After a fair amount of ear movement Antsy shook her hand. "Pleased to meet you, Cow."

"He knows a few phrases," said Paul. "But his Standard is limited to what he needs for trading with humans."

Antsy turned his head, rotated his ears forward, and flared his nostrils. "Supper?"

Jasmine saw the same type of ring in Antsy's ear as Paul's. "Those rings in your ears; are they decorative?"

Antsy leaped to his feet and made for the door.

Paul stomach growled, and he covered it with his hand. "They are a sign of position. The more rings, they higher the responsibility. Some signify a specialty. Come. Let's eat." He pulled her in the direction of the entrance.

Not wanting Paul to think she needed to be carried to the kitchen den, Jasmine did her best to stay upright.

Den, burrow, neither was an accurate name for the semi above ground structure. While grass grew on its roof like any other den, large wooden panels that could be raised or lowered, depending on the weather, lined its perimeter. Inside, long narrow tables stretched from one end of the room to the other, broken only by the pillars that supported the roof. In the center of the den was the actual kitchen where the meals were prepared. Multiple chimenea shafts poked through the roof for ventilation.

Unlike midday meals brought to you where you worked, or morning meals where you picked up what you wished from the kitchen den and went on your way, evening meals were a time of fellowship and could last several hours.

Along the short walk to the kitchen, she recalled Fawsha's earrings and her first official introduction to him. Once Jasmine and Paul entered the den, she said. "Fawsha called you LutPaul."

"Lut is a prefix that goes with this ring." Paul touched the ring in his ear. He spotted a table and guided Jasmine toward it.

There were Kawokee seated on pillows or mats in groups large and small all around the kitchen den. The kitchen staff brought food boxes to each table allowing everyone to pass them along the line.

Jasmine sat down on a mat. "Does Fawsha have a prefix?"

"Kap. KapFawsha is how others who hold a position would refer to him."

"He introduced himself as Fawsha."

Paul sat next to Jasmine, but Antsy grabbed three meal boxes and sat across from them. "You have no responsibility to him. It would be odd for you to call him KapFawsha. He outranks me, so he calls me LutPaul and my brother LutAntsy. It's complicated."

With a new understanding, Jasmine looked around the kitchen den. A few others joined their group and Antsy scurried to the end of the table to gather more boxes.

"I see the females also have rings."

"Yes." Paul looked puzzled for a moment before a dawning of understanding reached his eyes. "Oh, that's right. Humans sometimes separate jobs by gender. Kawokee never do."

Jasmine was learning more in a few minutes than she had in a week. How many other things had she missed, not having a proper translator? Several incidents ran through her mind until she settled on one that puzzled her most. "So, I saw something in my first days here I still don't understand. A male and a female stood in the center of the village, and everyone gathered around. There was a long argument. Then the male tore a ring from his ear and gave it to the female. There was a lot of blood, but the male didn't try to stop the flow, and neither did anyone else. Everyone looked away."

Paul nodded. "It could have been many things, but it sounds like the male did something he shouldn't have. When it was decided he was in the wrong, he tore the ring from his ear as a sign of sorrow. He gave it to the other whom he had wronged. It will take a long time for that ear to heal. The female will decide when or if to give him the ring back and restore him. I'm guessing it was a pretty serious offense. Greed or laziness would be my guess."

"Those don't sound like serious crimes to me."

"Violence, Anger, Lying, these things hurt one individual. It's enough to give the ring to the one harmed. The offender is usually forgiven in a day or two. Crimes that hurt the entire village are more serious."

"Do they have a death penalty?"

"They do. But it's very rare. The Kawokee are more likely to cast one out rather than kill them. If you ever see a Kawokee missing half his ear lengthwise, he's probably an outcast. I'd suggest you avoid them. Everyone else will."

Jasmine pulled a box from the center of the table closer to her. The black lacquered box was colored with brilliant red and gold birds. The artwork that went into the outer surface of the dinner boxes still intrigued her. Before she could open the box with its familiar concoction of spiced vegetables, Paul switched it with a yellow lacquered box with red and gold flowers.

"You took the wrong box."

Her first reaction was to remind him she did not want special treatment. Then she realized it was the first time she saw black or yellow meal boxes. Previous box colors varied from deep purple to pale lavender. Jasmine glanced around the large room, but every meal box was either black or yellow. Another thing she noticed was that males took the black boxes while females took the yellows.

Curious of the difference she opened the lid of the yellow box Paul pushed in front of her. Inside she saw a piece of thinly sliced raw meat. "That's odd. I was beginning to think they were vegetarians."

"The red meat is for the females. The festival is approaching. You'll see more meat in the diet for the next few days. Organ meats are considered a delicacy." Paul pointed at her box. "If you prefer your meat cooked, you can take it over to one of the grills."

"Grills?"

"There are small heated iron grills set up in each corner of the room." Paul pointed out the one nearest to them. Two females were at the small stand with a black cone on top. One female laid the strips of meat on the surface of the cone then used a two pronged metal fork to put them back in her box. The other seared both sides of hers before removing them.

"Not everyone likes their meat raw. I've known a couple of females to char their meat into shoe leather."

Jasmine looked at her own box. The urge to go over to the grills and do just that was great. "Why do the females get meat? Did you get any?"

"No. Everyone eats more meat in the winter. Females get meat as the fertility festival approaches. It has something to do with their religion. It's the most important event in Kawokee culture." Paul devoured his vegetables and roots, but savored the bread. "This is one area where I am not an expert. Those here," he waved his hands around at all the Kawokee in the room, "grew up in the… villages and learned the customs. My brother and I came too late for the formal religious training."

"Is there a way I can find out more?"

"Of course. It's all written down. I don't think they have any sacred texts here, but they will at Gehnica. Antsy could translate."

"Me? Why not you?" Antsy's fur poofed out for a second. "I've got better things to do."

Before an argument could get underway, Jasmine asked Paul, "Can you read them?"

The brothers stared at each other in silence until Paul relented. "That I can do. I don't know if I'll understand it. Antsy would be the better teacher, but I'll be happy to translate for you. The priestesses would be quite pleased to tell you about their religion."

"Really?" Jasmine sat up straight at the news. She could not keep from smiling in excitement. "You don't know how important this is. I won't be able to remember it all. I'll need my equipment to record everything."

Antsy gave a low growl while Paul's face darkened. "No. I'm sorry. We're taking a big risk as it is."

Confusion mixed with her disappointment and frustration. Jasmine tried keeping her voice steady, but she still felt she sounded like a spoiled whining child. "It's all wasted if I can't send the information back. What are you afraid of?"

Antsy said something in Kawokee that she could not quite catch, but whatever it was Paul glared at him. He scratched the fur underneath his chin and studied Jasmine before answering. "Of you. Humans that is. Our numbers are dropping. Maybe not as fast as yours, but there used to be far more villages. Since humans came, our numbers are halved."

She remembered Paul telling her the same thing. Had so many of them turned their backs on their own kind to throw themselves at the feet of humans, or had humans taken a more direct approach on Kawokee?

"I wouldn't hurt anyone."

The fur on his body puffed again as Antsy's eyes bore into hers. His voice cut the air, silencing all conversation in the room. "If you tell the ship where the mothers and infants are, soldiers will kill them looking for your cure."

Jasmine noticed every head within the kitchen den turned toward her. Uncertainty crept up her spine like a cold, deadly spider. She opened her mouth then closed it. As much as she wanted to protest, Jasmine knew there were humans who did not value Kawokee lives.

"Do you think I'm wrong?" Paul put his hand over hers and looked around the room. His words had a certainty to them that was frightening. "Tomorrow. I'll show you."

Antsy and Paul shouted at each other in Kawokee. Jasmine couldn't understand one word. Her name was not spoken, and they did not look at her, but she was certain they were angry with her. It was so un-Kawokee to talk in front of someone as if they weren't there. The longer it went on, the more incensed she became. Before she could demand they talk to her, they both stood, took their empty meal boxes and walked away in different directions.

Jasmine felt confused and hurt. Did they want an apology? What had she said? The others watched her in silence until she left with her meal box untouched.

CHAPTER 10

Arluza breathed a little easier knowing Jasmine survived the Pox and appeared tired but healthy. The soldier's warning scared him, but nothing more happened after the man left.

There were the endless test samples forever ending with the same results. He found it hard to concentrate on Dr. Campion's words. Arluza compiled the data the man talked about. He had to remind himself that everyone was working together toward a common goal; to find a cure for the virus. It still grated on Arluza's nerves to hear Campion talk as if he had gathered the data all by himself.

"We have covered ten percent of the villages on both continents. All samples carry the virus. Using human standards, four percent of the samples were adolescent. Some females showed hormones indicating they were lactating. This proves there is a way to combat this disease. It's time to move on to the next phase of the project."

Arluza looked up in surprise, his mind attentive. There was no such data. His first thought was that Campion misread the report he sent, but Arluza could not think of how that could be possible.

"Since the virus isn't found in the haploid cells, we

need to know when it's passed to the fetus and how to prevent it from causing fatal changes to cell differentiation. This has already been tried, studying infected women, but the number of carriers donating their eggs was very small. Even with the advances, there is some doubt that artificial wombs mirror natural processes."

Arluza had heard this same speech word for word on a news feed. The whole human testing mess created a public outcry on Earth. Why Campion was saying what everyone already knew was beyond him.

"The cost of growing human fetuses and the limited supply of natural ones makes this impossible on Earth. We've decided to try a different course, and we will begin to gather Kawokee subjects, use artificial insemination, and harvest the fetuses."

The reason for the diatribe was clear, and it chilled Arluza to the bone. He waited for Campion to ask for questions, but that invitation never came. He called to Dr. Campion as the man turned to go. "Where are you going to find Kawokee volunteers?" Arluza learned his lesson last time and made sure he was in the front row. He could hear the shuffle of many feet behind him and hoped others would also ask questions.

Campion rolled his eyes and turned off his mic. "The Kawokee prostitutes should serve the purpose. We're not going to harm them."

"You're going to force them into pregnancy and kill their babies. Do you think they'll be happy about it?"

"As a scientist, you should know better than to attribute human values and feelings to an alien species."

"And you are assuming no values or feelings at all." Arluza could not comprehend the callousness of the man before him. Campion always came off to him as an insufferable prat, but what he was encouraging everyone to do was beneath any respectable scientist. Not to mention illegal on the hundred plus inhabited worlds. "When Earth finds out about this, they'll fry you."

Campion jumped off the stage and was inches from Arluza's face. "I will be a hero with a cure. You clearly do not see the gravity of this situation."

Arluza's blood pounded in his ears. He shoved the man back. "Nothing can justify what you're doing. If our species would stoop this low to survive, then it deserves to die. Better we die with dignity."

Campion looked around the room. "That was assault. I will see you ruined for that."

"Then I might as well get my money's worth." Arluza swung his fist, but Campion caught his arm and pinned it to his side. Campion's fist drove into Arluza's abdomen, dropping him to his knees. Arluza's head almost hit the floor as he curled up in a fetal position.

"Insufferable little twit."

Arluza could not draw a breath, but with the air he had, he managed to glare up at Campion and say, "You falsified data. I can prove it."

"Good luck." Campion stepped back up onto the stage. His shoes clicked on the hard surface. The noise stopped as the sound of a door rolled closed behind him. The room was quiet.

Someone close by said, "That was foolish. Take a slow, deep breath."

It hurt to breathe in. He blew out a long breath and took in another. This time it was easier.

"You're in a lot of trouble."

At first, Arluza did not recognize the face he was looking at. The man was out of uniform. The scar on the man's face was the giveaway. "Hintz." Arluza realized his mistake and hurried to make an explanation. "That's what the Kawokee call you. Are you here to make threats?"

"Threats? No, doctor. I made no threats. I was warning you before, but you still walked into a pile of crap. The name is Macalister." The man helped Arluza to his feet and steadied him into a chair. He kept his voice low as he talked. "We have to move fast. You said you have proof.

Give it to me fast. In ten minutes, your office is going to be stripped bare. Can you stand?"

The pain receded, and Arluza nodded.

Macalister pulled him up and shoved him toward the door. "Hurry, doc."

Arluza could barely keep his feet under him as Macalister dogged his heels. Once in the lab, Macalister looked around, grabbed the comm-vid, and ran to the door. "Start making a backup."

The loss of the comm-vid worried Arluza. He hoped Macalister was on his side. If what the man said was true, he did not have time to think, and did as he was told. The soldier returned in seconds.

"Where is my comm-vid?"

"Safe. Where's the data?"

"Here." Arluza hesitated before handing him the chip.

"Now, make another. Just keep copying it over and over until someone arrives. I don't think you'll have to wait long."

With hands shaking, Arluza searched the drawer for another chip and heard the door close. Macalister was gone. Arluza didn't understand what was happening, but he couldn't see how another copy could hurt anything. He put the chip into the hub and was in the middle of another backup when the door burst open.

"Hands on your head."

Stunned, Arluza watched as the soldiers poured into his lab with their guns drawn.

"You are under arrest for assault. Come with us."

Before Arluza could put up his hands, they were twisted behind his back and handcuffed. The soldiers marched him through the ship past shocked and worried coworkers who scurried out of the way. The guards shoved him into one of the smaller conference rooms, but did not follow. Arluza heard the door lock behind him.

His mind raced. What could they do to him? He never actually hit Campion. And he could prove the falsified data charge, or at least make a good case for it. All the scenarios he could imagine played out in his mind, and he grew more afraid with each minute. His arms ached after an hour, and he needed to go to the bathroom. As the second hour closed in, he thought they were trying to scare him into silence. Frankly, it was working.

The door unlocked, and two soldiers entered. One unlocked the handcuffs. "Come with us."

"I have to pee." Arluza rubbed his wrists as he spoke.

They hauled him into the closest bathroom and stood while he relieved himself. Giving him no time to wash his hands, they dragged him down the hall and shoved him into another larger conference room. Campion sat with his feet up on the table and cup in hand. A pitcher of water surrounded by cups was in the center of the table.

"I might excuse the assault charge, but I think we need to have a long talk about who is running this project. I've been given charge of this mission from the top rung of the government. I take your charges very seriously. Why do you think there is falsified data?"

"For one thing." Arluza's voice was raspy. He reached for the pitcher.

Campion nodded and pushed it toward him. Arluza felt much better after the first sip and downed the entire cup before sitting down. "You said some Kawokee were lactating. There is nothing in the data I collected to indicate that."

"I see. And you think you have all the data?"

"Were there other scientists analyzing blood?" Arluza hoped he did not sound sarcastic, but neither did he wish to sound frightened or uncertain. "I thought I was the only one."

"Hmm. I see." Campion's eyes narrowed, and a hint of a smile touched his lips. "Did you check with any others? No. Of course not. Is that all you've got?"

Uncertainty scraped at the edges of Arluza's mind, but his scientific training had him rushing back to the data, or lack thereof. "In your first speech, you said the Kawokee population was stable. How could you know without knowing their lifespan? Where are the records from sixty years ago? I've not been able to find any detailed studies of how many villages there were or their size."

"Then you didn't do your research." Campion waved his hand in a dismissive pattern. "That's not my problem. Anything else?"

"Yes." Arluza had never been accused of not doing his research. If anything, he spent too much time at it. Anger replaced his fear freeing him to point out the careless mistakes Campion had already made. "Who decided on taking blood samples? You said that was suggested. By whom? It was a dangerous and careless move not to mention the inherent flaws in that sort of data collection. You don't send untrained personnel to gather critical information. That always results in crap data." Arluza had other things on his tongue but Campion's chuckling broke his concentration.

"Guard." The door opened. "Is his lab cleaned out?"

"Yes, sir."

"Throw him out."

The soldier hauled Arluza out of his seat. Once outside the room, the soldier released him. Arluza trembled. What was Campion going to do to his career? He felt sick when he opened the door to his lab and found everything gone. What happened to his equipment? One item remained; a floor cleaner. It belonged in the closet down the hall. After the soldiers left, he walked back out into the corridor. Arluza listened to the soldiers receding footsteps. When no one else appeared, he crossed the hall and opened the closet to find his comm-vid.

CHAPTER 11

On the vid-feed, Macalister watched the pudgy little scientist enter the room with Campion. On an emotional level, Macalister wanted to cheer the man on for taking a poke at Campion. The logical part of his brain wanted to scream and tell him to stop giving away information.

There was nothing Macalister could do as the scientist raised the cup to his lips, but in a life full of hard choices, there was always a cost. In this case, the scientist, Arluza. Not that he was the only one. Without this recording, the logs showing Campion taking viral samples was circumstantial.

No sooner was the scientist hauled from the room, then Campion took surgical gloves and a plastic bag out of his pocket. He slipped the cups surrounding the pitcher, including the one Arluza drank from, into the bag and sealed it.

Macalister had to switch surveillance feeds several times as Campion walked the hallway to the nearest empty lab, put the bag in the biohazard vault, and vaporized the evidence.

Four other scientists were now infected. In each case, Campion did it out of petty motives. Macalister hoped these recordings would be used to bring Campion down this time instead of just blackmailing the man. He encrypted the recordings and sent them to his superiors; the nameless men who ruled worlds.

Macalister copied the unencrypted feeds onto a simple memory chip and put it in his pocket. He was tired of waiting for justice for men like Campion and himself, tired of hoping the end was worth the price. Perhaps he would not live to see it, but giving Arluza the chip would be enough for now.

CHAPTER 12

Jasmine was up with the sun after a fitful night. Her mind would not let her rest, being so close to a goldmine of information yet unable to carry anything out. She helped in the kitchen den, preparing for the morning meal. Usually it was fresh chopped vegetable salsas that filled the large bowls. Baskets of fresh breads and dried fruits sat at either end. Today, fresh berries filled brightly painted bowls. Biscuits dripping with a sweet golden sticky syrup replaced the fresh bread. Thin, crisped wafers were baked that morning. Small molded gray squares set atop each cracker with a single green leaf between them.

The thought of eating one of the gray squares made her want to gag. Jasmine had watched the preparation of the animal liver. The odor from the boiling pot made her queasy. Watching Miwi grind the thing up after she pulled all the pieces out of the pot was not so bad. Even with the additions of several herbs and spices, Jasmine could not imagine the gray lump tasting very good.

"Jasmine?" Paul's voice was soft, almost apologetic.

She looked at him framed by the morning sunlight that came in through the open panels of the den. "Good morning, Paul. Sorry I was upset last night."

"It's understandable. We did a lot of talking last night. Me, Fawsha, and Antsy. Would it help if you could take notes and pictures and not transmit them until later, after it's reviewed by one of us?"

She knew it would slow down her progress a hundred times, but it would work. "Yes. Of course." She held up her arm to show him her wrist computer. "My wrist-com would be all I need. It has a camera, but I promise not to use it until you tell me it's okay."

Paul nodded. "There are some things we can let you take pictures of. Under no circumstance will you be able to take pictures of the location of the city. So just check with me first if there is a question."

"Thank you. When do we leave?"

"We'll leave after the morning meal. Both Miwi and Fawsha can operate the comm-vid. So, if Arluza has any urgent messages, he can tell them. Or vice versa." Paul grabbed a few items off the table, turned, and walked out of the den.

Only then did Jasmine realize his shorts just covered his front. The image lingered in her mind for several seconds. She felt the heat in her cheeks and reminded herself that she told him not to change his customs for her, but it made her nervous. Growing up in a conservative household, Jasmine had never seen a man's bare chest unless it was at the pool or in a movie her parents would consider scandalous. College had been an eye opener and her marriage a complete disaster. The last thing she needed to do was make an utter fool of herself.

It would have been nice if Paul had stayed and talked longer. His sudden departure made her wonder if something was wrong.

Kawokee came and went from the den. Some sat at the low tables and talked while most wandered off to fulfill their duties. Jasmine watched over the table and filled cups with tea and plates with snacks. The gray lumps disappeared quickly.

"Have you eaten?" Miwi's soft voice startled Jasmine.

"I've tried the sticky rolls. What was that on top?"

"Honey and nuts. Ground very fine. I make it for special times like this. Did you like it?"

"They're delicious."

Miwi smiled and held up one of the gray lumps on crisp bread. "Did you try?"

"No, I…" Jasmine's voice trailed off. She did not want to insult Miwi. "I wasn't sure if I should take any. Paul said something about meats being a part of a religious ceremony."

"I am too old. You can have mine."

Jasmine was not sure what Miwi meant by being too old. She knew if Miwi gave up something the Kawokee considered a delicacy, she was being more than kind.

"Are you sure?" She took the lump from Miwi's hands.

"Yes."

With a silent prayer she could eat the thing without making a face Jasmine bit down on the crisp. The rich buttery taste was as unexpected as it was delicious. Her eyes went wide as she took another look at the remaining piece that still clung to the crisp.

"Is good. Yes?"

"Amazing." Jasmine stuffed the rest of the crisp into her mouth and wondered if there was any way she could abscond with another.

Miwi smiled and patted her arm. "It will do much good for you."

Most of the cleanup was already done and Jasmine had little else to do to get ready for the trip. Curious about what Paul was doing, she left the kitchen den and wandered over to the edge of the animal pens. Carts were being converted to wagons. The sides detached and reattached like benches covered with long, narrow pillows. The cloth covers became a waterproof sunshade over the top. Among the other supplies, each finished wagon had a basket of the soft fibers used to make pillows. If they were for something else, she couldn't guess.

Jasmine concealed herself behind a large tree and watched Antsy and Paul work. When they finished the last cart, they sat and ate. As if on cue, the Kawokee lined up near the wagons.

Jasmine jogged to the den to retrieve her backpack. She was tempted not to leave the comm-vid behind, but she knew doing so would bar her from every village.

When she neared the pen again, she noticed several familiar faces. Jasmine had no idea how old they really were, but she guessed the majority were younger than her. If her count was correct, the females outnumbered the males three to one. Most carts carried six people. Jasmine's cart held two others. It looked like the journey might be hard on her backside, but she thought the view where Paul rode ahead of her might make up for it. It was foolish to think he might be interested in her with her arms covered in fading Pox marks.

There was no fanfare or farewell as the caravan moved out of the village. Their horse needed no driver but followed Antsy's. Jasmine concentrated on the excited small talk of her companions. They happily taught her many new words about male anatomy and bodily functions. She couldn't bring herself to add to the conversation but was happy just to laugh with them. To her surprise, they found Paul almost as interesting as his brother. None of the male Kawokee had approached Jasmine. She wasn't sure if she should feel hurt or relieved. When she was propositioned by one of the town prostitutes it shocked her, but she found none of the loose morals in the villages she had read about in her studies.

When they made the first rest stop, the first cramp hit. Jasmine's period always came at the worst times with no rhyme or reason to its timing unless medically encouraged. She did not like being stuck on the road with a mess to deal with, even with using absorbent undergarments. One of her companions stood up and threw away the bloody fibers she was sitting on. Jasmine looked down at the basket of fibers in realization. The females in the caravan were influencing each other's cycle. The meat in the diet, the basket of fibers, they knew this would happen.

They were only on the road for a few days when they stopped at a tiny village just off the trail. Jasmine suspected there was only one den. She would not have known of its existence if not for the elder Kawokee that stood by the trail. His fur was pure white, and he leaned on an ornately carved cane. A chain connected the earrings he wore in both ears, and the shawl which draped around his thin shoulders held the same four colors as his beaded necklace. The elder welcomed the caravan and even tried to help with the horses.

When Paul unhooked the horse from Jasmine's cart, he said, "Ride with us. You should take pictures as well." To the others in the cart, he spoke Kawokee. Jasmine translated enough words to understand their meaning. They were not going far, and no one should worry.

Antsy and Paul led her off the trail through the pathless forest for about an hour. The horse radiated heat beneath her and sweat dripped down her neck. She did not want a repeat of the first time she rode a horse, but she was not about to complain. They came to a straight path lined with broken, long-dead trees. Here saplings and bushes grew, but no tall trees. They turned east for a few kilometers and came to a mountain of crushed stone. The remnant of a collapsed den was still visible at the base.

With a shaky hand, Jasmine took pictures as Paul confirmed what she thought happened here. "This was a Kawokee mining village. The machines came one morning, their giant wheels ran over one of the dens, killing everyone inside. They started digging while the Kawokee were still working in the mine. In minutes, the exits collapsed. They say the entire mountain crumbled within a day. Those in the mine were never seen again. The machines came and went day after day. You can still see their path that leads to a flat plain where nothing grows."

Jasmine took pictures of the flattened den and the shattered stone. "The machines are remotely piloted. Didn't anyone warn the Kawokee, or persuade them to leave?"

"I doubt anyone so much as asked the mining village about excavating anything. The last time any human bartered for mining rights the Kawokee refused. The humans dug anyway. But not before rounding up every priest they could find in Homebi and pushing them off a cliff."

"What?" Jasmine turned to Paul, her eyes wide. "They did what?"

"Homebi was a religious center high in the mountains. Unfortunately, those same mountains contain a lot of minerals including silver. The place was centuries old and said to be one of the first places Kawokee ever built. It was destroyed in a matter of hours. Humans value metal and coal more than Kawokee lives. How much more important is this cure?"

Paul's voice wasn't loud, but it held the hard edge of anger. He was doing his best to sound objective.

Not wanting to believe what she heard, Jasmine looked down at her wrist computer. There in tiny print underneath her most recent picture were his transcribed words. Her eyes focused on the word destroyed. The tightness in her chest made it difficult to breathe. If the Kawokee world were part of the union instead of out on the frontier she doubted the mining companies would have done something so bold.

"I've never heard of Homebi." Her words escaped her before her mind could stop them. It was far too easy to hide atrocities like this, when so few cared and little attempt was made. "I want to interview witnesses to what happened here. I'm sure I can find humans who would care and bring those responsible to justice."

"You might still find a few survivors scattered among

the villages who remember. The elder back at the den is the only one I know of."

By the size of the trees growing up around the edges of the rubble, it had been many years since the devastation. Only the Kawokee remembered. There was nothing she could say as the tears ran down her cheeks.

The argument over bringing her equipment came back to haunt her. If she found a cure in a plant or a mineral, humans would swarm the place and consume it all without a thought to the consequences for another species. She choked out her words. "I'm sorry. I didn't see the danger."

Antsy was already on the move. Paul led his mount at a slow pace. "You've already saved many lives by warning us of the soldiers."

She pushed her horse faster. Though whether to keep up with Antsy or to stop Paul from talking she did not know. Did she hurt humanity by helping the Kawokee? But the Kawokee also faced annihilation. How could she ask for their help if it meant their extinction? "Did you hide the children from the soldiers taking blood samples?"

"Yes. We've been hiding the children for decades, but you will see them. You understand now the trust they are placing in you?"

"I do now, and it terrifies me." She was torn. What if saving millions of human lives cost the lives of all the Kawokee? What would she choose?

"They have a plan for saving both races. You may not like the plan in the end, but it's the only way they can think of. If you become angry, please remember we only want the best for everyone."

This cryptic warning worried her more every time she heard it. "You've said that before. I still don't understand what you mean." She waited for a response, but he said nothing more. Even when they rejoined the caravan back at the village, he seemed to avoid her.

That evening they spent in the warm den where both food and drink were plentiful. Jasmine was surprised the elder knew Standard, and she asked him about the mining village.

"I remember." His ears lowered, and he bowed his head. "So much death. The Vaw was getting his revenge on our ancestors; and still is."

"The Vaw? Who or what is the Vaw?"

"There is an order to everything. The Vaw does not like order. It tricks us when it can. Blinds us today and removes the clouds from our eyes the next day."

"I don't understand."

The elder smiled, nodded, and patted Jasmine's hand.

The Father God told the people, "I will make you a great canoe and stock it with all you need to travel the rivers of the barren sky. As you travel, plant seeds to bring life to the barrens, so that your sisters may follow and harvest what grows. All the people will flourish if you follow my instructions."

The people bowed to the Father God and said, "We will do as you command. Your wishes will bring much joy to all.

The Father God made the great canoe and filled it with all the magic of the stars. The people who entered the canoe he called Kawokee. The Kawokee traveled the barren sky and wherever they found an island, they planted a seed. This went on for many, many years.

One day the Vaw said, "I'm jealous of the Kawokee. They travel the rivers and plant seeds for their sisters to harvest, and the seeds they plant grow strong and true. I will throw stones at their canoe and tear its bark."

So, the Vaw threw his stones and tore the bark of the canoe. The Kawokee scolded the Vaw for throwing stones and patched the holes the Vaw's stones made. They continued to travel and plant the seeds Father God commanded them to plant, but watched the banks for the Vaw and his trickster ways.

But the Vaw was not content to throw just stones. He tried to steal their seeds and replace them with pebbles. When that did not stop them from planting, he pulled the ears of the Kawokee, and pinched their sides. The Kawokee told the Vaw, "We will tell the Father God and let him reprimand you."

The *Vaw* did not wish for the Father God to know what he was doing, so he burned the message the Kawokee had written to the Father God. To keep the Kawokee from sending another, he tormented their young.

Mother God heard the cries of the Kawokee young and asked, "Why do you cry?"

The Kawokee answered, "Oh Great Mother, your son, the *Vaw*, insists on plaguing us. We've patched our canoe and soothed our bruises, but we cannot keep our young from crying. What shall we do, Great Mother?"

The Mother God's sorrow was great. She said, "I cannot keep my son from wronging you, but I can help you hide your young from the *Vaw* so he can't find and torment them. But if I hide them from the *Vaw*, they must not use the magic of the stars."

Sorrow filled the Kawokee hearts. "How are we to raise our young and not teach them the magic of the stars? If our sisters do not see them when they come for the harvest, they may mistake them for the mice of the fields and chase them from their burrows. But what choice do we have? We cannot keep the *Vaw* from making them cry."

So, the Kawokee came up with a plan. "We will write on bark and skin the knowledge of the ancient of our people so they will not lose all the magic. Our sisters will see the writing and gather our young."

"You are wise to do so," said the Mother God. "But the *Vaw* may try to burn your writing. What will you do if he succeeds?"

The Kawokee answered, "We will carve the words in stone on the highest mountain, and paint them on the wall of the lowest cave."

"The *Vaw* will try to pull down the mountain and flood the cave," said the Mother God.

"Then all is lost. Without the words our young will not flourish. When our sisters come for the harvest, they will find nothing but bones bleached by the sun." The Kawokee wept at the thought.

Disheartened by the Kawokee tears, the Mother God made a long, beaded necklace and wrapped it around the waists of the Kawokee young. "I give this to you as a protection against my son the *Vaw*. Keep its colors true always. If one bead is lost or a color *switched, the Vaw will find you and torment you with anger greater than the expanse of the heavens."*

The young bowed to the Mother God and said, "We will do as you say and keep the colors true."

The Mother God covered the Kawokee young with a blanket of the softest skin, and they ceased their crying.

The Vaw searched for the young but could not find them. Angry with the Kawokee, the Vaw tore a great hole in their canoe, making it sink into the barren river, drowning all who clung to its sides.

The Vaw searched again for the young of the Kawokee, but could only find what he thought were the mice of the fields. Sometimes he would torment the mice, but mostly he would let them run. The Vaw did not recognize them as Kawokee because they stayed hidden by the Mother Gods soft blanket and protected by her necklace. There they must stay until the time of the harvest.

The elder took the long, beaded necklace he wore from around his neck and placed it around Jasmine's. The thing was so long he had to loop it around her neck three times. As he did so, he said, "May the beads of the Mother God protect you from the Vaw and his ways. May your eyes see, your heart welcome, and your mind understand."

With the last strand placed over her head, the elder stared deep into Jasmine's eyes. "The harvest is here."

A chill crept up her spine and would not let go.

The elder leaned back against the pillows on which he sat, and his breathing became labored. "Awkae, build your bridge."

Jasmine frowned and was about to ask what he meant when she realized he was no longer breathing. "Elder?"

One of the nearby Kawokee came over to check the elder. They closed his eyelids and placed a pillow beneath his head. They said something in Kawokee Jasmine could not understand.

"Paul?" Jasmine stretched out her hand in his direction but did not take her eyes off the elder's corpse. "What is she saying?" At the first touch of his hand, she turned to Paul and repeated her question in a near hysterical tone.

"What is she saying?"

"The elder is dead, Jasmine. Calm down. He was old."

"What did she say? She said something after she closed his eyes."

Paul asked the Kawokee what she said, and he translated it for Jasmine. "The elder is dead. He will go back to the earth." Paul pulled her up from the pillow on which she sat. "They'll bury him in the morning."

"The last thing he said to me was, Awkae, build your bridge. What does it mean?"

"I don't know." Paul asked the Kawokee female. Jasmine caught a few words and phrases but waited for Paul to translate.

"The elder was one of the few priests who survived the massacre at Homebi. The only reason this village is even here is because he refused to leave. He was hoping to meet the Awkae before he died."

"Who is the Awkae?"

Paul shook his head. "I don't know enough of the religious text to tell you. And I don't think anyone here can tell you much. I can't say for sure, but like the Vaw, the Awkae must be a lesser god. I don't think I've ever heard of him."

"Who would know?"

He shrugged and guided her toward a sleeping pillow. "Someone should know in Gehnica. We can ask when we get there. Sleep now. We will leave in the morning."

The elder's body remained untouched on the pillows until the carts and horses were ready. Jasmine watched as four Kawokee carried the body from the den and placed it in a freshly dug grave close by. Everyone stood around the grave in silence as a layer of dirt was pushed over the body. A second Kawokee stepped up to the grave with seeds and placed them within the earth, and the last layer of dirt covered them.

Silence would have ruled the morning if not for the low murmur of chanting Kawokee and the click of beads as they worried the long necklaces they wore.

When the burial was complete, the villagers gathered their things and headed down the path from which Jasmine and the carts had come. Paul watched and nodded his approval as Jasmine attached the horse to the cart and climbed in. She couldn't be sure, but he seemed somber. Whether it was for the elder, or from what he had shown her, she did not know.

It felt good to be riding in the cart and not on the horse. Jasmine had been too worried about missing the funeral and took no time to clean up that morning. She smelled of dried sweat and horse.

"I stink," she said in Kawokee.

Her companions were more amused than offended. "Take off clothes, no stink."

The idea had a tremendous appeal. Jasmine had stopped wearing a bra weeks ago and couldn't imagine ever wearing one in this heat. It was not like she needed to wear one anyway, she was never that big. Her eyes watched Paul as her hands wavered at the buttons of her blouse then fell to her lap. Jasmine didn't have the words to explain her reluctance to her companions. They whispered to each other then stood and lifted her blouse over her head.

The feel of cool air across her skin overcame her embarrassment. Paul may not have cared, but her own upbringing scolded her. As she chatted with her companions, she tried to decide if she would put the blouse back on once they stopped for the night.

Jasmine's growing vocabulary enabled her to understand most sentences, but putting that together with the culture was still a challenge. She wished she could record her conversation with her companions so she could go over them later.

The dark brown female Jasmine came to know as Louy, stroked the white spot between her breasts. "I wish the ceremony was an hour and the sowing a month."

The light furred one called, Halan said, "You have only one ceremony. When you've had as many as I, one day of sowing is enough." She touched the thinning patch of fur on her upper arm. "I think this will be my last ceremony."

Halan looked up at the sky before turning her attention to Jasmine. "I say that every year. Then I go back the next." She rubbed her belly and smiled.

Based on their previous talk about males, Jasmine was sure sowing meant sex, but it was not like them to use euphemisms. Despite their open and sometimes frequent sexual encounters, she had not seen one get pregnant.

Jasmine arranged the words in her mind. "Will the sowing give you a baby?"

"I hope so." Louy nodded enthusiastically.

Jasmine was thrilled by the answer. If she understood, it would prove her theory and provide clues about a cure.

Halan removed the ball of fibers she sat on. There was only a hint of blood. "Yes. I think this will be my last. I've been given many children."

Jasmine tried to listen to the rest as she rehearsed each new word in her mind and made a note in her wrist-com with a temporary translation as pregnant. As soon as she could, Jasmine formulated her next question. "You've had a baby?"

"Yes," Halan said with a smile. Kawokee smiles looked like a snarl as their mouth muscles were not the same as humans. "I've had three females, and four males. I see them now and again."

Jasmine had so many questions and no way to record the conversation. By the time she understood what was said, another sentence needed translating. She could not even formulate a question fast enough.

Paul might be willing to explain. Since he was more Kawokee than human, he probably would not feel awkward talking about it. In reality, it was Jasmine's own reluctance that made the subject seem taboo. Anthropologists were not supposed to let personal sensitivities stand in the way of discovery.

"What was it like, the…" Jasmine racked her brain trying to remember the word they used for when they gave birth. "Nest?"

Louy closed her eyes. "It was a frightening and exhausting time, but I will do it again. You get used to it. New things are always frightening, and no matter how much it is explained to you, the first time is always the worst. But you forget the pain. Once you see their faces, nothing else matters."

Halan turned to Jasmine. "Have you ever had a child?"

"No." She struggled to remember the word for miscarriage.

When Louy tilted her head sideways and gazed at her, Jasmine gave up trying to remember. Her shoulders slumped, and she willed her eyes to cease tearing with little success. "Three times."

Her companions looked at each other, their ears twitched back and forth. Halan took Jasmine's hand and patted it. Louy sat at her feet and rested her head on Jasmine's knee.

Jasmine brushed away the tears she could not control. They could not understand the pain of a cheating husband, or the looks of friends who suspected she had the disease. Then again, she didn't need words. She put her hands on their heads and drew them close. "Thank you."

The cart slowed and stopped. Jasmine remembered her blouse and attempted to untangle herself from her friends.

Before she could do so, Paul stood beside the wagon. "There is a stream behind those trees. The horses need water and rest." He walked to the next wagon without a reaction. Feelings of insecurity scratched at the back of her mind. Most of the Pox marks had faded. Had it left blemishes on her face? She had no mirror in which to look at her reflection and wondered how bad her face was scarred. Arluza said nothing the last time she had talked with him.

Jasmine hesitated, debating on leaving the blouse in the wagon and joined her companions as they led the horse to the stream. In the end, she rinsed the shirt and hung it over the side of the wagon to dry.

The next day, when everyone piled back into the wagons, Jasmine practiced her question before speaking. "What happens at the ceremony?"

"The ceremony is boring." Louy threw back her head and let her tongue hang from the side of her mouth.

Halan huffed and waved off the theatrics of her younger companion. "The females go to a big house and listen to stories of the gods. At the end, we make a sacrifice to the Mother God and receive a blessing from the priestesses."

Jasmine shifted in her seat and thought about what that would entail. Some ancient human rituals were unthinkable to modern eyes. She was willing to do almost anything but wanted to be prepared. "What kind of sacrifice?"

Halan touched her shoulder where several small scars were visible through the thin fur. "A small cut. It is nothing."

The relief Jasmine felt at her words eased her tense muscles but lowered her spirits. None of this sounded like it would help with a pregnancy. "Is that all? Do you eat or drink anything?"

Halan cocked her head and sniffed the air. "No."

Jasmine had considered the cure might be administered as part of the courtship rituals or even given in the meals. "Is there special food you eat?"

"Yes. We eat more meat during the week of ceremony." There was an edge to Halan's voice as if she was trying to answer, but frustrated not seeing the point.

Jasmine did not want to irritate her companions and decided to wait and see for herself. She hoped she wasn't being too obvious pushing the conversation back to Louy's favorite subject. Though only slightly curious, she knew it would put them in a better mood. "Tell me about the courtship ritual."

Louy's body jerked as if she were waiting for this moment. "This will be my second time, but females find males by wandering the city and talking to them. You choose by giving a token. We can give as many tokens or as few as we like." She smiled and wiggled in delight.

"Just don't forget to give at least one of your tokens to someone outside the village," said Halan.

"I won't." Louy's ears shifted down, and she looked off into the woods.

The stern look Halan gave Louy was ignored, but Halan explained, "Too many fathers from one village can result in an unhealthy child."

Incest in humans and every other animal Jasmine could cause all sorts of problems, and she assumed it was the same for Kawokee. With so many things about the Kawokee she discovered already which debunked registered documents, she was not surprised they understand the concept of recessive genes.

Unable to construct her next question well enough to receive a coherent answer, Jasmine gave up and searched for a different subject.

She had not seen any unusual items with the wagons or her companions. "What are these tokens? Where do you get them?"

"You make them. It could be anything. A ring is good. It could be a piece of string." Halan reached into a bag and handed her three wooden rings, each had the same symbol carved into them.

"I don't think I will need many." She turned to the younger Louy. "If you're smart, you'll put the burrow number on your tokens so they can find you. Males have a very poor memory." Halan shrugged. "At least for me."

Jasmine was more interested than she expected. "Are there rules for the males?"

Louy's snout and ears lowered, and she crossed her arms. Halan smiled and answered. "Males should take no more than four."

CHAPTER 13

Arluza could not enter any hallway without an alarm going off and doors locking. He could only go to the common areas and his quarters. After his first trip to the cafeteria, he stayed away from the common areas. Everyone knew of his present status and treated him like a pariah. No matter how civilized or nonjudgmental scientists were supposed to be, they feared guilt by association. Arluza was a prisoner in his room with no one to talk to. Fear kept him from contacting Miwi. He was not even sure if the old Kawokee female would answer his call. Hiding the comm-vid underneath his bunk behind an extra pillow may not have been the safest place to put it, but neither was leaving the small black box in the janitor's closet. Social by nature, Arluza was willing to risk going to the surface if only for the change of scenery.

His door chimed, making his heart race. Excitement over talking to someone, anyone, mixed with the fear of further torment from Campion and his goons. "Enter."

When the soldier who spoke to him in the lab walked into the cabin, Arluza panicked. "Captain? What's wrong? Did something happen?"

He shook his head and frowned. "Just call me

Macalister. Soldiers aren't stupid, but we aren't scientists, which is why I've come to ask your help."

"Help?" Arluza could not fathom why any of the soldiers would need his or any other scientists help.

Macalister produced the memory chip. "You said this had proof the data is falsified. I need someone to check other reports for me. You may not be alone in your suspicions."

The sight of the small chip gave Arluza a glimmer of hope. "All my access is revoked. But even if it wasn't, a first-year student looking at the raw data would know something was amiss. The collection of samples by untrained personnel and lack of even the most minimal of documentation would send up warning flags for those who bothered to look. The problem is getting anyone to look closer. Campion has a name and a long shadow." Arluza shrugged. "You can see what happens when someone tries to question him."

"You've been reassigned," said Macalister and tucked the memory chip in his shirt pocket.

It took a moment for Macalister's words to register in Arluza's mind, along with everything else the man said.

"You have access to your old lab again. Let me know of anything you need. Right now, you only have read-only access to all the raw data files."

"I didn't think Campion would allow that."

The twitch of a smile crossed Macalister's lips. "He wouldn't if he were in charge of security. Will you help me?"

"Gladly."

Macalister handed Arluza another chip in a sealed sleeve. "This is an insurance policy for both of us. If something happens to me, read it. There is a file with your name on it. Otherwise, keep it hidden. You understand there is a risk in helping me."

"I'll hide it under my mattress." Arluza tucked the sealed chip in his pocket. "I've already had my reputation ruined and may go to jail. What more can Campion do?"

Macalister opened his mouth as if to say something, then shook his head. He handed Arluza a set of dog tags. "You could end up dead. This will give you access to the shuttles. I may need you to go to the surface from time to time."

Arluza took the tags and stared at them. The black matte surface absorbed the light. "If it will fry Campion, I'll do it."

"Good. Just to be clear, ending a political career is not my goal. Understand?"

"Understood." After placing the tags around his neck, Arluza made an attempt at a salute.

"Come with me down to the surface." Macalister headed for the door.

"Now?"

Macalister stopped and turned. "Do you have any pressing social commitments?"

The thought of getting off the ship sounded wonderful despite the threat of disease. "What do you need me on the ground for?" Arluza wrung his hands, but followed a bit confused. When they turned down a corridor away from the shuttle bays, he expected to hear the alarm, but nothing happened.

"It's difficult to explain." Macalister held the door open to a locker room. "I've got a uniform that should fit you."

"I'm not a soldier."

"You are now. For safety's sake, you'll address me as Captain, and I'll address you as Private."

"Yes sir." Arluza did his best to snap to attention and salute.

Macalister's eyes narrowed. "Don't try so hard. I'm not a general." He handed Arluza the clothes and opened a locker. "This one is yours."

Arluza put on the uniform and put his own away before closing the locker.

With a few minor adjustments, Macalister inspected

Arluza. "Make sure you have your shirt well wrinkled. Dirty will also be an improvement. Don't come here unless I'm with you. And whatever you do, don't go near the real soldiers in this uniform. I don't want them to spot you. There are twenty-four of us. Some have served together. If they see you, they'll know something's up. This getup is only to get you past the Civs."

"Civs?"

"Civilians. Regular people look at the uniform and not at the person. Do non-scientists question you when you wear your white coat? Or just when you don't wear it?" Macalister placed a hat on Arluza's head and pulled the bill down to his eyebrows. "Keep your head down."

Arluza glanced down at his soldier's disguise and thought about what the man said. No one ever questioned his integrity at the pharmaceutical company he used to work at, even with his mid-level status. Social parties were another story, but he had always chalked it up to ill-informed personnel. His mind was full of questions.

Macalister picked up two boxes from beside the locker. "Carry these, Private."

Arluza took the boxes. They were as light as a feather.

"When we get to the surface, you'll help me carry these into the facility."

"Yes sir." He followed Macalister with the boxes into the shuttle. The cockpit was small but the copilots chair was comfortable. Arluza did not dare touch the console in front of him and kept his interlaced fingers in his lap.

"Tell me what you know of the Godiva Trials." Macalister hit a few buttons, and the ship slipped out of the docking bay.

"It was a government research project to find a cure for the Kaw Virus. It shut down when the half a dozen doctors assigned to the project were accused of infecting women so they could use them as test subjects. The details were all a bit sketchy. But I didn't have time or the inclination to consider it at the time."

A low pitch shuddering filled the air, and Arluza grabbed the armrests of his chair. He did not like the turbulence caused by the uneven heating of the outer shell of the shuttle as it collided with the plasma of the planet's ionosphere.

Macalister's voice rose above the noise of reentry. "And how does Campion enter into that?"

It was a few minutes before the noise dropped below a deafening roar. Arluza let out the breath he was holding but kept a death grip on the padded armrests. "I remember seeing him on the news condemning... the doctors." Arluza remembered Campion's words in the meeting. They flared in his mind like fireworks on a dark night. "He condemned those doctors, yet he's starting the same thing over again."

"Campion designed the Godiva project, hired the researchers, and I'm sure he paid someone to alter data. He was never questioned or linked with the project."

The shuttle's vid-screen showed the landscape below rushing by, but Arluza was not paying attention. The puzzle pieces slammed into place like heavy stones. With it came the realization of why so many top-level scientists avoided primary slots and offered to take second and third year shifts on the current project. They would rather clean up Campion's mess than drown in the cesspool he would create. "He has some powerful friends."

Macalister unbuckled his seat before the ship finished decelerating. "In very high places."

Arluza waited until the ship was down firmly on the ground before he risked unbuckling his seatbelt. "How do you beat someone like that?"

"You don't want to know."

Arluza picked up one of the boxes and followed Macalister out of the shuttle. As they walked across the landing pad in the middle of a dilapidated town, Arluza gasped at the devastation. If someone told him a war wiped out the town instead of a virus, he would have believed them. They walked toward the only one that was clean and stood straight. On closer inspection, it appeared someone had pieced together several large shipping containers.

The first thing he noticed when they entered the building was the odor. Arluza recognized part of the smell as alcohol. The other odors might have been due to the filthy man who sat in a chair against a wall near another door. Next to him, a Kawokee female with patches of dried mud on her legs and matted hair on her arms fidgeted in a chair. Arluza was not sure what to make of the female. She reminded him of a junkie he once saw back home.

Arluza copied Macalister as he put down his box, stood, and waited.

"I'm hungwy," the Kawokee said in a child-like voice.

After many conversations with Miwi, it still took a moment before Arluza's brain corrected for her pronunciation, but this one seemed to accentuate the problem.

"You said I could have a dwink," Her voice was shrill.

The man curled his fist in the female's face, and she cringed back.

The door opened, and one of the scientists from the ship entered.

Arluza ducked his head as the doctor looked at him, but there was no recognition in his eyes. The childish thought of hiding behind Macalister had him shuffling his feet. Curiosity warred with the desire to hide, and Arluza peeked out from beneath his hat.

The scientist regarded the female before turning to the man. "That's five." He held out an energy cell to the man.

The man snatched the energy cell out of the scientist's hand and was at the door in less than a second. "Pleasure doing business with you. I'll bring more next week." Without a backward glance, he hurried out the door.

The scientist reached into his pocket, put on gloves,

and grabbed the female's arm.

She winced in pain and tried to pull away from his grip. "He said I could have food and dwinks."

The man pulled the female through the doorway. "Yes. Yes. This way." He looked back. "You two. The supply closet is back here."

They followed the scientist and the squirming Kawokee female down a short, narrow hallway into the next room. Macalister led the way to a storage room. Out of the scientist's line of sight, he pointed to a camera in the lab above the storeroom door. Once inside the storeroom he tossed the box onto the floor. Arluza followed suit. With a touch to his wrist-com, an image of the exam room floated above Macalister's hand and the word recording appeared below. The scientist put on a mask as the female stood beside an examining table.

She shuffled closer. "Why do you weaw that on your nose? I don't smell bad."

"Take off your clothes and put them in this bag." The scientist handed the female a biohazard bag.

When the Kawokee feigned a seductive smile at the scientist, Arluza's stomach churned. Her child like voice did not help his disgusted reaction. Not wanting to witness some twisted game he looked away as the female stripped off her clothes by an examining table. "You like?"

The scientist examined the female's eyes and tongue. "Up on the table."

She leapt up onto the table, but drew back from the gloved hand holding a swab. "You said I could have a dwink."

"Fine." The scientist left the room.

The Kawokee jumped from the table, picked up the biohazard bag, and ran for the door. She tried the handle a few times, but it refused to budge. Her head turned as if hearing a sound, and she hurried back to the exam table, throwing the bag underneath. The man returned and handed her a cup. The female downed it as one would expect an alcoholic to drink a shot of whisky. She coughed and gagged. "This is water."

"There is no alcohol here."

She let out a high-pitched whine. "Food?"

"Yes. After the tests." He put the swab near the female's bottom.

She drew back her feet and shuffled to the far end of the table. "No. Now."

The scientist's growl was barely audible over the video feed. Arluza heard a loud crack as the man's fist connected with the female's jaw. If the shock of the violence had not rooted his feet to the floor, Macalester's grip on his arm would have prevented him from moving. With eyes wide, Arluza watched in horror. The man grabbed the Kawokee whose whimpers turned into screeches as he threw himself on top of her. The camera only showed the man's back until he straightened. Arluza's gaze riveted on the restraints that secured the female to the table by her hands and feet. Three other straps held her torso in place preventing her from moving.

Though blood trickled from the female's nose, she screamed and cried out with a string of garbled pleas and curses until the scientist grabbed her muzzle and wrapped it with tape.

The scientist opened a drawer under the table and removed several devices in a metal tray.

The female's head turned away as the man brought a syringe close to her. Her chest fur bristled. The man stuck the needle into her arm and as the syringe filled with blood, her body shuddered. When the needle pulled free, her chest heaved, and her neck arched back.

The scientist put a label on the tube he took from the syringe, placed it on a tray, and typed something into a computer attached to a movable tripod. He then grabbed what looked like a soldering iron from the table and held it close to the Kawokee's ear. The female screamed through her taped muzzle as a curl of smoke drifted up from the table. Arluza thought he could smell her burnt flesh though he was not even in the room.

The scientist returned to the tray of tools and placed four sampling test tubes beside the blood sample and attached labels. From one of the test tubes, he removed a swab.

Arluza's legs trembled as he watched. Macalister's grip on his arm tightened.

The Kawokee thrashed and whimpered as the man adjusted the table so that the female's legs were raised and her knees bent. Arluza was not sure what the scientist was doing, but she squirmed, and her back arched against the restraints.

She squealed and convulsed as he yanked out the swab and put it into a test tube. Her chest heaved, and her cheeks darkened wet with tears. Again, she tried to scream and fight her bonds as he repeated the procedure with a second and third swab.

The scientist lifted several tools from the tray and haphazardly cleaned each one with an alcohol swab.

Tears obscured Arluza's vision, and he wiped his eyes.

The Kawokee's head stopped thrashing, and she craned her neck to see what the scientist was doing. Her eyes followed the first device the scientist picked up.

Her chin almost touched her chest as he pulled a rolling chair over and sat down. He adjusted the speculum before placing his hand on the Kawokee's thigh. Her fingers and toes tightened into balls.

The female's head snapped backwards hitting the table with a thump, and her fingers and toes spread wide and vibrated. Foam appeared around her gag.

The scientist straightened and lowered an optical device from the ceiling, positioning it between her legs. He cursed and jumped back when the Kawokee defecated.

He left her on the table lying in her own filth and pressed a button on the nearby laptop to write notes.

Macalister closed the image and whispered, "Keep it

together, Doc." He led Arluza out the storeroom door. Macalister pushed Arluza behind him when he stopped two approaching soldiers. "We've got this one."

The soldiers nodded and returned the way they came.

He gripped Arluza's arm again, "Don't say a word," and pushed him into the examining room right up to the table where the now still Kawokee lay in a puddle.

The scientist did not look up from his notes. "Take this one to fifty-seven."

Macalister handed Arluza a pair of medical gloves and donned a pair himself before he released the straps from the Kawokee's arms and torso. Arluza released her feet.

As Macalister lifted her shoulders, her head hung backward.

Arluza tried to lift her from the table by her legs but his hands slipped, and her backside crashed down. She remained limp in his hands as he tightened his grip and pulled her off the table. She didn't weigh as much as he thought. Their fur made them look larger than they were. This one looked to him so much thinner now.

As gently as he could, Arluza carried her, but Macalister was pulling her quickly through swinging doors.

The stench hit him like an arm around his throat. He lowered her feet to the floor, and Macalister's eyes narrowed as he let her down. Arluza tried to catch his breath and control his stomach. Row upon row of cages, not large enough for a Kawokee to stand up, filled the room. Most were empty. He wanted to ask Macalister how they would rescue the female. Mindful of his instructions, he bit his tongue and lifted her feet.

They passed a cage where a hollow-eyed female sat naked on a stained pad. Underneath the cage, a tray held her scat. The number on her cage was fifty-five.

Macalister cocked his head at cage fifty-seven.

Confused, Arluza opened the cage and Macalister pulled the female they held into a sitting position and let her fall backward into the cage. Folding her legs into the cage, he closed the door and clicked the lock shut, then took Arluza by the arm and pushed him toward the swinging doors.

Arluza looked back at the cage over his shoulder. "You're not going to leave her here?"

Macalister's grip on his elbow stung as he pulled him to the exit.

The scientist who had examined the Kawokee pushed through the doors in front of them, and Arluza almost screamed. The man did not seem to notice as he spoke. "You there. Dispose of fifty-five. Be careful. She has every STD we have a name for and some we don't."

"Yes sir."

The moment the scientist was out the door, Macalister looked at Arluza. His eyes softened, and he whispered. "Sorry, Doc. I didn't want you to see this yet."

"You're not going to kill her; are you?"

Macalister's eyes hardened. "No choice." He marched over to a carrier and wheeled it under the cage.

The female inside stirred as the cage lifted. "No. Please?"

Arluza trembled as he followed. "You can't do it."

"Quiet," Macalister snapped. He pushed the cage out a back door while the Kawokee inside thrashed and kicked at the bars of the cage. Blood matted the fur of her feet as the skin tore.

"For God's sake."

Macalister turned and hit Arluza in the stomach stopping his words. "If I have to, I'll break your jaw. You might get yourself killed. It will be a loss, but you are replaceable. I'm not. I don't have time to be gentle. It's time you grew up."

Arluza staggered as Macalister pushed the carrier out the back door and pulled him along.

The yard behind the building had a long trench dug into the earth. Dirt covered over one end dotted with new weeds. As he positioned the cage over the trench, the

Kawokee, in a quavering voice, sang.

Macalister grabbed Arluza's shirt and pulled him to the edge of the trench. "Look."

Below was a tangle of Kawokee bodies. Arluza fell back from the trench and landed hard on the ground. He watched as Macalister took out a pistol and ended the Kawokee's song. Macalister unlocked the cage and rolled her into the trench. He emptied the tray on top of her and kicked in some dirt to cover the body.

Points of light swam in Arluza's vision.

Macalister stood over him. "I'm sorry, Doc. You may think I'm the devil himself and you'd be right. But I'm the devil that's going to stop another devil. Good men, men like you, have tried, failed, and died. You will do things my way, or I'll put you down. You've seen the worst of it so far, but I've seen worse than this."

He grabbed Arluza's jacket and pulled him to his feet. "Now, get a grip and follow orders. We need to do something right now. There might not be a second chance, so don't screw this up. You are to watch and say nothing. Is that understood, Private?"

Tears made it hard for him to focus and made his nose run. Arluza hated the man, but ground his teeth and spat. "Yes, sir."

"Good." Macalister touched his wrist-com and tapped the record button. The urge to push Macalister in was strong, but it did not take long to scan the trench saving Arluza from his impulses.

After wiping his face, Arluza focused on Macalister's back. They walked into the cage room, past half a dozen comatose females, and into the exam room where the scientist was cleaning up.

Macalister stopped in front of the scientist. "Doctor? I have a list of questions about your report."

The scientist threw down his gloves and crossed his arms. "Not again. I've explained everything in as much detail as I can. It can't be any clearer." He huffed. "Get it over with."

Macalister touched his wrist-com, and a list of questions appeared. "You've paid settlers for ninety subjects, yet your report shows only sixteen. What happened to the rest?"

"Half were disposed of because of disease. The biobots in our bloodstream don't eradicate the diseases we carry. They only limit the effects. So, the Kaw contract every disease we carry. I've tried antibiotics, but we burned that bridge centuries ago. The few we have are government regulated, expensive, and tend to work better on the less resistant strains."

Macalister flipped through pages and pointed at a graph. "Then why are the number of subjects still dropping?"

"It's keeping them alive long enough for the fertility drug to take effect that's been a challenge. I lost several to suicide. But I'm preventing that now by removing their clothes so they can't strangle themselves, and I put them in every other cage so they can't euthanize each other. A few tried to starve or poison themselves by eating their waste. I had to put them into a coma and feed them intravenously. I'm afraid we won't be able to keep them going long term. We'll be lucky to have two harvests from them."

"Is it true you are paying one cell for five instead of increasing it to eight as directed?"

"If Campion thinks he can negotiate a better price, let him come here and do it himself. I've lost half my suppliers when I increased it from four to five. For that matter, let someone else do it. I've worked triple shifts because Sanders has turned half the scientists against the project. I can't even get enough soldiers to keep the cages clean and carry out disposals."

"Sanders, huh?" Macalister made a note. "I'll see if we can't put more pressure on them and get you some help."

"See that you do. Are we done?"

"Yes. Thank you."

The doctor turned his back and put on new gloves.

CHAPTER 14

After many days of travel, the grinding boredom affected them all. Even with the pillows to soften the boards, Jasmine's backside still ached. Periodically everyone would walk instead of ride, just to do something different. Conversation stopped days ago. Excitement stirred in her companions as they grew close to the journey's end. At her first sight of Gehnica, Jasmine's breath caught in her throat. The winding narrow ravine stretched into a wide valley filled with tall, black, twisted rock spires. The spires rising from the river were at least fifty meters tall. In the center of the valley, a wide river followed an irregular path and reflected the orange early evening sunlight. Far larger than the Kawokee village she came from, Gehnica dwarfed the human settlement she saw.

"How?" She did not mean to say the words out loud, so it startled her when Paul answered.

"You can't see it from above. And ever since humans showed up, unsheltered light is banned within the upper city limits. They don't want anyone to find them."

As the caravan wound its way down the path, the city disappeared from view hidden by towering trees and smaller stone spires until they arrived at a wide beaten trail that meandered along the river. The trail ended where a ferry waited. Its rectangular wooden platform was large enough for the entire caravan. A thick rope spanned the river attached to stone spires rising from the water. It was linked to the floating platform by pulleys. Rudders on the corners of the platform used the river's current to push it across. By human standards, it was a small thing, but it was the largest machine she had seen on this world.

As the wagons rolled onto the ferry, Jasmine braced herself expecting to feel the platform shift or sway. Though the wagons moved from one end to the other, she felt no movement of the floating platform.

Antsy and the ferry operator spoke briefly.

Jasmine's eyes scrutinized the far shore but could see nothing. The last rays of the setting sun reflected off the water, giving a mirror image of the rock spires that rose from the river like twisted trees. In the middle of the river, the ferry's main rope was anchored to one of these spires. As the ferry passed by, Jasmine could see the rock up close. She was not a geologist, but it appeared to be very porous igneous rock.

When they crossed the river, no one spoke to the ferry operator. If the Kawokee had money or a barter system, she had yet to see it.

On this side of the river, she felt as if the Kawokee had advanced several thousand years. Jasmine could make out a road as wide as three wagons, sheltered under dense trees. It rose past a high levee wall and up the embankment. The caravan crossed another road which traveled the levee wall lined with low buildings and wide archways.

The thick foliage of the surrounding trees blocked what little sunlight remained. Jasmine thought they would be traveling blind if someone did not light a lamp soon until she spotted the soft glow up ahead.

The farther they moved from the river, the more detail she could see along with an increase of activity.

It was odd to see so much movement and hear laughter at this hour. In the previous village, everyone went into the dens at sundown and talked or played games for hours. Here, numerous Kawokee moved about along roads and through stone archways guided by shuttered lamps and lines of phosphorescent stones.

The road curved and headed under one of the larger archways and through a long tunnel. When they exited the other side, Jasmine felt like they had entered a parallel universe into a fairytale forest. There was a glow along the sidewalks made by long tubes with small flames under reflectors, protecting the flame from wind and rain. The road was smooth, and the wheels of the cart left no markings.

Long buildings with walls of hanging fabric, and roofs covered in living plants and flowers were most common. The walls of one depicted creatures. The next blended in with the hanging vines from the roof. One building had open shutters, and the interior had the familiar sleeping pillows and hammocks. Another looked like a workshop or storage facility. Jasmine looked up but could only see more buildings and crisscrossing walkways. A virtual cathedral of archways within archways covered with living plants.

"How?" she breathed.

"Parts of the city are built on top of itself," Paul explained. "The deeper the buildings, the safer it is to use light."

"But with so many here, how do they feed everyone?"

Paul reached out to one of the hanging plants, pulled off a leaf, and handed it to Jasmine. "Some products are shipped in, but much of the vegetation that hides the city also feeds it."

She had to adjust her estimate again of how advanced the Kawokee were when she saw one of the fountains. Water sprayed from center, powering a clockwork, of ornately carved stone fish which surfaced and submerged.

Copper paddles, green and pitted with age, caused ripples that bent the image of the fish, making them appear to swim.

As people passed by, they stared at Jasmine. There was no panic, only interest, and even that was short-lived.

Antsy stopped the caravan at a long house and went inside. He came out minutes later with a female. In his hands was a bowl of ornate earrings. He handed the earrings to everyone in her wagon. "We are part of Burrow Ninety-two Den Salmon. This is SaoAlise."

Jasmine took the offered earring as did the others.

She stopped Paul as he repeated Antsy's words. "I understood." Jasmine watched as her companions fitted the wires into their ears. The shape of their ears made losing it unlikely, but the ring would not fit around her ear.

"Let me help you with that." Paul reached for the earring.

She gave it to him, and he bent the wire. When he turned his head, she saw he had joined an identical ring to his own earring. "So, this signifies us as belonging to Burrow Ninety-two Salmon? Is SaoAlise the person in charge of the burrow?"

"Right on both statements." He turned her head gently. She felt his warm hand at odds with the cold wire.

"There."

It fit comfortably and did not fall out when she tugged on it. "Thanks."

His voice was thin. "I'm sure you're tired. This will be our den for a while. Go in and rest. Antsy and I will see to the horses."

Everyone climbed out of the wagons, gathered their few bundles, and entered the long house. SaoAlise helped Antsy and Paul lead the horses away. When Jasmine entered the long house, conversations grew silent. All eyes were on her. There were so many faces she did not know, and they made her self-conscious. "I am Cow."

Her traveling companions spoke about how she came

to their village and answered the questions of those already within the den. Jasmine singled out a sleeping pillow convenient to her size and fell onto it. She was more sore than tired and was glad no one asked her direct questions. Jasmine prioritized her inquiries about the city for the next time she encountered SaoAlise. The most important thing was learning about the ceremony, but Paul's lack of religious knowledge was a problem. Her handle on the Kawokee language bothered her and feared that it was still too weak for a detailed conversation. There was a nagging sense she was forgetting something crucial.

She spent time listing and cataloging questions in her mind until Louy caught her attention. A large circle of females watched them as Louy stood over Jasmine and said, "They want to know if you will take the ceremony."

Paul said she could watch and learn. He never said she could participate. The scientist part of her knew the benefits of taking part over observing any ritual. No longer tired, she sat up on the pillow.

Everything she learned about the ceremony from her traveling companions seemed harmless enough, but she doubted they had told her everything. *Could a Kawokee cure work on her? How could she know unless she tried to get pregnant?* "Would they let me?"

Her concerns grew as several Kawokee voices clamored to be heard. Some appeared angry while others looked happy. Too many voices mixed and mingled for her to understand what was being said.

Would her joining the ceremony mean that someone else would be left out? The question stuck in Jasmine's mind. The Kawokee shared everything. In her short time with them, she never heard or saw anyone want for anything. What was it about the ritual that was different?

Paul's form appeared over the crowd of Kawokee. Jasmine heard someone say SaoAlise's name and knew she was somewhere in the den. The crowd moved away from Jasmine toward the far side of the room.

Though Jasmine could not see her, SaoAlise's voice rose above the din. "Cow may take the ceremony."

Silence followed as if a bubble popped and removed all sound from the air. There was not one word of objection from the circle of females. Jasmine was surprised and somewhat disconcerted at the response. The decree had the tone of a command, but was it to stop infighting, or something else? Would she offend them if she decided not to participate? The distress of not knowing every little detail had her wondering if she even had a choice in the matter.

SaoAlise sidestepped the circle and approached her with Paul and Antsy in her wake. Paul knelt beside her, "If you're not too tired, SaoAlise would like to give you a tour of the city."

"Really?" Relieved to have a distraction from the current situation, Jasmine leapt to her feet. "Yes," she said in Kawokee.

The female leader stepped forward and took her hand. The soft fur of the top of SaoAlise's hand was thin and tinged with gray. Antsy stayed behind, and Paul took Jasmine's other hand as the leader led them out to the street, already talking.

Jasmine resisted the urge to ask all her questions at once and focused on trying to understand the female's words. As Paul spoke, Jasmine was pleased she already understood much of it.

"SaoAlise oversees all of Burrow Ninety-two." He pointed over Jasmine's head, and she turned to see poles towering over several the buildings. "The symbol is also on the door fronts." Jamine didn't recognize it at first, but the weaved tapestry that covered the door matched the pattern in her earring. She had no doubt that a similar carved shape or flag topped the pole. "The burrows are laid out in a grid. Each street within a burrow is numbered, and the dens named. Although you could sleep and eat anywhere in the city, it's considered rude to stay too many times in a different burrow."

"How many burrows are in the city?" asked Jasmine.

"Four hundred, but less than half are still used."

Jasmine almost asked why until she remembered him telling her about the population drop. How many had they lost, and how was their society still able to function? The plagues of Ancient Earth devastated populations by killing anywhere between thirty and sixty percent of the people. Not wanting to face the answer, she squeezed Paul's hand. "Thanks, but you don't have to translate every word. How about I ask you when I don't understand SaoAlise?"

Paul smiled and nodded.

Even in the dim light, Jasmine was surprised how much detail she could see, and wondered how much more she could find in the bright light of day. She noted the posts at the street corners and examined the closest one, wishing she had not left her notes on the Kawokee written symbols back at the border village. The numbers were easier. There were only a few she remembered by heart. Here, she needed to memorize as many as she could or risk becoming hopelessly lost. Some buildings she suspected were for storage. Others, like kitchens, were recognizable by the flues that poked through the roofs.

"This is our kitchen." SaoAlise passed the building with her head held high and her back straight. She gave the impression of being proud of the city and her place in it.

Jasmine noted how many of the buildings incorporated the rock spires into their construction. The kitchen was one. Buildings with hanging fabric walls were more common here than underground ones. Not that she could tell that any one building was truly underground. As she walked by them, the uniformity and precision of the supports caught her attention. She felt along the length of one and felt a seam. The lower piece of carved wood was the same height and diameter as the one above it. Something held these pieces together well enough to support a heavy roof.

SaoAlise turned as Jasmine paused to look closer. "The wood comes in from cities near the southern forests. Metals and other things come from other places. This city makes machines and building materials for trade." The burrow leader gave her hand a gentle pull and quickened her pace.

Jasmine had many questions but combined them into one. "Who decides who gets what?"

SaoAlise touched her earring, which was the same as Paul's, but with a simple silver ring woven into it. "I talk with the other Sao, and we agree what to give and what to take from what is given by the Kap of the city."

A disturbance in the distance had SaoAlise quickening her pace.

Jasmine jogged to keep up. The sound of many Kawokee making their characteristic wheezing laughter floated on the breeze. The city block ahead had no buildings, but a covering blocked the sky high above. Whether it was thatched panels or weaved cloth Jasmine did not know. Many Kawokee stood facing down a mild slope. As they neared, the crowd made room for their little group. The audience looked down on a stage with a play going on complete with props. The burrow leader attempted to explain but stopped as Jasmine could not take her eyes off the spectacle. It was while she was looking at the first row of the audience that Jasmine noticed several small Kawokee through a break in the crowd. They were still and quiet like the adults, which made her doubt, but they were small and looked like children to her eyes.

The words of the actors were too fast for Jasmine to catch. The crowd laughed leaving her to retrace the words looking for the joke. Paul never missed one, but did not explain, and she did not ask. Sometimes, caught up in the moment, Jasmine laughed with him. What she figured out was that the play was a silly story about the misfortunes of an inept artist whose true gift was painting through the eyes of the Vaw. Jasmine would have called the pictures caricatures. She remembered the term, Vaw, as an unfriendly Kawokee God. The story added meaning to the word. The Vaw was dangerous, yet not evil. Chaotic and unpredictable, it lived within its own set of rules.

When everyone clapped their hands, SaoAlise looked at the canopy high above them. "Tomorrow, I will show you—"

Not understanding the words used, Jasmine rolled them around in her mind trying to figure them out. She then whispered them to Paul who answered, "The engineering burrows."

Jasmine looked at the Kawokee who gave her a wide berth as they dispersed. Which things, like clapping hands, were human contamination and which came naturally?

On the way back to their own burrow, Jasmine asked SaoAlise, "Who told the ones on stage to do this?"

"I don't understand." SaoAlise glanced at Paul.

"Do you want to know why they don't use money?" Paul took Jasmine's hand as they walked.

"Yes. I am looking for the social hierarchy and what regulates trade on a group and personal level."

"The Kawokee find the concept of money to be evil. There are only two reasons a Kawokee would not give to someone who asks. Either you are poor because you are lazy, or you wish the other to starve. Both are extremely serious offenses. They measure greatness to those who give much."

Though knowledgeable of other systems, the concept remained alien to Jasmine, having grown up in a capitalistic society where accepting from social programs carried a stigma. "So, the Kawokee on stage do it for the status they receive? Individually or for their burrow?"

"Each actor gets status within their burrow, yes. But no, the burrow gets nothing more from the other burrows by putting on a play. The play serves as an emotional need more so than a physical need for the actors."

"Interesting." There were many human structures that resembled what Paul described. All had vanished into Old Earth history. If she researched each one, she doubted any of them would be a perfect fit. The Kawokee were, after all, not human, and Jasmine could understand how the system worked with small groupings. Everyone would know everyone else, and a new face would be easy to spot. But how did they keep the system stable within a large city? Jasmine recalled what Paul told her about those who refused to obey the law. To her, many of the punishments did not fit the crime, but to sustain control on such a system, strict codes needed enforcing.

The thought had her wondering if she had broken any rules or insulted those around her. As cautious as she tried to be, had she been careful enough?

Jasmine thanked SaoAlise when they returned to the burrow, and she received a Kawokee smile. The evening meal was being served and Louy and Halan waved to her. The crowd parted, allowing for her to join the pair. One brave female reached out to touch her arm. Jasmine stopped, smiled, and raised her arm to touch the other's hand. Her actions caused an avalanche of hands touching her along with whispered comments.

Halan handed her a meal box. "They want to know what it is like to travel the sky."

Jasmine knew if she opened the box, the food inside would be cold by the time she finished, so she hurried through the polished description she thought would make the most sense to them. She had questions of her own, but could not squeeze them in and eat between explanations.

When Paul and Antsy made a show of climbing into hammocks and covering their ears, she apologized and told the crowd she needed to sleep. However, Jasmine was too excited. She tried closing her eyes, but her mind would not let go of the possibilities. There were children here and an answer to their existence somewhere in the city.

Morning had Jasmine's eyes wide open, too energized

to stay still. She didn't remember sleeping, but she did not feel the drain of a sleepless night. The moment Halan lifted her head from her own pillow, Jasmine crawled near her and whispered. "If someone takes a male but does not go through the ceremony, can she have a baby?"

Halan closed her eyes again, plunked her head back on the pillow. "I do not think so. I have had many males, but only have babies after the ceremony."

Jasmine had asked about the details of the ceremony several times during the journey, but Louy always turned the subject to the mating and token giving. Although Halan gave in to Louy's interests, Jasmine hoped the older female would be more serious while the younger slept. "Do you eat or drink anything special during the ceremony?"

"Stop worrying."

"I'm not worried."

"You've asked me that question at least three times." The older female opened one eye and whispered. "Everyone wants to know if you will give a token to Paul."

The question startled Jasmine. Though the thought of going through the ceremony thrilled her to no end, she had not fully comprehended what she was getting into. This was a fertility ceremony. It required sleeping with a male, and the only other human she knew of in the city was Paul.

Jasmine could feel her ears burn with embarrassment. How could she have made such a foolish blunder? "I don't know. I mean, yes, I should. He's the only human male here, but I... I really didn't think this through."

The thought of laying with Paul sent a thrill through her, but would he want to? The way he touched her was overly familiar, but he did not look at her or say anything that told her he was interested. Then there was the thought of sleeping with someone not her husband. What would her parents say? If she went to a fertility clinic and picked out a donor for an embryo grown in an artificial womb, the grumbling about how hard it was to raise a child alone would never end. But if she could identify the father? If her family found out the child was not conceived in a laboratory test tube, but flat on her back, on a pillow, on a quarantined world?

The desire for children clashed with her upbringing only to drown within her fear of rejection.

There was nothing to the ceremony that sounded like a cure, yet children existed within the city. What were the odds of it working for the Kawokee? Certainly, better than zero. Could whatever they did work on her? Would Paul even be interested? If he was not, would he go through the motions anyway because there was no one else available? Jasmine did not think she could bare sleeping with someone who did not love her. Not again. When her ex-husband told Jasmine he only wanted her family connections and never cared for her, it hurt more than everything else he had done. She did not want to go through that again.

"Would he want me?"

Both Halan's eyes opened, and she rolled to face Jasmine. "You wish a Kawokee, perhaps? Some of us are going to meet males this day. Would you like to join us?"

"No. I…" Jasmine struggled with what she wanted to say. "You're right. I should give a token to Paul."

Halan smiled and reached out to pat Jasmine's hand. "Good." She poked the female next to her, waking them up, and said, "Cow will give LutPaul a token."

The heat in Jasmine's ears returned as the news spread with each waking female. As if fate were setting her up. Paul awoke and climbed out of his hammock. He was not close to Halan and her friends, but Jasmine did not want him to overhear their conversation. She hurried to him and rambled with anything that came to her mind. "This is a lovely place."

He grabbed a towel, a homemade toothbrush, and headed toward the giggling females. Not knowing what else to do, she took his arm and led him toward a different exit and tried to ignore the curious look he gave her. "Have you been here before?"

"Many times."

Once outside they headed for the bathing area. Jasmine followed racking her brain to figure out what to say next. For a moment, she felt like she was back in high school, hoping the captain of the lacrosse team would ask her to dance.

"I often bring caravans from villages near human settlements. It's not like I can do anything if the humans attack a caravan, and I've never had to interpret. I guess it makes them feel better to have me around."

Without removing his scant clothing, Paul stepped onto a platform and pulled a hanging cord. Water rained down on him. He scooped soap powder out of a container nailed to a post and lathered up. As he did so, he turned away from her and faced the lavatory.

Unlike the village, this one had a roof and three walls and could accommodate six people. Water ran beneath the row of seats and carried away the refuse. Jasmine watched the soapy water from the shower run into a nearby drain. She had asked about the sewage system in the city. The roads and the sides of buildings had similar drains. The water system rivaled any human city of the Iron Age.

Jasmine had not bathed since arriving in the city and sniffed discretely to make sure she did not stink. Her blouse might need airing, but she was not about to let him see her without it again. The memory alone was too embarrassing.

His shower did not last long. Paul pulled the cord again and rinsed off. He stepped down and dried himself with the towel. "Would you like to continue the tour? SaoAlise offered, but she's extremely busy now, so I told her I'd take you around."

"I'd like that. When would you like to go?"

Paul shrugged. "Now?" He hung his towel over a hook

in the bathhouse wall. His toothbrush he pushed into the side of his loincloth. The action made Jasmine smile. Paul left wet footprints on the road, which quickly vanished in the morning sun. Daylight revealed a road of crushed shells held together by a hard resin. The substance might not stand up to the weight of human vehicles, but it was more than sufficient for carts and foot traffic. "You have to see the manufacturing they do here."

The word caught her attention, and as curious as she was about learning what Kawokee manufactured, questions about the ceremony were at the forefront of her mind. She wasn't sure why, but it felt awkward to ask him about it. As they walked the streets, people turned and watched. "I would think they would react to us more."

"They used to. I'm well known here."

"A hero?"

Paul chuckled. "Not as much as you. I'm old news. I'll bet if we ask, they'd all know who you are."

"Don't be silly." Jasmine looked at him to see if he was kidding.

He crossed his arms and looked around. Taking a few steps toward a crowd of passing females, he pointed at her. "Do you know who this is?"

"Cow," they answered as one.

Paul looked at Jasmine and grinned. Turning back to the bevy, he asked, "Where are you from?"

"We are from Sialthia," said a female. "It is six days journey to the east."

Jasmine found it hard to believe. She traveled longer from the north to get to the city. That simple fact raised several questions in her mind. How did news travel? At what detail? Was there some general broadcast for the common people? There were no newspapers.

Another female took her hand. "Thank you. You saved many lives."

"You're welcome." When she and Arluza told Fawsha what the soldiers had in mind, she didn't think there was that much danger to the Kawokee. She only wanted to avoid panic and ill feelings. Not to mention avoid getting kicked out of the village. After seeing what happened to the mining town, she could see why they might have a different view. Would the soldiers hurt any of the Kawokee? Jasmine was no longer as sure as she once was.

"You see?" Paul grinned as he turned west toward Burrow Eighteen.

The urge to verify his statement had her calling to the females who were walking away. "Do you know him?" Jasmine pointed to Paul.

Their ears twitched, and several whispered between each other until one female answered, "Paul."

"What did he do?"

They were silent. The one who knew Paul's name shrugged as the others drifted away.

"You see? It was before their time." He pointed down the street. "There it is."

Jasmine followed his gaze to a line of buildings that covered more area than all of Burrow Ninety-two. Built around three rock spires, large trees grew on the roofs. These buildings, unlike most others, had a combination of hanging cloth walls and stone barriers. Most of the coverings were rolled up into the three-story ceiling. The inside was a maze of machines and pulleys reminiscent of pictures she had viewed of the early industrial period of Old Earth. She stared in amazement.

"I can't believe humans could think the Kawokee are savages if they've ever seen this."

"This place is a heavily guarded secret, as are all large cities. Even before humans, it was their custom to hide these places from being viewed from above. It's as if they feared an evil god."

Her mind raced as Paul talked. Ancient human civilizations believed the gods watched them from above. They carved images that could only be seen from the air and built giant structures in their honor, but the Kawokee did the exact opposite, why? Possibilities tickled at the back of her mind before she pushed them away with a reminder to not compare humans to Kawokee. Instead she focused on what Paul was saying.

"Buildings too large for an underground area or needing constant ventilation are hidden under branches of trees with vines woven to cover everything." Paul pointed to one of the canopied areas above them. What looked like one thatched panel was actually the branches of several plants weaved together to form a blanket of greenery. The edges supported by the roots of the plants that wrapped around the trees or twisted down to the ground formed a new pillar rooted into the dirt.

"Why spend decades weaving the branches of trees and vines rather than make a wooden structure in a few weeks?"

"Those trees and vines have withstood the elements and repaired themselves for a hundred years. Look what a human city looks like in one lifetime. Workers trim back or move vines and branches. Everything is alive. Parts that die feed the living."

A caravan several times longer than their own, passed along the street. The wagons contained many males and females.

Paul waved to the caravan leader who returned his salute, but asked Jasmine, "So, what goes on at the ceremony?"

Shocked at his words, she looked up at Paul. "I was going to ask you for details."

"Men aren't allowed."

"And have you never asked?"

He shrugged. "There are some things that would be impolite. I think they would have made an exception in my case since I'm not mate material."

"You're not?" Jasmine felt uneasy about asking him such a personal question, but her curiosity was as unfounded as it was illogical. "No one has ever given you a token?"

Paul's posture tensed. He did not say anything for several breaths. "Let's just say I'm no one's first choice."

CHAPTER 15

Arluza heard the chime through the cabin door again. There was still no answer as he stood in the empty corridor hoping no one would walk by and see them. He would have given up after the first try, but Macalister was not about to let him escape. "Talk to him."

After shuffling his feet, Arluza took a deep breath. He did not want anyone else hearing him yell in the dim hallway and leaned closer to the intercom. "Doctor Sanders? This is Doctor Arluza and Captain Macalister. We would like to discuss your concerns with the direction of the project."

The hard stare Macalister gave Arluza demanded he continue, and he focused on the sliding door that was the entrance to Doctor Sander's living quarters. "I compiled the raw data and can prove Campion is lying to you and all the other scientists."

He shrugged and tried to turn away from the door, but Macalister's hand caught his shoulder and held him in place. The intercom crackled with an old man's voice. "Are you the one that took a poke at Campion?"

If there was one thing he did not want people to remember him by, it was that. Arluza choked back the bile in his throat and said, "Yes." Even to his ears, his response sounded more whine than admission.

The door opened. A barrel chested senior man sat in pajamas on the opposite side of the room in a padded chair. "If it were anyone else but you, Dr. Arluza, I wouldn't have opened the door." Sanders leaned forward and made two unsuccessful attempts to rise before gaining his feet. He extended his hand and tottered forward on unsteady legs. After they shook hands, Sanders waved them to a couch as he turned and shuffled back to his chair. "Campion is threatening to destroy my credibility for criticizing the way the project is being run. All I did was ask a few researchers to reevaluate the data."

He collapsed into the chair. "Make yourselves comfortable. I heard what happened and wished you'd hit him. The data is invalid because the collection method is flawed. The data is not representative. Even an undergrad would see it."

Arluza glanced at Macalister and gave him a quick smile. A dark glare was all he received in return. He placed the comm-vid he had been cradling in his arms, on the floor and sat opposite the elderly scientist with Macalister taking a seat near the door. Arluza nodded. "You're right about the poor design of the data collection method. He's clearly making a show of it. But you're wrong about everyone seeing it. They see what they want to see. What tipped you off?"

"It's not possible for the Kawokee to be infected with so many human venereal diseases. The chances of them all being zoonotic between species is astronomical. On Earth, only half of the pathogens can transfer between human and animal. The percentage goes down with the native species of other planets. At least until we introduce too many Earth animals in. And the terraformed worlds fall somewhere in between."

The news came as a surprise to Arluza, he hung his head with the fear of making a grievous mistake. "But the

STACY BENDER & REID MINNICH

venereal disease data is correct. I tested the samples. The part he forged was the evidence that females were lactating."

Sander's chin rested on his chest. He raised his head. "I assume you're here to help me stop this madness?"

Arluza folded his hands between his knees. "No. Actually, we're here to ask you to back off."

"Not you too? They got to you." Sanders banged his hand down on the armrest. "No. I won't back off. We're being manipulated."

As much as he wanted to sink into the chair and disappear, Arluza wanted more for Sanders to understand. He raised his hands, palms out. "No. He hasn't got to me. And yes, Campion is leading the other scientists down a dangerous path."

Sanders leaned forward. His face a mass of both wrinkles and anger. "Then why can't I warn them?"

Macalister barely let Sanders finish his question. "Because Campion and most of the scientists are sure they're on the right path. If you think anyone will see the flaws in the data and jump ship, you will be disappointed. Even those with doubts will bow to peer pressure. I've seen it before. I was personally connected with the Godiva project."

The old man's eyes locked on Macalister. For a second, he looked ready to strangle the younger man. "If I back off, the insanity will continue."

"Before you can stop Campion's project, you must have something to replace it with, and the other scientists must be willing to abandon what they're doing. Data is a poor weapon against strong belief. Do you have an alternative theory?"

Sanders sunk back in his chair and folded his hands under his chin. "I don't have a theory. All I know is the Kawokee should have died out. I don't even know where to start looking for a replacement project. There isn't enough data."

Arluza saw his chance and leaned forward. "I'm already gathering data and working on an alternate plan."

Sanders stared at him in disbelief. "You are? How?"

"I've been speaking directly to the Kawokee, and we have a researcher on the ground, Jasmine Char, gathering data as we speak. My Kawokee contacts insist there are births, and their numbers are stable." Arluza stopped and thought about Campion's current methods. "Or will be, as long as no one starts massacring entire villages. They've been hiding their young from humans. They won't tell me where, but Dr. Char is hoping to gain their full trust."

"What's her theory?"

After taking a deep breath, Arluza articulated Jasmine's theory as best he could, all the while trying to gage Sander's reaction. He did not want to leave anything out, nor did he want to misspeak. Once done, Arluza braced himself for the tongue lashing he expected.

"Do they have uninfected females?" asked Sanders.

The relief Arluza felt had him expelling the breath he had been holding. "They can't answer those questions. If we can ask the right questions, we might be able to build a theory. I know the Kawokee have a solution, but it's not a cure like what everyone else is looking for."

The old man's eyes brightened, but for a moment Arluza thought he saw something else. "This is fantastic. What in their culture could affect a virus?"

Arluza sat back on the couch. "As a prominent immunologist, I was hoping you could tell me. Would you be willing to run a separate research facility on the ground?"

"Why not bring the samples up here?" Sander's snapped his eyes shut and waved his hand in the air. "Scratch that. Campion would notice too many shuttles and the soldiers being overextended; wouldn't he?"

"Yes, and there is another reason." Arluza looked at Macalister. The soldier rose from his seat and knelt beside Sander's chair with his arm extended. Arluza already knew what was on the video surveillance. He saw it. The knots in his gut returned as he heard Campion's voice.

In the video, Campion leaned back in his chair. "So, what you're telling me is, none of the Kawokee subjects can carry past the first trimester?"

Arluza recognized the off-screen voice as the scientist from the land base research facility. "The virus is fatal to the fetus, just as in humans."

Campion shrugged. "Then we must begin again with wild Kawokee. I'll order the soldiers to round them up and deliver them to you."

Macalister stopped the recording. "That happened less than an hour ago. I know these creatures, Dr. Sanders. They will be at war with us within days of the first kidnapping. How many settlers remain on the planet? Thirty thousand? Or maybe a hundred thousand. No one's bothered with a census. Does it matter to you that their lives may be in danger? We've no idea how the Kawokee will react. But I know how I'd react if someone, some alien, tried kidnapping my family for a scientific experiment. I'd kill every one."

Sanders sank in his chair, and his face grew pale. "I can't believe it. This is the Godiva project all over again."

Arluza nodded. "This mission was created to avoid controversy."

Macalister silenced both men with a wave of his hand. "There will be time enough for this later. Right now, we need an answer from you Dr. Sanders. Will you go to the surface with us?"

There was no hesitation. "Yes."

Macalister's hard eyes bore into Arluza. "Dr. Arluza. It's your turn. Make it convincing."

Arluza grabbed the comm-vid and pulled over a small end table on which to set the device. He pointed the view screen toward Dr. Sanders, and like Macalister, knelt beside the old man's chair. After he pressed the call button it felt like an eternity until Miwi and Fawsha's faces appeared on the screen. "Why have you called?"

"We bring terrible news and must ask a favor," Arluza began.

CHAPTER 16

Every day, the city became more crowded than the previous one. Jasmine spent two days wandering the city with Paul. He took her to a huge building called the Great Hall, crammed with people. Arched ceilings and stone pillars held frescos which adorned both ceiling and walls and mirrored the activities they looked down on. Taller than the Kawokee, Jasmine could see over the crowd. There were many events happening. Her first impression was an athletic competition but there was also poetry, singing, dancing, and even a science fair. Being neither engineer nor chemist she was both fascinated by the beauty of even the simplest of machines and concerned over the safety of the more explosive endeavors. Males and females participated in all events. No one cared who was the best. When she witnessed a few males receive rings or scarves as tokens, she realized the entire production was the equivalent of speed dating.

Today, she struck out on her own. Her exploration of the city never failed to turn up new surprises. These people worked hard, but played hard. There was music and singing on many street corners.

She loved to stroll through the mazes, both above

ground and below. There was a tangle of gardens built around areas of closely packed rock spires and connected by narrow pathways draped with fragrant flowers. It took her most of a day to learn how to navigate the smallest of these sections in the city. She was never afraid of getting lost. There was always someone who would lead her out, but she delighted in plunging into the tunnels of hanging moss and rock to emerge into a new feast for her eyes. The memory of the crystal garden deep within the ground still lingered in her mind's eye.

But the most exciting discovery was when she saw a dozen children swimming in a shallow pool near the riverbank. They were the size of teenagers and acted the part, full of energy and loud voices. They fell silent and backed away from her as she walked toward them, except for one scruffy little fellow who called to the others and spoke her name. His heroic stories made her blush, but she was glad when they came back to her. "May I ask how old you all are?"

They all talked at once. Her mind focused on the numbers. Most said they were six. "Were you born in this city?" At this question, they fell silent, abandoned their swimming fun, and left as a group. Jasmine let them go. She trusted Fawsha's promise that all would be revealed.

As she walked through the streets, she noticed everyone was hurrying in the direction of the river. She paced one of them and asked, "Where is everyone going?"

"The Priestesses have arrived."

She followed the Kawokee until they reached a crowd lining the street. A caravan of animals and carts came toward them, and the crowd cheered. Many of the carts contained dozens of caged birds. At first, Jasmine mistook them as clockworks because of their metallic green feathers, but their movements and squawks told otherwise. As in other caravans she had seen, only the lead animal had a driver.

Jasmine heard the cheering from the crowd before she

saw the four carts with the six priestesses in each. The only thing that set them apart from any other Kawokee was the headdress of bright metallic feathers and long necklaces they wore. As they drew closer, Jasmine saw that the strands were not necklaces but a chain attached at both ears. The high-pitched cheer from the crowd stung her ears. Other carts followed, but the crowd boiled away as people ran from the street. Jasmine guessed the crowd was hurrying back to their burrows, so she jogged toward her own designated den.

News had already reached her burrow, and Paul rushed toward her. "They're here."

"I know." Jasmine pointed down the street and was about to tell him what she saw when he pushed her wrist-com into her hands.

"Good. Let's go." Paul looked worried and spoke quickly. "The priestesses are preparing everything. The ceremonies will start tonight. Normally, no one is allowed in while they're setting up. But you've been granted special access to take pictures and ask questions."

He led her at a pace that had her legs aching despite her recent conditioning. They arrived at the Great Hall where workers were rearranging the interior to be three auditoriums of tiered benches around a stage. One wall was taken down to allow fast access for a steady flow of carts. A sleeping building was being assembled against another wall away from the auditorium.

Jasmine took pictures of the carts of caged birds. One of the Kawokee unloading the carts looked in Jasmine's direction and came toward her. She bowed to her and to Paul. "You must be Cow and Paul. I am Ingwa." A small feather of the fancy headdress still clung to her head entangled in her fur.

"Yes." Paul returned the bow.

Jasmine copied him. "I am pleased to meet you, Ingwa. Are you a priestess?"

"I am." The petite female brushed the feather from her

head. "I'd be happy to answer all your questions."

Jasmine took a close-up of a bird. "What are the birds for?"

The priestess put her hand near the bars. The bird came close to her fingers and bowed its head allowing the priestess to scratch at its feathers. "These birds say when a female is pregnant."

Paul stood ready to translate, but most of the time, Jasmine needed him for only the occasional word.

She was impressed anew with the Kawokee. It was only a few millennia ago when humans detected pregnancy and other medical conditions based on changes in the scent of a person. "Can you tell me how this ceremony helps females keep the baby and why females who don't have the ceremony lose the child?"

Ingwa looked down at the ground. "Not in a way a human would understand." She looked up again at Jasmine. "But I must try." She returned to the cart and helped the others unload the cages but continued to talk. "The Mother God created our ceremony to hide us from the Vaw. Long ago the Vaw became jealous of us and killed our babies."

Paul lifted two cages from the cart. Jasmine also took one, careful not to stick her fingers through the bars in case the bird bit. They followed Ingwa to where she and the other priestesses stacked the cages. Since she had never seen a pregnant Kawokee, Jasmine suspected a reason, but no Kawokee had yet given her an answer to this direct question. "Do you mean you hide the babies or the mothers?"

Ingwa did not hesitate. "Both." She set down a cage and went for another. "We've been hiding pregnant females and their babies from the Vaw since time began. It's only by following the sacred ceremony precisely, that a female can hide her child from the Vaw."

Jasmine stifled the urge to compare the Kawokee gods to that of Old Earth or the menagerie of human beliefs.

"What happens at the ceremony?"

"We teach the sacred stories, make sacred cords, and blood sacrifice."

"What if a female does two of the three?"

"The ceremony will not protect unless performed accurately."

Of all the elements to the ceremony, the blood sacrifice was the only thing Jasmine thought had a remote chance of changing a pregnancy. "Tell me about the sacrifice?"

"A small patch of fur is shaved from the shoulder. Many times, a female will do this on her own before the ceremony. During the ceremony, a small cut is made to the shoulder with a sharp, clean knife. The cut is then cleaned by a special salve that is rubbed into the cut."

That had to be it. Something in the salve must affect the virus long enough to protect the baby. The Kawokee clearly understood that sharing specific body fluids transferred immunity. She wouldn't have known this but for something Arluza said when discussing pre-bionic medicine. Humans had not used such practices for hundreds of years. The Kawokee were very knowledgeable about this world around them. "Can I have some of this salve?"

"Yes. If you go through the ceremony."

The answer had to be there. But there was a lingering doubt she might be wrong. Her desire to obtain the sacred salve was tempered by her fear of insulting the priestess. "Can I have some of this salve to take with me?"

Ingwa's forehead wrinkled. "There is only enough for the ceremony," Paul translated. "If you took some away, you would deny others their portion. We should be ready for an evening ceremony. Will you take part?"

Jasmine felt the pressure of having to decide. It would have been easier if Paul weren't standing right there. Confronted with that question when he was so near sent her heart racing as muscles tensed. If she wanted to find her answers, there was only one way. Jasmine could not bear to look at Paul as she responded. She did not want to see his reaction written on his face. "Yes, but can Paul stay with me? I may need an interpreter."

The priestess frowned and shook her head. "Males may not be present. Don't worry." She smiled and squeezed Jasmine's hand. "You will understand everything. It's not hard."

A thought occurred to Jasmine, but she doubted Ingwa could answer. "If one hundred females go through the ceremony, how many of them will get pregnant?" She was already devising a method to collect the data. If she made it a game, she hoped the females of her burrow would all join in.

There was no hesitation in Ingwa's answer. Jasmine understood most of what the priestess said but asked Paul to interpret to help convince her unbelieving ears.

He confirmed, "In seven to ten days, sixty two percent should be pregnant. Thirty eight percent of those who don't get pregnant within that time are pregnant within the following week. Of the ones that do not get pregnant, most are too young, too old, or had too few males."

Before Jasmine could string another sentence together the priestess said, "Now, if you will excuse me, I have much to do."

"Of course." It was odd to hear Ingwa speak in mathematical terms as if her religion were a science. Then again, the Kawokee language used the same word for both.

Jasmine took pictures of the rooms. The placement of the stage and the benches were the same in each chamber, but different things appeared on the stage. The first room had an empty stage, while the next had baskets filled with beads and a table of long cords. In the last room small sharp knives and jars of salve sat on low tables.

She looked around for Paul and realized he had wandered off. He was always easy to see, even in a crowd, so it was odd that she could not find him. The last she remembered seeing of him, he was talking to Ingwa.

A line of people entered the first auditorium. No longer did she see them as alien. The Kawokee were people, not the least bit less human. Was it because they acted so much like humans, or because she spent so much time with them? Could she objectively see the differences anymore?

The excited crowd funneled into the first auditorium. With every shaking step, she forced herself to go to the end of the line. Her stomach was in knots as she took one of the last spots on the highest bench. Hundreds of chattering female voices fell silent as a priestess took the stage wearing her headpiece and ear chains.

She spoke loud enough for all to hear. The first story, Jasmine remembered hearing from the old priest she met in the tiny village just outside the destroyed mining town. The second was new to her.

Jasmine tried to concentrate, but there was no way she would remember a tenth of the stories with any accuracy. Not that it mattered. The religious tales could be translated and studied by others who had less pressing mysteries to solve.

Story after story was recited. Jasmine took pictures more to stay awake than for their content. All the while, the crowd sat in rapt attention, or at least quiet. After the fourth or fifth tale, the priestess directed them to the next auditorium.

Here they each received a cord and sat in small groups around baskets filled with beads. Jasmine drifted to the far side of the room and sat with a group of females surrounding four baskets. Each basket held red, green, white, and black beads. The priestess told them the order of the beads and held up a basket of the color she described. The process made little sense to Jasmine since she didn't understand the story she heard an hour ago. What she did understand was how important the chain of beads was to the Kawokee. The strand had to be perfect or the unsuccessful female could not go on to the next part of the ceremony.

Rather than say a color, the priestess assigned a letter to the beads. She tied a knot in the cord, and everyone copied her. She called out the first bead. The crowd sat with the prescribed baskets of beads in front of them, ensuring everyone could reach for the right color of bead. Jasmine was uncertain if she could remember which color went to what letter. This part of the ceremony was even more mind numbing than the last as the string of beads grew heavy and unwieldy. Jasmine was ecstatic when the priestess told them to tie the cords closed. The long strand in her hands reminded her of the old priest she had met and the string of beads he had wrapped around her neck. That necklace was back at the burrow, but Jasmine swore it was a duplicate to the one she made.

The crowd filed past the priestess who examined each string of beads against her master copy. No one in line in front of Jasmine made any mistakes. Jasmine felt a moment of tension as the priestess checked her beads. That tension did not ease as the priestess waved her on to the next room. Here, they took seats on benches and waited until everyone was seated. At a signal from a priestess, the first row stood in line. Several tiny blades stuck out from shallow dishes. The priestess pressed the tips of the blades into the shoulders of the females then rubbed the salve into the wound with a flat wooden stick. Used blades were placed in a steaming pot heated over a flame from a larger pot. The used sticks they tossed into the fires.

The Kawokee had a decent understanding of sterilization and unlike the reports Jasmine studied, more advanced than they first appeared. They merely used naturalistic methods rather than chemical or electrical ones.

Jasmine took many pictures of this part of the ceremony, partly out of nervousness. Her mind was racing, looking for a reason to run when her row stood and stepped before the priestess. She shut off the noise in her brain and forced herself to stay calm.

There was almost no pain, and the salve did not sting. That salve could contain a medicine. There was no way she could analyze it, and there was only one way she could test to see if it worked on humans. Now that the ceremony was done, Jasmine would have to make the last and most difficult decision.

Outside the Great Hall a crowd of males stood waiting. Jasmine stopped, a little nervous at the overwhelming sight. None of the males paid her any attention, but descended on the females who came after her. Jasmine was pushed away from the building by the pressure of the frenzied males.

She took a long way back to her burrow, but with a wrong turn she ended up in one of the mazes. Jasmine sat alone in the crystal garden and thought about what she should do. Paul was pleasant on the eye, but the thought of having a child to raise was intimidating. She let the thought linger. How hard would that be compared to living with the stigma of having the Kaw virus? If the government on her homeworld had its way, anyone infected would be unable to adopt. Even if Jasmine could get back home, life in a concentration camp of aging people was all she had to look forward to. Child or no child, how would she live? The minute chance to have a child was what she came to the planet for. Over sixty percent of the Kawokee would get pregnant with in the next two weeks. The priestesses saw a correlation between those odds and the number of males the females slept with. Jasmine would only have one and only if he agreed. She still had not asked him. Her biology was different than the Kawokee. What were her odds? She could only imagine it being far less than sixty percent.

Her thoughts ran in circles until a pair of lovers entwined on a bench nearby. She felt guilty for watching them. They did not care about her presence, and this was not the first time Jasmine had seen Kawokee mating. She imagined herself in the female's place. When they finished, the couple cuddled for the longest time. This too, she observed and daydreamed about. When they left, she felt painfully alone. She could not give a reason for the tears that blurred her vision.

Jasmine stood and noticed the glow lights were lit. Her stomach growled, confirming it was late evening. With a rough draft of an apology on her lips, she hurried out of the maze toward her burrow.

As she passed each block, the music from dozens of singers and musicians blended with the sea of Kawokee laughter. Everywhere, people were dancing and singing. The smell of food drifted in the air. Jasmine witnessed several barrels of alcohol rolled into cradles and tapped into as the previous casks ran dry.

When she reached her own burrow, there was a party like all the others she passed. Trays of food were everywhere and glasses of sweet wine. She nibbled at the food while searching for Paul. Jasmine wandered the burrow looking for him when Antsy stopped her. "We were worried. Paul is looking for you."

The feeling of guilt, paired with humiliation over acting so foolish kept her from looking Antsy in the eyes. "Where did he go?"

Antsy pointed. "He said he would check the Great Hall, but that was long ago." He caught her arm as she turned. "I think you should wait here. Paul will return. He wanted you to have this." Antsy hurried to Paul's pack and returned with a scroll.

Jasmine unrolled it and saw Standard. She read several lines and recognized it as the first story from the ceremony. She rolled through the scroll until she came to a large blank area followed by the next story. The scroll contained all the stories told by the priestesses. It must have taken hours to translate and write them all down. Jasmine looked up to thank Antsy, but he had melted into the party. Putting the precious scrolls in her pack, she paced around the burrow, waiting for Paul's return. Fidgety and feeling too guilty to wait any longer, she hurried back toward the Great Hall.

The streets overflowed with people dancing, some of it gracefully choreographed, but most was drunken and stumbling. The cold night air mixed with so many other smells had her feeling light headed. It was an ordeal to get to the Great Hall, only to find it quiet. The priestesses were surprised to see her. Ingwa's muzzle pulled in a Kawokee frown. "You should be celebrating. Why are you here?"

"I'm looking for Paul."

"You did not see him? He left here long ago. Did he give you the scroll?"

"Yes. Thank you. Do you know where he went after he left here?"

"No. I'm sorry."

Jasmine felt sick to her stomach for the thousandth time that day. How could she screw this up so badly? Paul had to return to the burrow at some point, and itwas useless scouring the city for him. She sprinted back the way she came.

Jasmine was still several blocks away from the burrow when she heard Paul call her name. He fought his way through the throng of celebrating people toward her. The apology on her lips vanished as he encircled her in his arms and hugged her close.

"I thought something had happened to you. Are you going to meet someone?"

The question took her by surprise. He must have read her expression, because he frowned and asked, "You never gave me a token, and we didn't make any plans. So, I guessed you either wanted to be alone, or you had other ideas."

She shook her head and struggled to think of how he could come to such conclusions. "No. Neither."

"Oh." Paul stood there clearly disoriented.

Jasmine took his arm and pulled him toward their burrow. "Sorry. I took a stroll and lost track of time. Thank you for the scroll."

"My pleasure. I always wanted to know about their religion, but getting near a priestess is difficult even at the best of times."

"Did it make sense to you?" Jasmine turned and looked straight into his eyes.

"Nope. Not one bit."

Jasmine's stomach growled as she fingered the wooden ring in her pocket. Every time she came close to Paul, she froze. This was as close as they ever came to talking about tonight. Now it was here, and she could not bring herself to do or say anything.

"You missed dinner." Paul lengthened his stride. "It's a special dinner. There should be plenty left. But there are a few special dishes you'll never see except tonight. There is a fish that's incredible. I hope you like spicy food."

Her legs ached trying to keep up with him. "I love spicy food."

"And you have to try the desserts."

As they passed burrow after burrow, Jasmine could see that the activities were becoming more festive, almost riotous. There were no musicians now. No one could hear them if there were. She slowed to watch someone blow out a blue flame over a glass before drinking the beverage. "What is that?"

"I don't know the name, but I remember tasting it. Funny. I'll bet I've asked the name every time I've tried it, and yet I never remember."

Paul swept her past the sleeping burrow to the kitchen. He searched every pot and covered dish. "The fish is gone. So is almost everything else. I'm sorry."

"It's not your fault. I was the one who was daydreaming. These desserts look nice." She picked up a fruit cup and popped several pieces in her mouth to appease her stomach. The combination of sweet fruit and tangy syrup made her finish the container off quickly and take the two remaining cups. The fruit also made her thirsty. Jasmine noticed Paul give her a funny look as she downed the last piece. "Do you think our burrow has that drink with the blue flame?"

"Are you sure you want more alcohol?"

"What?"

He pointed to her fruit cup. "That stuff is fermented. Why don't we find something else for you to eat?" Paul chose several of the desserts and the few remnants of dinner and put them in a basket for her. "The drink you were asking about goes fast, but I think I know where I can find one." He pulled her back to the sleeping burrow.

With an evil smile, Paul waltzed up behind Antsy who watched three females dancing around the fire pit. He lifted a basket placed upside down near his brother. Under the basket sat a filled glass.

Antsy turned and grabbed for the glass, but Paul held it away from his brother's flailing arms. "That's mine. Give it back." Antsy's slurred hiss was loud enough to be heard at the other end of the room.

Paul pointed to Jasmine. Whatever he said after that appeased Antsy.

Once back at Jasmine's side, Paul said, "He's already had several. He won't even remember I took this one." Paul took a twig from the fire pit and held it over the glass. A flame flickered on the surface before becoming a crown of blue flames. "Be careful not to shake it until after the top layer burns off, or you will ruin the effect as well as the taste. When it sputters, blow it out and drink it hot. That's when it is nicest."

Jasmine took the glass, and watched the flame. The stem of the glass felt cold in her hand. The dance of the flame was like the dance of the females around the fire pit. A male reached up to one of the dancers, and she fell into his embrace. The other two dancers, having lost their rhythm, turned and pulled each other close. They sank to the ground.

As if Jasmine's drink imitated the dancers, the flame died down.

The chiseled features of Paul's face were illuminated by the blue flame. "Now."

At his command, Jasmine blew out the flame and took a sip, unsure if it would be hot or cold. To her surprise, it was both. The warm, sweet syrup of the bottom was the same as the fruit she loved, but the cool alcohol was the perfect counterpoint. A warm, sweet glow fill her chest. She could not stop until the last drop fell from the glass.

"That was incredible. Thank you for the drink. And thank you for the scroll." Jasmine leaned into him and gave him a light kiss on the cheek.

"My pleasure. As I said, I always wanted to know about their religion."

She looked at his face. "Did it make sense to you?"

"You already asked me that question."

"I did?"

"Yes."

Jasmine lowered her gaze. Both her hands pressed to his chest, in one hand wrapped around her fingers was the wooden ring she forgot to give him. She focused on the ring trying to figure out when she removed it from her pocket, but her brain could not recall.

"Do you want a child?" His words were soft.

"Yes."

"Is the token for me?"

"Yes."

She closed her eyes and felt his warm fingers on her back. There was a chill in the air, but her skin grew hot as she felt the hairs of his beard travel the length of her torso. Warm kisses burned into her thigh. She opened her eyes, surprised to see the rafters of the burrow high above her.

"I should take off my clothes."

Paul chuckled. "No more blue flame for you."

CHAPTER 17

Dr. Campion leaned back in his chair. "What do you have to report?"

The man reeked of over confidence and joy. Macalister knew better than to sit in the chair next to him in the large conference room. Campion considered him an underling, so Macalister took a chair across the table. "I've started separating the dissidents from the other scientists. Next, I'll weed out the soldiers who we can't count on."

Campion smile turned to a scowl. "But you didn't isolate them as I ordered."

What did Campion think he would do? Hang a sign on a shuttle that said, 'deserters enter here'?

"Confining one man to his quarters would work, but eight scientists refused to go back down after their first visit to the settlement. I wish you had discussed the setup with me before you assigned shifts. I could have cut the number of dissenters in half."

"Discuss with you?" Campion chuckled and looked down his nose at the captain.

"Have you learned nothing from your failure with the Godiva project? You should have assigned each doctor a single task. That way each one would feel the others were more responsible for any atrocity they saw. They may view the Kawokee as just a bunch of animals, but it's a little disturbing when those animals can talk."

Anger flashed in Campion's eyes, and he slammed his fist on the table. "You've no right to talk to me like this. I've been given complete authority over this project."

There it was, Campion's massive ego. Macalister could not resist turning the screw and letting the air out of the old windbag. He let the flicker of a smile cross his lips before he spoke. "Yes. You have authority over this project. But need I remind you that the ones who gave you that authority know your weaknesses? You cost them a fortune last time. They're growing tired of cleaning up after you."

"What are you talking about? You know nothing about me, or my superiors."

"The people who put you in charge hired me to make sure you didn't screw up again. You know what they'll do to you if you fail, so stop wasting time and resources."

"I don't believe you."

Macalister clasped his hands, put his elbows on the table, and leaned forward. "I have a job to do, and I will do it. Over your dead body if necessary. You will discuss your plans with me from now on."

"Like hell I will." Campion jumped up from his chair and stood fuming. His confidence was crumbling, or he would not have stayed in the room. "You're just a rent-a-soldier."

"Sit." The thought of shooting Campion raced through Macalister's mind. But it would only give a few minutes of fleeting satisfaction. Managing a group of scientists was like herding cats, and Campion knew what made them tick. He was also good at manipulating public opinion. The man's fists clenched and unclenched.

"And if I don't discuss my plans with you?" Campion slid back into his chair.

Macalister shrugged and sat back. "Then I can't discuss

mine. We'll blindly threaten each other's plans. If you work with me, we can increase our chances of bringing home a cure. For my part, I offer what I've already done. I've isolated two scientists and have them chasing a theory that will keep them busy, but ignorant of anything else that's going on. They won't be spreading discontent. And I'll have a place for others to go if they become too unreliable."

The look in Campion's eyes was all Macalister needed to see. The rat was already trying to turn the situation to his own advantage.

"I'll consider your offer."

"Don't think on it too long." Macalister stood and walked out the door.

CHAPTER 18

Tension ran high in the party. None of them trusted humans, not as a group. Watching their settlements from the high cliffs was less stressful than being right outside their walls. Fawsha wanted to trust Alooza and Sandawz but experience refused to allow him to let down his barriers.

The metal canoe floated down from the sky like a feather. It was easy to see how the Fallen would see these tall beings as gods. The canoe settled on the rock circle like a bird on a nest. A door opened in the side of the craft, and three figures emerged.

Though the lenses of the spyglass were not as good as human-made, it was good enough to recognize the one called Alooza. The fat one would be Sandawz. As the third human descended, Fawsha could just make out the scar that gave the male his nickname. He was first seen during the early raids, and was only spotted once after that. Not being known as a troublemaker did not make Scar a friend.

Fawsha was disobeying orders by not joining his troops as they prepared to attack the death camp. The decision to hold the death camp scientists hostage assumed the sky leader cared for their lives. Worse, it made the Kawokee soldiers vulnerable. Instead, he sent Cow's box. Fawsha's own runners would warn the Adwals of the sky leader's plans. The Adwals would change their strategy and send their fastest runner to the north, but it would be too late. Now that Kawokee villages were targeted, they needed to stop, or at least delay the sky leader until Cow became pregnant. This was still their greatest hope, but it took time and might not work. For now, all he could do was hope and lose as few Kawokee lives as possible.

Fawsha handed the spyglass to one of his soldiers and removed the short-bow from his arm. He nodded to Miwi along with his two bodyguards. To the rest of the party he said, "Watch and be ready."

Fawsha, Miwi, and the two bodyguards walked from their concealed position toward the gate. He reached through the metal bars, feeling for the latch. Why anyone would think such a thing would bar any person with half a brain was beyond him. Once Fawsha slid back the bolt, he opened the gate wide enough for everyone to slip through. He half expected to hear the high pitch squeal of metal on metal, but the gate swung open in silence. He hurried everyone inside and closed the gate but left it unlatched in case they needed to make a quick exit.

They kept to the shadows and hurried through the empty streets to the house of the Fallen. As they climbed the steps of the house, many eyes followed them from the dark windows. The large main room was filled with a strange array of clutter. Huge cushioned benches, many of them torn or stained, lined the room.

The Fallen surrounded the four of them and assaulted them with questions. Fawsha found it disturbing they could not speak or understand their native tongue, but he didn't need to speak human to know what they were saying. There was not a female among them. For weeks, the reports of females being taken away did not alarm him until news from the spies in the north accounted for them. Knowing what the humans planned next, he shared their fear.

Miwi delivered the news to the Fallen of what happened to those who disappeared. There was nothing he could do for them as their grief took hold. Fawsha focused on the safety of his interpreter and the information he needed. He stood by a window and watched.

The Fallen fled to the back of the house as Alooza's team approached. Fawsha preferred to limit contact to the machine. When viewed on the talking box, he could imagine them being his size. To be in a village with so many humans made him feel weak and vulnerable.

Alooza and the fat man sat on one of the cushioned benches, but Scar stayed near the door. Alooza handed Miwi another talking box.

Scar introduced himself, not by his unpronounceable name, but by the Kawokee nickname for him.

Miwi spoke with Scar for several minutes then turned to Fawsha. "Their leader does not negotiate. He does not care about the lives of the humans at the northern facility."

The thought of having such an evil being floating somewhere in the sky high above them disturbed Fawsha. It also solidified his decision. He took the talking box from Miwi and pushed the buttons that would connect him to Jasmine's box. In seconds, the face of his runner appeared. Beside him was the face of the Kap assigned to watch the human settlement to the north. Fawsha cleared his throat before saying, "Wait until nightfall. Rescue any females who live, replacing them with the dead. Burn the settlement to the ground with the humans dead in their burrows."

The Kap's ears flattened back on his head, and he bared his teeth. "My orders are to take no lives unless necessary."

"I have new information. The old plan will get us all killed. We must make this look like an accident. I will take full responsibility."

The other Kap lowered his eyes as his ears rotated

forward but stayed low to his head. He nodded. "I understand."

Fawsha turned off the box and handed it back to Miwi. "As long as no Kawokee are harmed, you and any you bring here will be safe. We will help you in your search where we can."

Sandawz spoke to Miwi, and she answered him.

Miwi shrugged and turned to Fawsha. "He asked if the Pox kills Kawokee. I told him it was rare."

Fawsha was not concerned about the Pox. There were more pressing things to consider. He motioned in Scar's direction. "Ask Scar if soldiers will come to our villages from the sky."

Fawsha was glad to hear their word for no. "Ask how long it will take to rebuild the facility if destroyed."

Her fur bristled at Scar's response, and Miwi turned back to Fawsha with the answer. "He can rebuild it in a few days, but he does not have enough soldiers to guard it. He will have to use the settlements' hunters to guard and to bring in females. That will take him two or three weeks."

"Now ask if the sky leader expects an attack."

Scar spoke in small sentences and paused to let her translate. "No. Their leader does not expect the attack. Scar understands that we have no choice and did not warn their leader."

Fawsha placed his hand on the black box. "Ask him if we can have more of these talking boxes?"

Scar spoke without being asked.

"If Scar gives them to us, their leader will soon know we're using them. He will hear our words and will know Scar betrayed him. We can have this one, but no more."

Fawsha feared Scar, but respected his intellect. "You help us against your own leader. Can you remove this leader?"

Scar was quick to answer.

"That is unlikely."

The translation of Scar's words remained disheartening but expected. Fawsha needed to hurry this news to a meeting of the Adwals. With a long journey ahead of him, and a lot to answer for, he concluded his business with Alooza and Sandawz and hurried his party out of the settlement.

Once safe and back with his soldiers, he ordered them to see Miwi back to their village. Fawsha mounted a horse and headed west. It was a hard day's ride to the relay point where a fresh horse waited. He had argued against using Cow as a weapon against her kind, but things would soon be desperate. The first time a settler was killed trying to take a female from the village, or the first time a Kawokee was killed trying to stop it, the tenuous peace would end. Even if most of a settlement favored the Kawokee, it only took one fool to ignite emotions.

Accusations would be quick to fly and many, human and Kawokee alike, would be itching to retaliate. In the past, if even one human from a settlement receiving Kawokee aid attacked a nearby village, that settlement would get no food or medicine. These rules kept the peace for several years. The offer of a bounty on Kawokee lives in exchange for their precious power cells would force the settlements to choose. It was against Kawokee values to kill unarmed humans, but one human with a charged weapon could annihilate an entire village. Could anyone dare take the risk?

For hours, he tried to imagine how to prevent the coming war. It did not take long to discard each new idea. The only thing he was confident of was the correctness of his decision to destroy the northern settlement. It would delay things for a few weeks, giving them time to prepare for the new attacks.

At least the humans would not be dropping from the skies. This meant the border villages could pull back to protect the cities, and the small villages evacuated to better, more secure sites. Even that solution meant hardship and could not guarantee peace. The thought of a power weapon reaching one of the hidden cities had Fawsha wondering if they should be emptied. Each possibility had benefits along with negative aspects.

If the Adwals knew what Fawsha had planned as a backup, they would cast him out. Perhaps he could not do it. His decision to destroy the northern settlement would cause him enough trouble. Demotion would be the least of his worries.

At each relay point, he ate a hurried meal and rode toward the setting sun. Each fresh horse knew the way to the next stop where he could get a few hours of sleep before continuing. But thoughts of the days ahead fueled his nightmares.

Movement in the corner of his eye attracted his attention. In the time it took to blink, a bird swooped down upon a snake. His eyes followed the bird as it flew up. The outline of the snake twisted in its claws. Silhouetted against the clouds, he saw the snake's head strike the bird's neck. The bird's flight twisted in the air and fell to the ground near Fawsha, but he could not find them in the underbrush and wondered if it had been a dream.

In that moment, Fawsha felt the Mother God answer him, and the response cut his soul. A groan was the only thing to escape his screaming mind. *'Please, no. Not this. Not me.'*

Fawsha knew the Mother God would not change her mind. What he planned would be easy. He could kill them all and end the terror for his people, but only at the cost of his own soul. A cold feeling started in his stomach and spread through his legs and arms.

The numbness of mind and body made the journey feel much longer than it was. When he passed the sentries of the city, he left the horse at the checkpoint and walked toward the city center to report in.

"KapFawsha." The shout echoed through the streets.

The female voice sounded like someone shouting a curse, but how could she know what was in his heart? Had he confessed without knowing or had the Mother God somehow warned her?

"Adwal Molkat." Fawsha expected to meet her in the meeting burrow, not at the city entrance. Silver white streaks flowed over her fur as if a painter brushed them in instead of nature. While her eyes filled with concern her mere presence commanded respect.

Instinctively, Fawsha stood straight and touched the ring in his ear. He did not dare move until the Adwal said her peace.

"Your runner just told me the news. This is a disaster. If only we had known before we attacked the human settlement in the north."

There was no reason to hide what Adwal Molkat would soon know.

"I spoke with the Kap leading the attack before it happened using a human machine. I told him to kill them in the night and make it look like a fire destroyed the settlement."

Her chest swelled as she drew a long breath and let it out. "The others may be angry. I, for one, support your decision. You know it was not yours to make?"

Fawsha was surprised she approved of his decision. He bowed his head. "I am ready to face any punishment the Adwals think right."

The Adwal waved away his comment. "Some will have to overstep their bounds and make quick decisions for our kind to survive." She looked at Fawsha and pursed her lips. "There is much I want to ask, but it is inefficient. The other Adwals will be here by tomorrow night. Rest. Burrow Three East is expecting you. I will send for you when the others arrive."

Fawsha bowed, and they parted ways.

The cool welcome at the burrow was the tension they all felt more than any rumors about him. Bad news followed whenever these meetings were called. He tried to rest but had no memory of sleep when the sun rose. Fawsha was taking his morning meal when the summons came.

He hurried to the central burrow where he was ushered into the inner garden where the Adwals and many of the Kaps sat.

Adwal Molkat stood at the center of the group. In Fawsha's presence, she updated everyone on the news about the human leader's orders. The silence of those assembled could appear as indifference to the uninitiated. "Despite our efforts, the raids on our villages increase. So far, the loss of life has been small, but it will not be long before this war overwhelms us. There are many decisions to make, but one emergency request deserves our immediate attention."

She held up a scroll and read. "Bridgewater Village requests reinforcements to attack the nearby human settlement. They have surrounded it, but the humans have a tunnel which we cannot find, and they continue to attack the caravans."

Adwal Molkat lowered the scroll. "In the past, we've called on Paul to intercede before we made any decisions. This new ship has given the human weapons teeth again. Most settlements know the ship that supplies them today will eventually leave and have maintained their allegiance to the villages near them. This town, outside Bridgewater, has been against us for a long time. Do we risk sending Paul before he has completed his mission?"

One of the regional Adwals spoke up. "It's been three days since the full moon. By the time a runner arrives, Paul will already have succeeded or failed. I say we send him."

"Opposed?" Adwal Molkat's question was answered by their silence.

Another regional Adwal said, "I recommend doubling the number of soldiers we used to send with him since the humans are more powerful."

"Would that do any good?" asked a Kap.

Soon the room filled with noise. There were some who wanted three or four times as many soldiers. While others voiced other concerns.

"The difficulty of amassing four hundred troops from the area would leave the villages vulnerable." The Adwal had to shout above the growing noise, and arguments.

"Silence." All stilled at a single word from Adwal Molkat. "We cannot risk an attack on other villages. We should have them send what they feel they can afford. Is everyone agreed?"

A brief silence answered Adwal Molkat before her motion passed. Fawsha looked around the room at the graying heads and relaxed. This was no time for panic, but measured response.

The Adwal's next announcement had Fawsha wishing a hole would open in the ground and swallow him whole. "Kap Fawsha has taken responsibility for exceeding his authority and ordering a change to the action against the death camp."

Her words gripped his stomach. He tried to appear impassive as she related the events and her opinion of his actions. To his relief, no one disagreed, and a few offered their commendation.

Adwal Molkat's stern warning of the risk he took was delivered in a monotone, but she added, "You will lead the troops against the settlement near Bridgewater. Please leave immediately, and proceed with all urgency."

CHAPTER 19

Jasmine lifted her head at the noise of the parrot and watched over Paul's chest as it threw a fit when a female walked by the open cage. Another of Jasmine's burrow-mates was pregnant. She would soon be whisked off to the Nest, wherever that was, to give birth.

There were less than half as many females in the city now, and Jasmine was one of the ten remaining females in her burrow. What had gone wrong? Did Paul count as one male or four? Why was she so disappointed? In her estimate, there was less than a fifty-fifty chance. And if she got pregnant, there would be problems she couldn't guess. Perhaps it was better this way.

When she was in Paul's arms, Jasmine could forget who she was and why she was here. But was she deluding herself? She enjoyed him. As much as she did not want to admit it, she liked being with him, and it was more than just the sex. It had been a long time since she had a man, but Jasmine knew deep down it would be hard to let him go. Each day she looked for any sign of his feelings. Did they have a future together? Jasmine reminded herself she had a duty to find the cure. That was the reason she crossed the galaxy. Now, the fear of failure grew hazy as if it was no more than a dream until her doubts pounced on them, scattering them like frightened birds. She daydreamed about not going back. Could she stay by Paul's side? Would he want her?

As if in answer to her thoughts, Paul rolled over. "Do you want to walk around the city?"

The city was losing its festive atmosphere and becoming like a small version of a human city. "I've seen enough. I need to know everything about the Nest."

He pulled off his blanket and sat up. "If you become pregnant, you'll see it for yourself."

"If." Jasmine looked at the bird now back in its cage. She checked her shoulder. Dry skin was all that remained of the small cut she received. "It's been a week. The priestess said the potency of the ceremony only lasts a few days. Would they let me go there if I wasn't pregnant?"

He kissed her, making her forget her train of thought for a moment until her scientific self resumed control.

"Should I ask the priestess if I can visit the nest?"

"You could ask, but I doubt it. There are things they're very strict about."

"Have you ever been there?"

Paul felt around in his pack and pulled out his toothbrush. "No. That is one place I'm not allowed to go."

"They don't trust you?" Jasmine thought it odd, considering everything else they appeared to trust him with.

He stood up and stretched. "It's not a matter of trust. It's their religion. From my understanding, few males ever go to a nest, and they're usually priests."

Jasmine followed him to the shower, determined to understand what things the Kawokee would allow. "I know you don't know much about their religion, but what is this Awkae the elder mentioned? The one back in the mining village."

He slipped out of his shorts and shivered as the cool water hit him. "You didn't ask before the ceremony?"

Jasmine liked the view and took advantage of Paul's lack of inhibitions. "I was preoccupied. The only reason it's important now is boredom."

"I'm not entertaining enough?" Paul gave her a questioning look, and she scowled at him.

"You know what I mean. I've read the translated text a hundred times and done everything the priestesses have told me to do." Jasmine looked away and bit her lip to keep her tears at bay. "It didn't work." She looked back up at Paul. "I need a distraction."

"Sorry. I've never heard of it. You could ask the priestesses. There are a few still in town."

"I'd rather hear it from someone who doesn't speak in fairy tales. When do I get to go back? I've got a lot of reports to send." She slipped out of her pants and was about to join him in the shower when someone called his name. Jasmine turned and saw an unfamiliar face.

"You're summoned. It's urgent." The male turned and ran off.

Paul left the water running. "Your turn." He jogged naked after the runner.

Jasmine almost called after him. It would not have done any good. A summons would trump her wishes. She showered and afterward did her laundry, leaving them to dry in the warm sunlight. When she walked past the caged bird, it did not react or ruffle a feather. Halan looked depressed since Louy left for the Nest. If nothing else, their language was getting easier to understand.

Not long after he left, Paul returned with three Kawokee. Each wore a single earring. Paul threw all his things in his pack. "There's an emergency. I have to go."

"I'm going with you." The words were out of her mouth before she could think of any good reason she should leave with him.

"The village of Bridgewater is having problems with the nearby human settlement. They massacred another caravan."

"You negotiate between the Kawokee and humans. I can help. They know you're with the Kawokee. If I say I'm a scientist from the ship, they'll assume I'd be on their side. Who do you think they will trust more?" For a spur-of-the-moment response, Jasmine thought it was a decent excuse.

"You might be right." Paul threw on his pants and put his pack over his shoulder. "I'll have to check it with Fawsha. But we need to leave right now."

"So, what's the situation?" Jasmine was a little startled Paul agreed. She didn't have much to collect, but had everything in her pack before looking around the near empty burrow for anything she may have missed. When she nodded that she had everything, Jasmine hugged Halan goodbye, and they set a blistering pace toward the river. As expected, the details were thin. They only had the Kawokee side of the story.

When they arrived at the stable, a dozen armed Kawokee, both male and female, waited for them.

Paul was a man of few words before the ceremony, but he had been chatty since they were together. It disturbed Jasmine that he was once again quiet. She did not presume to know him well, but he seemed worried. As they traveled along the trail, Jasmine attempted a few questions. "Have you handled situations like this before?"

He nodded. "A few times. There have always been a certain number of killings on both sides. Every village remotely close to a settlement has problems, but this one is worse than the others. The town near Bridgewater was a mining town, but that seems to have stopped. The town is one of the oldest and was the largest until the Pox outbreak which they blamed on the Kawokee. Bridgewater is the spot where it's easy to cross the river. After humans started shooting at trade caravans, Bridgewater became a border village and holds the crossing, but the humans get around it. They must have a tunnel and use it to attack from the south. This is the sixth attack in a month. It seems like the work of a few individuals, but the town won't do anything to stop them. If they don't stop, we'll have no choice but to attack the settlement. Thanks to the ship paying in power cells, they're well armed. Which means the odds are in their favor."

"Making enemies of those who outnumber you doesn't seem very smart. Don't they rely on the Kawokee for food and medicine like the others?"

"They don't trust Kawokee food and don't allow us in. All the other settlements conserve what little power they have, but this one's lights still burn bright."

"So, what's the plan?"

"I was going to stand alone outside the fence and hope they come out to talk. But they're more likely to shoot at me. Hopefully you're right, and they'll talk with you. If they don't assume you're on their side, maybe they'll think you're at least unbiased. Even so, it will be dangerous. If fighting starts, they might use the tunnels to attack us on two fronts."

She expected Paul to say something like, if fighting starts I want you to go somewhere safe. That would be the human thing to do, but he was very Kawokee in this way. "What if we can get the other settlements to fight on the Kawokee side? A few individuals can be bought for a power cell. Most rely on the Kawokee. I would hope some of them would fight with us."

Paul nodded. "If we could get a dozen humans with pulse rifles, we'd have the advantage. But time is against us. It'd take a long time to visit the friendly settlements and gather volunteers. We might find anyone willing to risk their lives for us, but we don't have any power cells."

"I left six spares at the border village where I was staying."

"Really? Why?" Paul's forehead wrinkled as he looked at her.

"That particular comm-vid is quantum coupled. I couldn't risk losing the signal and couldn't be sure of staying in range of the ship's RF.

His mouth hung open. "Well, it doesn't solve the time problem, but it'll help. If we could show them we have serious firepower, they might negotiate."

Paul turned and faced the trail once again. "How we proceed is up to Fawsha."

"Fawsha?"

"He's responsible for the eastern border villages. We're to meet him at Bridgewater."

When they came to a river, they entered a small fishing village where they traded the horses for boats. At night they rested and ate before moving along the river. This went on for several days until they came to a narrow part of the river. The soldiers loaded bolts in the crossbows attached to their arms.

Jasmine asked, "Are we expecting an attack?"

"It's possible. The human settlement is less than an hour downstream." Paul pointed to a wooden covered bridge with stone pillars. "And there is Bridgewater."

A trail led up a hill to one side of the bridge. While a large party of soldiers camped on the other embankment.

Fawsha stood apart from the soldiers and walked toward them as they docked. "Cow? Why are you here?"

Paul helped her out of the boat as their party unloaded. "Where else would I be?"

His ears tilted forward. "You wanted to see the Nest."

"The priestesses wouldn't let me go unless I was pregnant, so I decided to try to help Paul."

Fawsha grunted. "I'm sorry. I hoped things would turn out different." His eyes lowered. "I have an urgent request for both of you." He led them to an empty burrow and told them everything that had happened while they were at Gehnica.

Jasmine knew what the scientists were doing with the females. Every detail of the Godiva project was repeatedly broadcast to all inhabited worlds. "I'm sure some doctors refused to participate. Not all humans are evil."

"I know. Alooza and several others now live in the settlement near where we first met. They seek a cure independent from the others. They ask questions I cannot answer. You are the only one who can help them. You must hurry back to them. If they can find a cure, perhaps war can be averted."

Paul leaned forward. "KapFawsha, Jasmine has an idea that might help with the mining settlement."

She watched Fawsha's reactions as Paul discussed their ideas.

Fawsha sighed. "It would take too long to get humans to aid us. For the war, yes. It would help to have as many humans on our side as possible. But I fear time, in this case, is not—" Fawsha's head snapped up. "You have six power cells?"

"In my backpack at the border village."

"You both need to help Alooza. But first, we must deal with the mining settlement. I have an idea of what we can do."

CHAPTER 20

Jasmine walked from the safety of the trees. Dread ate at her confidence, and she wished she was back in the burrow at Bridgewater. Held within Paul's strong arms, she felt as if anything were possible. In the weeks of waiting and planning, the danger seemed far in the distance. The nervous tension turned to pure terror when the day arrived. Everything started with her. For the first time since she met Paul, Jasmine was certain of what he felt toward her. All that morning he refused to leave her side, and on the trek toward the settlement Paul would not let go of her hand. To leave him proved harder than walking the weed covered path toward the settlement.

With every step, she braced herself for the pain of an energy pulse. Strained nerves already had her stomach tied in knots and unable to eat anything all morning. So many things could go wrong with this plan.

The barbed wire that crowned the stone walls on either side of the gate did not keep out animals. The settlers were ready for a fight. Jasmine passed the high gate and saw six men with an assortment of guns standing in windows of the nearby buildings. Two followed her down the street, keeping their distance.

The moment she walked into the tavern, she was confronted by men holding knives and pistols. The only female she could see in the room was an old woman who tended the taps. Her voice was akin to breaking glass as she demanded, "How did you get past the Kawokee?"

"I am one of the scientists from the ship. The Kawokee offered to give me data for my research in exchange for negotiating with you. And they offer to withdraw if you close the tunnels."

"We're ready for them. It's time we finish them," said one man. He snarled and spit on the dirty floor.

"Quiet, Buford." A thin, older man silenced the others. "I am Harmon Jacks, mayor of this town. Everyone calls me Jacks." He reached out to shake her hand. "Welcome to Forsaken."

With some reluctance, Jasmine shook his hand. "Forsaken?"

"The company that set this town up thought it was sitting on top of a deposit of rare earths. They dug a tunnel and found a reactor shield from some old ship. There were no mineral deposits, only debris. Another company beat them to the rich coal fields. They promised to come retrieve us so we could work somewhere else. Bastards never did. Maggie, pour this woman a drink."

"Before or after I spit in it?"

Jacks glared at the old woman who grumbled but poured the drink. He grabbed the glass before she could carry out her threat and handed it to Jasmine. "I'm surprised they didn't send Paul."

"I met him. He said you would kill him rather than speak to him." Part of Jasmine wanted to ask Jacks how a company could make such a mistake, but Jasmine knew it would be too dangerous to get distracted.

"Certainly not." Jacks looked down his nose at Jasmine. "We'd torture him first then kill him. He's a Kawokee puppet."

"I thought he was cute."

As Jacks barked a laugh at her response, Jasmine sniffed at the contents of the glass and wrinkled her nose at the acrid stench. She could not imagine drinking the cloudy mix and asked a question to keep from doing so. "What's your gripe with the Kawokee?"

"Beside them being murdering, thieving, disease carrying animals?"

Jasmine forced a smile, "Yeah, beside that."

"They sold us contaminated grain that killed half our animals. We charge cells in return for fresh meat. Since your ship pays for Kaw females with cells, the hunters stopped bringing anything to us. We depend on the hunters. What they do outside is not our business."

"What the hunters do is your problem if they use your tunnels to attack the Kawokee villages and hide behind your walls."

Jacks turned to address the half dozen men. "We can defend this town." Everyone in the tavern grumbled their agreement.

After setting her glass on the nearest table Jasmine tried to sound nonchalant as she spoke. "Well, they also have well-armed humans on their side."

Her words gained everyone's attention. The mayor's cocky smile turned to a frown and looked around before asking, "You saw them?"

"I heard them talk about four humans with guns. I didn't see them."

Jacks crossed his arms. "Who are these people who're fighting with the Kawokee?"

She shrugged. "Volunteers from towns that are dependent on the Kawokee; I suppose."

Jacks motioned the old woman behind the bar to pour him a drink. "Well, I don't want to get into a fight with the other towns." He swilled down half the contents of the glass before eyeing Jasmine. "You say they'll leave us alone if we close a tunnel?"

Before Jasmine could ask if there was more than one

tunnel, a filthy man with angry red claw marks on his hand jumped up. "No. You can't. The Kawokee have us bottled up. That tunnel makes this town a central hub for all of us. Those cells keep us alive. Not just this settlement, but all of them."

Jasmine tried not to stare at the man's wounds as she spoke, "There are other ways to hunt. Bow and arrow can be just as effective."

The filthy one grabbed her arm. "She is one of them."

"Hey. I'm just delivering a message." Jasmine pushed him back, breaking his hold. Filth lunged at her again, and she leapt out of reach.

"She's going to tell them how many guns we have and that there's only one opening."

"Shut up you idiot." Jacks backhanded the man sending him to the floor. "Even if you hadn't opened your big yap, I had no intention of letting her leave."

Another man grabbed Jasmine from behind and shoved her into a chair. "Maybe she can give us some information. How many Kawokee are out there?"

"I didn't count. Look. I'm not part of this. I just need data."

Filth pulled himself off the floor and shouldered his rifle. "We're taking the fight to them before the Kaw lovers get here." The men in the room cheered. He glared at Jacks and grabbed Jasmine's wrist. "And we're taking her with us."

"How do you know the traitors aren't already out there with them? You attack them and they'll attack us for sure." Jacks stepped forward ready to take another swing at Filth, but the man was faster. He put a pistol in Jacks chest and pushed him into a chair.

"Don't ever hit me. The next time you try, I'll make sure it's the last." With the pistol held high, the man pushed Jasmine toward the kitchen. A dozen armed men followed as he shoved her out the back door and down the street. Her forced marched ended when a man jogged forward and threw open a shed door. Jasmine thought they would confine her or worse, but the sight of a stairwell leading into the ground had her rethinking her predicament. Boxed in, they forced her down the steep stairs.

The angle of decent required Jasmine to grip the handholds which protruded from the walls. Once she reached the bottom, she clasped her arm wanting to keep the camera in her wrist-com from shaking. The clearer the picture sent from her wrist-com the better Fawsha and Paul could identify where she and the tunnel was. Not only had they retrieved her energy cells but the comm-vid. Without it, Jasmine doubted she could have convinced either one to let her step inside the settlement. "What will taking me with you accomplish? I'm just another human to them."

Filth laughed. "Somehow, I doubt that."

Her eyes adjusted to the dim light. A smooth circular tunnel with a thick cable running down the center stretched into the distance. Bits of broken rock rolled underfoot along the hard-packed dirt floor. They half pushed, half dragged her along for at least a kilometer where the tunnel appeared to end at a black wall. As they drew close to the wall, the sides of the tunnel widened.

The black wall turned out to be the drill that carved the tunnel. A narrow crack between the machine and the rocky wall allowed the group to squeeze around to the front of the machine and enter a wide cavern. A chunk of metal shone bright where the drill tried to bite into it. One side of the metal was melted but the other side was still smooth with straight edges. As they climbed over the rocky floor of the cavern, the group passed close to the seared metal. In the faint light from the lamps rigged along the path, Jasmine saw lettering on the pitted surface. The symbols were not Standard but some version of Old Earth. The realization stunned her, and she walked in a haze to wherever the men pushed her. Paul's words about the hidden cities echoed through her head and consumed her thoughts. "It's as if they feared some evil god." She snapped out of her shock when they neared an elevator platform. The others readied their weapons.

As the platform ascended, Jasmine rubbed her sore wrist. "I'll scream and let them know where you are."

"Go ahead. We want them to know we have you."

"Then I won't scream," she spat.

"You'll scream." He twisted her arm behind her back. The force of which made her wince.

The platform stopped, and the walls of the cylinder dropped away. They stood in the middle of a sandbar near a stream. The call button for the platform was camouflaged by the bark of a fallen tree. Jasmine did her best to make sure she got a decent image of the spot until the man shoved her into the stream. Water soaked her shoes as the rock infused streambed made walking difficult.

"Why can't we walk the bank?" asked Jasmine.

"They're not tracking us back to the tunnel. No way."

When the group left the stream, they tramped through the woods for a long distance. Unlike the hunters, Jasmine made as much noise as possible as she dragged her feet through dead leaves and kicked at dried sticks and small stones. When the village of Bridgewater came into view, the hunters leveled their weapons and marched forward. Filth yanked Jasmine along with one hand while holding his pistol in the other.

Desperate to warn the guards to their presence, Jasmine screamed in Kawokee at the top of her lungs. "Run." The village was too far away to see anyone, but it was unlikely they would, seeing as the village had already been evacuated to temporary lodgings. Within seconds of her shouts, the hunters fired at what they thought was a thriving village. Plumes of black smoke shot up from the above ground buildings and surrounding trees. The burrows would need to be within a closer proximity for the energy weapons to damage more than entranceways.

A wooden bolt protruded from the nearby tree with a pop. Jasmine could not see the Kawokee who fired the errant shot. She dropped to the ground and curled up into a ball as best she could while Filth tried to haul her up by her arm.

Several more bolts flew through the trees to sink into human flesh or protective heavy leather.

"Where are they?"

"I don't know. They're all around us."

Filth released Jasmine's arm to shoot a wild arc into the trees. His actions ignited the dry underbrush.

A crossbow bolt buried itself into a hunter's face, and he fell backward. His head hit the ground, right in front of Jasmine, but he didn't get back up. How long she stared at the feather bolt protruding from his eye socket she did not know.

The village was obscured in thick smoke but the men around her continued to fire their weapons. Whether it was on the village or in the directions of the defending Kawokee, she could not tell. An explosion sounded from the direction of the village. She was certain a hunter tripped a well concealed booby trap.

Jasmine knew she needed to get as far from the fire fight as she could, but Filth's frantic shooting kept her planted to the ground near his feet. Thick smoke and the encroaching forest fire spurred her from the ground. Using her body weight, she threw herself on Filth and tried to wrestle the rifle from his hands. He nailed her across the face for her efforts. The force of the blow had her back on the ground and seeing stars.

When Jasmine could focus and look up, it was to see Filth's head explode. Thinking one of the other hunters was shooting blind, Jasmine stayed planted on the ground. The whine of energy weapons continued to fill the air along with men's screams. Only once the noise died down did Jasmine dare rise to her hands and knees and look around.

She thought about the name of the Kap in charge of the forces near the village but could not remember the name and called out, "Kap? It's me, Cow. Are they all dead? I think they're all dead." Jasmine's voice sounded weak even to her own ears. She coughed and squinted into the thick smoke of blazing fires. With a quick prayer she was heading in the right direction, she scurried through the forest keeping low to the ground. The thought of getting her directions crossed and stumbling over a tripwire or falling into a pit lined with sharp wooden steaks kept her from running full tilt away from the carnage. An explosion somewhere behind her had her wondering if the forest fire ignited a trap or if it was a hunter bent on escape.

Jasmine screamed and jumped as she felt someone grab her arm and pull her back.

"It's me, KapAnu. We need to get to the stream. It will be safer there." Heat from the fires seared Jasmine's skin. She let KapAnu lead her through the forest as smoke threatened to choke them both. Far above them, the black cloud rose and obscured the sun.

Her head throbbed, and her chest burned. Jasmine took a deep breath as her feet touched the wet sand of the stream. KapAnu pulled Jasmine into the water until she stood waist deep. Other soldiers stood in the water or on rocks. KapAnu turned to the others and asked, "Did anyone check the bodies on the ground? Was anyone still alive?"

"If any hunter lives, the fire will take care of them. As for our own, the injured were taken to the other side of the stream."

Jasmine did not know the name of the soldier who spoke to KapAnu, but she tried regaining the Kap's attention. "KapAnu, where's Fawsha and Paul?"

"They're attacking the settlement. I was assigned here in case the hunters attacked KapFawsha's flank." KapAnu pointed up stream. "Fawsha is there on that ridge. Can you contact them on your device?"

With the fear induced adrenaline rush burned away Jasmine almost fell into the stream. If it had not been for KapAnu steadying her until she could get to a smooth rock to sit on, Jasmine would have ended up underwater.

"Thank you," said Jasmine. Used to having the thing kept in Paul's possession, Jasmine still felt foolish for not thinking of her wrist-com.

The wind picked up clearing the air of smoke. Jasmine hoped the gusts was strong enough to turn the fires back on itself or if nothing more bring rain.

A few deep breaths helped clear Jasmine's mind. She touched her wrist-com and took it off mute. "Fawsha? Paul? Can you hear me?"

The face of a Kawokee Jasmine recognized but could not remember their name filled the tiny screen. "Cow? You are well, Yes?"

"Yes, I'm fine. Where's Paul and Fawsha?"

"Humans attacked. Everyone is fighting. I was told to wait here until I heard from you and KapAnu. What of the hunters?"

"Dead, and I know where the tunnel entrance is."

A loud boom came over the wrist-com speaker and was echoed through the air. The Kawokee on the screen cringed and clapped his hands over his ears. A series of smaller explosions followed before the Kawokee on the screen looked up. "Show KapAnu. I go now."

The Kawokee did not shut the comm-vid off or touch it in any way. Through the tiny screen Jasmine could just make out the smoke filled detail as flashes of light dotted the screen. Whether they were from human held energy weapons or Kawokee modified guns, Jasmine did not know.

Unable to shoulder the largest of the weapons, the Kawokee mounted it on a horse-drawn cart. It had reminded Jasmine of the one carried by the hunter who killed her first guide. Her shiny energy cells were in sharp contrast to its weathered stock and tarnished barrel.

Another gun must have been buried too long. The casing had cracked allowing water to seep in and short the electronics.

The other weapons were small enough for a strong Kawokee to hold, but they still looked like children playing military.

"I should have asked about Paul. If he's all right."

KapAnu put a hand on Jasmine's shoulder. "LutPaul will be fine. Show me the tunnel entrance."

CHAPTER 21

Arluza heard the sharp ring of the comm-vid. Excitement mixed with worry as he removed his protective gloves and scurried toward the black box in the next room. He jammed his finger on the answer button hoping that whoever was on the other end could wait. Jasmine's smiling face filled the screen, and the sound of her voice sent a wave of relief through Arluza's tense muscles.

"Hi there. It's just me."

"Jasmine, you're back? Did you find the cure?"

"No, but I've made some exciting discoveries." Jasmine looked down at her wrist-com and touched the surface. "I am downloading details of the ceremony and a translation of all related religious teachings. It'll take time to search the documents. I think the answer's in a salve they put on the females. Somehow it must inoculate them long enough to give birth. I'm not sure if it'll work for humans, but it's a start. At least we know the Kawokee reproduce. I saw children. A small group, about six years old. For some reason, they hide their young in places they call nests. The practice predates the settlements. I think there are at least three such places in the area, but they keep the location secret. Other than the priests, males aren't even allowed near the place. At least that's the impression I got. Only pregnant females can go there. Not being pregnant, they wouldn't let me anywhere near a nest. From what I understand, children get their basic education there before they're sent out to the cities."

"Cities?"

Jasmine looked up from her wrist-com. "You should see them. They're amazing."

"Kawokee don't have cities. In the sixty odd years of human settlement no one's ever seen one."

"Or they've never told anyone." Jasmine stopped talking and stared down at her wrist-com. Her voice lowered. "No one in sixty years."

"Jasmine?"

She looked back up at the screen and bit her lip. "They invited me there. What would happen to someone who stumbled across one?"

Arluza was not sure what was going through Jasmine's mind but it made her face go pale.

"They're hidden. Hard to find unless you know where you're going. Though I didn't see any, I'd guess the trails are guarded. But that's not the weird part."

"Weirder than secret cities?"

She nodded and continued. "You can't see them from the sky." Jasmine looked straight at Arluza and asked, "What makes an entire race that doesn't have the power of flight, hide entire cities from the sky? And I'm not just talking a city, I'm saying every one around the globe. Old Earth had multiple governments well after the first wave of migrations. This planet has a single authority. How does that happen? What makes a non-space going planet unite."

Arluza was not sure how to answer and grasped at the first thought that came to mind. "They live in burrows. Wouldn't they do the same for larger settlements?"

"The city was different. Look at the pictures, and you'll see what I mean. Gehnica held around ten thousand Kawokee. During the festival, the population had to be four times that much, if not more. Would they have hidden them because of the ship?"

"Our ship?"

"No." Jasmine shook her head. "An ancient ship. There is, or was, a human settlement north of where I'm at. The residence called the town Forsaken. The mining company that set it up left the workers and equipment after the site proved worthless. Seems what they thought was a rich field of ore was actually the heat shield and other debris from an old ship."

"And no one reported it?"

"Maybe the mining company folded before they could. Or they covered it up for some reason. What's more likely is they filed a report and no one bothered to read it."

"There are ships out there that fail. Most break up and burn before they hit a planet's surface."

"Look at the picture." Jasmine touched her wrist-com, and the comm-vids screen shifted. The scorched metal plate filled the screen. Jasmine must have had someone else take the picture because she stood with her hand planted on the metal surface.

He leaned close to the screen. "That's bigger than you. What is that? Seven? Eight meters across?"

"And just as high. Look at the next photo." The screen shifted, and a series of faded letters on a pitted surface appeared. "What do you think?"

"It's not standard." Arluza sat back in his chair. "Are we talking about a third race of beings? Someone that came in and scared the Kawokee underground?"

"No. I'm sure that heat shield came off a human vessel. I've seen similar characters in my studies. Just don't remember where."

The picture disappeared, and Jasmine returned to the screen. "If that thing fell sometime within the last hundred years, a mining company wouldn't have made such a grand mistake, would they?"

"I would think the surveyor would be lucky to get a job

with cleaning bots after a mistake like that. Besides, wouldn't something that big effect the environment?" Arluza scratched his head and frowned. "I know it's not my field of study, but something that size, somebody's going to notice."

"My thoughts exactly. Do you think you can find out what ship this thing belongs to?"

"I'll do what I can. We've made some discoveries too."

Jasmine raised an eyebrow. "We?"

"Didn't Fawsha tell you? I'm down here, on the planet. It was the only way to get away from Campion. A dozen other scientists are here with me. I don't know why, but Campion hasn't noticed a few of us have jumped ship. We've mapped the Kawokee genome. Do you want to add more to your weird pile? We're close enough to crossbreed."

He held up his hand before Jasmine could ask a question. "Wait. There's more. The most astonishing thing is the amount of evidence that the Kawokee DNA has been altered. We're working on the theory of a terraforming ship coming here, altering the Kawokee, and making the Kaw virus."

Jasmine waved her hand, and she shouted at the screen. "That's it. The heat shield. It was Old Earth writing. And the size, wouldn't that match the size? Weren't they monstrous? But why would a terraforming ship alter alien DNA or create a sterilization virus?"

Arluza's mind raced with Sander's current theory and arguments, adding in Jasmine's discoveries. Sander's would want to see the heat shield she found, perhaps even bring it back to their work site.

Something still did not fit. "Could it have been an accident? I'm mean, terraformers were supposed to turn dead planets into living worlds, not massacre entire civilizations. And if they tried to kill the Kawokee, why did the Kawokee welcome the first colony ships? Wouldn't they have tried killing them on the spot, fearing another attack?"

"Good point." Jasmine scowled and drummed her fingers on a table. "Could that be why the cities are hidden along with their young? Maybe the terraformers wore suits, and they didn't recognize the settlers as being the same species."

"We're forgetting something."

"What?" She stopped drumming her fingers and looked at him.

"The heat shield. If it's buried under a bunch of rock, where's the rest of the ship? What happened to it?" When he noticed Jasmine's distracted look, Arluza asked, "What is it?"

"If something that size fell into a planet's atmosphere, could it destroy a civilization? Say, turn an industrial culture back to stone age?"

"They did use radioactive power sources. Like I said, that's not my area of expertise. But I would think it would mess with environmental factors in all the worst ways. Why do you ask?"

"Because the Kawokee are not the savages everyone thinks they are."

"You care to elaborate?"

"Humans looked at their laws and thought they were cruel without asking why they had the laws. We saw their homes and villages and thought, because they weren't like us, they were simple. Nobody saw the machines."

When Jasmine paused, Arluza did not dare speak. He did not want to break her thought process.

"The Kawokee don't have a pre-tech society, it's post-tech. Or at least post-industrial."

"The religious text you sent. Does it pre-date or post-date a terraforming ship? I'm mean, the possibility that ancient texts might still exist that mentioned anything about a human terraforming ship, would be too good to hope for. And even if it did, anything written from their perspective would be suspect. Wouldn't it?"

She shook her head. "I don't know, but if the religious stories predate terraformers, or are connected to them, there might be old records that would help to undo all this."

"How old are these religious writings?"

"I don't know, but I'll ask." Jasmine backed away from the camera and gestured to a man standing beside her.

The sudden tug of jealousy felt strange to Arluza as Paul's arms encircled Jasmine. The following twinge of fear of someone interfering with a lifelong friendship had Arluza shifting in his seat.

"You remember Paul?" asked Jasmine.

"Hello. Alooza," Paul corrected the mispronunciation, "Arluza. The Kawokee call this the year 1453."

Arluza did some rough calculations based on the Kawokee solar year. "It's possible that piece of ship you found is from a terraformer. We'll have to date it to be sure. But the Kawokee calendar year falls within the correct date line of Sander's theory. Are there any ancient holy places; anything that might help prove our theory?"

"There are a few," Paul drawled, "but the ones I know of were either destroyed by the first missionaries, or mining corporations. There's still the monasteries where they train the priestesses. But visiting one would take getting the consent of the Adwals."

"Adwals?"

"Kawokee rulers." Paul pulled at the ring in his ear.

"How long would that take?"

"Don't count on it happening in our lifetime. Remember what I said about the first missionaries and miners destroying the monasteries?"

"Yes."

"They murdered religious leaders. Priest and priestess alike."

The thought of a civilized person doing such a thing made Arluza cringe. Memories of Campion's facility flooded his mind, making his stomach churn and threatened to purge his lunch. He felt guilty for asking. "How long would it take for you to go to one of those destroyed sites? The oldest one. Maybe there was something missed? I hate to ask, but if the terraformers did something, they'd make sure there was a record. Something that would last for centuries."

Paul shook his head. "That would be a long journey, and I don't know where they are. I'll ask permission to take Jasmine to one of the current monasteries and the locations of the desecrated sites. Someone should know how old each of them are. We don't have time to visit every site. The Kawokee will need me if there's another fight. And I'm sure there will be."

Jasmine looked away. "Fawsha told me about the scientists killing Kawokee females."

Arluza folded his hands to keep them from shaking. "I know. We were the ones who warned him. Our little group is made up of people who refused to take part in Campion's torture chamber. I'm still waiting for Campion to have us killed, but none of the ship's soldiers will obey him or protect the new facility. It might be because one of those soldiers helped put this group together. His name is Macalister. The Kawokee call him, Hintz."

Jasmine's head turned. "That means scar."

CHAPTER 22

Campion slammed his fist into the table. "You knew they would attack? Why didn't you tell me?"

Macalister's opinion of the man dropped another notch. "I made the terms of my help clear. You didn't value my opinion or pay for my services."

Campion pointed a thick finger at his face. "You let your own men die?"

A yawn escaped Macalister. He hated working with people who acted like pampered children when they did not get their way. "They were soldiers killed by other soldiers in a war you started. You killed them; not I." He stood, but did not turn away. "I assumed you were ready to meet my terms."

Campion looked at the floor. "Fine. What do you want?"

Macalister sat and folded his hands in his lap. "Must I repeat myself?"

The muscles in Campion's face twisted. "No. I'll lower the price of each cell to three females." He spread his hands. "Does that meet with your approval?"

"Yes. You will also pay a cell for pictures of bands of six or more Kawokee moving outside villages. The pictures must be dated, with coordinates. You'll also assign scientists not currently conducting research to monitor ground based tracking systems I set up."

"What good is that?"

"It will help us find places the Kawokee call nests. You would have an unlimited number of test subjects already impregnated. It would save months or years of research time."

"Damn it. You know how important this is to our mission. Why didn't you tell me this before? Who's side are you on?"

"I found out about it recently. It's the Kawokee's most closely guarded secret. As to sides, I have only one mission, to find a cure. I don't care who gets the glory or who is blamed."

CHAPTER 23

The cold morning air chilled Jasmine's side as Paul pulled away the blanket and put on his clothes. The pattering of raindrops on the tent told her today would be like the past three, overcast and gloomy. She pulled the blanket over her and tried to get another few minutes of sleep. As Paul stepped outside, a cold mist blew in. Antsy, who was dozing beside her, yanked the covers to himself and cursed, leaving her half covered.

With Antsy in the same bed, she felt too self-conscious to do much with Paul or respond to his affections. Not that Paul was as frisky as he was before Bridgewater. Both Paul and Antsy hadn't been the same since they arrived at the settlement where Arluza and Sanders worked.

There were warm buildings and real beds all around her, but Paul and Antsy wouldn't even try to spend a night in one. They complained about the smell. Having been away from civilization so long, she agreed there was a faint mustiness to the place.

It was an odd feeling coming back to where she started. Mayor Corbin was overjoyed to see her. The warm feeling it gave Jasmine, that a stranger cared for her well-being, evaporated when she found out the reason for his jovialness. It seemed he always bet the long odds, and he won a tidy sum with her safe return.

When Paul entered the tent, she expected him to get under the covers. Instead he sat on the floor and warmed cold hands over the small electric heater, his only concession to human comforts. "I'm worried. Fawsha has disbanded the border villages to reinforce the larger villages. The best we've been able to do is force hunters to grab females from outlying areas. Dozens of Kawokee die every day trying to protect their homes. We can't keep this up for long."

Antsy grumbled and covered his ears.

Jasmine sat up and pulled on her top. The rest of her clothes she shoved under the edge of the blanket to warm them. "You survived a major battle against a well-armed town. What is so dangerous about visiting a religious ruin?"

"With a quarter of this world's humans turned hunter with new weapons and charged cells, compliments of the ship, and dozens more paid to defend the research facility, dozens of Kawokee die every day trying to protect their village. We can't keep this up for long. Sooner or later, the ship will find a nest. The Kawokee will die out if that happens."

"Not if we find the answer first." Jasmine had those same fears, but for the first time in a long while, felt optimistic. "We all agree the evidence I brought back hints at terraformers and some positive relationship with the Kawokee. They would have left instructions, perhaps the viral vector itself."

When his expression did not lighten, Jasmine asked, "When this is over and the Kawokee are safe, what will you do?"

"Do?" Paul shrugged. "What I always do; I guess. I never thought about it."

"How about going off world? Go exploring? There are so many things I want to show you. My family and friends would love to meet you."

"There is more here I want to show you, too."

Antsy groaned, twisted into a ball, and mumbled, "Talk outside."

She knew Antsy understood every word they said although he never spoke Standard if he could help it. "And you are welcome to come with us." Jasmine slipped her bare feet under the covers and buried them in the warm fur of his back.

Antsy screamed a curse and thrashed, but she knew he liked it. And he liked her. She understood him now.

He sat up and looked at the roof of the tent. Jasmine knew she would hear the craft in a few seconds. A low sound like thunder heralded the arrival of the shuttle. Jasmine put on her shoes and followed Paul out of the tent.

Macalister said the shuttle would land in the morning. Jasmine would have preferred arriving at the settlement at first light, but she understood he had to work within his own restrictions. There was no way to contact the town near the desecrated site, and they knew very little about those who lived there. With the attacks on the research facility and Bridgewater, many towns were on guard. Shuttles from the ship were not as welcome as they once were fearing Kawokee reprisal.

She saw the glow behind the clouds announcing the shuttles arrival. When it settled on the pad and the hatch opened, Paul gathered the bags they packed the night before and stacked them at the edge of the landing pad. "Shall we wake your friends to say goodbye?"

"They can talk to us anytime. And Arluza's not good company until after several cups of coffee. It's more important we use the daylight we have to travel." Jasmine stepped back into the tent and picked up the remaining bags. "Antsy, get up. The shuttle is here."

Antsy cursed her, and she cursed him back. Her curses were feeble compared to his, but she saw Antsy hiding a smile.

All three headed for the shuttle.

A middle-aged man stood just inside the doors of the craft, out of the rain. He had a military bearing, and one of his eyebrows were split by a pale thin line. "Hello Jasmine, Paul. Pleased to meet you at last."

Jasmine was tempted to call him Hintz, but was not sure if he cared for the nickname. "Captain Macalister, thank you for keeping our little group of renegade scientists hidden from Campion."

Paul said nothing but followed her into the shuttle.

Macalister helped them secure their gear in nets at the back of the shuttle where two ATVs were strapped down. "These are for you if you want them. They can take you much farther and much faster than those things you call horses."

The bright colored machines looked brand new. "That's wonderful," said Jasmine. I didn't know the ship had any of these."

"I had them fabricated. They have enough charge to get you across the continent. I've included a wagon with tools in case of bad terrain." He pointed to the controls on the handle bar. "This is the on/off switch."

Paul waved his hand. "We don't want them. If we can't get horses at the town, we'll walk. I'll get my brother." He turned back to the tent.

Shocked by Paul's rudeness, Jasmine smiled, in apology. "This is very thoughtful. Thank you. He's uncomfortable with machines, but he'll change his mind. I'm sure this will cut several days off the travel time."

Macalister seemed unruffled. "I've made maps of the location specified. With these, you should be able to get there from the settlement in an hour. By horse, half a day."

He touched the memory chip to her wrist-com to transfer the data, but used a tablet to show her the images. "I ran extensive scans on the area and found some interesting shadows, thermal images, magnetic resonance, and the like."

Macalister's hand touched the floating image. "Here is the area where the ruins should be. And there's the settlement. There appears to be an old road which leads between the two. If that isn't odd enough," he touched an icon, and a new image overlaid the first. The outline of a massive foundation overlapped the image. The place was at least five times the size of the settlement.

"I would have been here to pick you up sooner, but I was looking for this." Macalister touched the screen again. "It's an aerial shot from a survey team before the nearest settlement existed."

The survey image showed a clearing one hundred meters wide surrounded by a white perfect circle. In the center rose a jet-black structure taller than the surrounding trees. The place would have been visible for miles. It was unlike the Kawokee to build above ground, yet this was before there was a human presence.

Jasmine flipped between the photos, both past and present. "That was a huge structure, and it's all gone. I don't understand."

"Neither do I. The magnetic imaging shows there is still something large underground. Don't be surprised if the entrance is blocked. Your mission is critical to all of us. Please give us regular updates so we know you're all right."

It seemed reasonable to her, but she knew Paul would object. He was highly suspicious of giving any information to humans. "I'll try."

Jasmine peered out the hatch. The tent was still standing. "We'll be ready to go in a few minutes."

She hurried out to Paul who stood with his arms crossed. "What's wrong?"

"I don't trust him."

"Macalister warned us about Campion's plans. Why don't you want the ATVs?"

"I can't explain it." He shrugged. "If you're sure there is no danger."

Paul made short work of the tent.

Antsy crept toward the hatch. "I never thought I would fly in one of these."

Jasmine guided him inside and seated him near a window.

"What do all these things do?" He pushed a few buttons experimentally, but the controls were not live. Only the seat controls functioned, but it was enough to have Antsy chuckling as he played with the chair.

Paul dropped their gear in the back and took the seat in front of Antsy and beside Macalister. "Didn't you commit treason by telling us of Campion's plans?"

Jasmine almost choked and wanted to clap her hand over Paul's mouth. She could not see Macalister's face, having sat behind him, but his tone of voice sounded amused.

"Yes. I did. Every soldier knows they share responsibility for the morality of the orders they obey. Campion has no training in either and a long history of failure in both. I've seen many men punished for obeying his commands." Macalister touched a few overhead controls, and the panel in front of him lit up. "I'm sure you've considered what would happen if you were ordered to kill humans for the Kawokee. Some would call you a traitor. How would you answer them?"

"I don't know. I have killed humans who were trying to kill me. But they risked their lives to continue to hurt Kawokee. And the Kawokee risked their lives to stop them." Paul's voice dropped in pitch. "If being a human means I must favor humans against Kawokee, then yes, I am a traitor."

Macalister continued to press buttons, and a low rumble vibrated through the shuttle. "Is your conscience clear?"

Paul cleared his throat. "I guess so."

"So is mine." Macalister pressed a few more buttons, and the scene outside the window changed as the shuttle rose and picked up speed.

Both Paul and Antsy gripped the arm rests as the shuttle rose higher. Their faces were glued to the window, watching the sunrise from above the clouds.

"What are the other settlements in this area like?" asked Jasmine.

"There are none," said Macalister. "This area had no mineral deposits or any other resources considered valuable."

As they reached altitude, the shuttle's acceleration increased, giving them the sensation of climbing. Only the instruments told their true orientation. The noise made conversation difficult. No sooner had she grown accustomed to the feeling, it changed again. The shuttle slowed and descended. It was not long before they saw the town.

The string of curses Antsy let loose interrupted any other questions. He pulled away from the window. "So many humans."

Jasmine assumed he was overreacting until Paul echoed him. Jasmine looked out a clear panel to see people hurrying into the buildings leaving carts and supplies abandoned in the streets. The first thing that struck her was the number of people. Forsaken had barely a hundred. In this town, there were at least that many scurrying away. The second surprise was to see a few children running for the shelter of a large central building. Jasmine thought they might have been playing in the central park. Everyone was completely covered, including gloves, hoods, and medical masks.

"Precautions against the virus?" Macalister echoed her thoughts as the shuttle touched the landing pad and powered down.

"That seems a little extreme." Jasmine spotted another figure carrying a small bundle. "But then again."

Macalister pointed to an old woman dressed in green, flanked by two young men. "Looks like that's our welcoming committee. Shall we? Paul and I'll get the ATVs unhooked while you say hello. Antsy should stay out of sight until we know how they'll react."

Jasmine nodded and headed to the rear bay doors. When she opened the hatch, the woman stepped forward. Her green jumpsuit had an insignia on the shoulder, but the lettering was too faded to read.

"I am Elder Sarah." In a sharp voice that sounded decades younger than the wrinkles around her eyes, the old woman demanded, "What is your business here?"

"I'm Jasmine Char, a scientist from the ship. We're sorry to come unannounced, but you have no comm."

Even with her face covered in the surgical mask Elder Sarah was easy enough to read. Her eyes bore into Jasmine. "We can't be tempted by greed or lust. We don't want whatever you're peddling."

"We don't want anything from you. I'm here to study the Kawokee culture. According to the Kawokee, the ruins of one of their most ancient holy places is only a few kilometers away from this settlement." Jasmine hoped to lighten the mood and whistled softly. "Your town is beautiful. It looks new. How is that possible?"

The old woman's posture relaxed. "We were one of the first settlements. Unlike the others, we didn't come here to take something and leave. No one here is infected with the virus. As you can see, our numbers are growing. We are members of the Church of Entangled Spirits. Our mission is to live in scientific study and devotion to the truth."

Jasmine had never heard of their group and disliked any mixture of science and religion. "We found Kawokee stories about sky gods. They may refer to a terraforming ship. That ruin may have been a landing site."

Elder Sarah barked a laugh. "You call yourself a scientist? The Kawokee are simple creatures. If there were any scientific writings, they would see only scrawling. But as I said, we have done extensive studies. There's nothing there. Their religion is full of meaningless fables. You're wasting your time. If there was any such evidence, we would have found it."

Jasmine touched her wrist-com and scrolled through the images until she came to the object in the tunnel. She turned the image to show the old woman. "We found a large piece of metal with Old Earth markings."

Elder Sarah shook her head dismissively. "That could have come from any ship. Many of the corporations used cheap relics as disposable transports."

It always disappointed Jasmine when scientists were quick to dismiss her thesis without looking at the evidence. "It should be easy enough to prove. If terraformers built the place and created the virus, they would have written the cure down in a way that would last for centuries. That ruin might hold important information on a virus which threatens all of humanity."

Elder Sarah nodded at the two men with her. "I must insist that you stay away. The Kawokee will not tolerate you defiling their site. We've heard about the heathens destroying towns. If you go there, this town may be next." The two young men stepped past her toward Jasmine.

Paul was beside her in an instant. His voice was soft, but not friendly. "The Kawokee will not be angry. We have permission from their leaders to visit the old ruins."

Macalister joined them. The young men sized up the new threat and took a step back, but the old woman pushed in front of them. "You expect me to believe that?"

"Antsy." Paul called.

"My name is Antsy. Pleased to meet you," said Antsy in a polite tone that was so out of character it made Jasmine want to ask who was impersonating him.

The elder cupped her hands over her face mask. "Don't let that thing out of the ship."

Jasmine was not sure what she felt at first. The elder's reaction to Antsy was extreme. Shock, hurt, and anger mixed together. Jasmine almost demanded an apology until she looked again at the woman's outfit and understood the reasoning.

The elder regained her composure, but stood her ground. "How dare you bring that thing here." Her bodyguards took handguns from behind their backs and pointed them at Antsy.

As if it were a dance, Macalister stepped and turned. The first bodyguard grunted as his body crumpled to the ground. The gun he once held was in Macalister's hand with the barrel pointed at Elder Sarah. "We will only be here for a day or two. Our destination is close by, and we will just take pictures and leave. This is extremely important to us. How far are you willing to go to stop us?"

Elder Sarah cackled. "We don't have to stop you. The Lord will put an end to the wickedness of the worlds. The righteous will rise and inherit the stars." She pointed at Antsy. "Keep that filthy animal in your ship or we'll shoot it. And be gone as soon as possible."

Macalister lowered his gun, and the bodyguard did the same. The guard holstered his weapon, grabbed his partner, and dragged him away. The trio retreated to a nearby building.

Jasmine followed Paul and Macalister into the ship. Macalister added two pistols to the carrier of one of the ATVs. He patted his own holster. "I'll keep this one to defend the ship. There's a rifle in one of the lockers if necessary. Their weapons can't scratch the hull of the shuttle. We're safe inside, but you're vulnerable. Use your radio if you have any trouble. This shuttle isn't designed to land on dirt, but if I can find a clearing, I can pick you up. I'm half tempted to fly you straight to the site, but we've already announced our presence. I'd like to keep a close eye on these people for now."

Jasmine nodded. "Thank you, Captain."

Macalister helped Paul position the ATVs at the edge of the bay ramp. "Keep Jasmine safe and hurry back. There's too much at stake to lose her."

"I will." Paul sat on the ATV and turned as Macalister

walked away. "Thank you."

"You're welcome. Now hurry." Macalister stood with his hand on the hatch button.

Paul took the lead. When they were out of sight of the town, Paul pointed and turned off the trail. He took the two holstered weapons from the wagon and strapped one onto his waist. The other he handed to Jasmine.

Even without the GPS, the old road was easy to follow. The forest undergrowth might have taken over, but new trees were few. The older trees on either side had stretched their branches toward the light, and in doing so, created an archway through the woods. Every so often they would come across breaks in the trees and encounter fields of near impassible brambles which slowed them. What should have taken an hour became almost three when they reached the coordinates. Jasmine took the radio from her pocket. "Macalister. We've reached the site."

"All's quiet on this end."

Paul pulled down vines on anything which looked like it might have been man-made. After ten minutes, they found nothing. "It's not like humans to build underground, and the Kawokee rarely make straight lines."

Jasmine looked around. "It might have been a human place originally." She thought about the sixty-year-old aerial picture and unhooked the computer tablet from the ATV. Using the GPS, she expanded the scan and overlaid it with their position. She closed her eyes and imagined what the place looked like and wished she had thought of bringing a 3D imaging set up. The equipment would have bankrupted her, but it would have made studying the ruins that much easier. Jasmine opened her eyes and touched the screen of the tablet.

"Assuming it's below us, there seems to be rows in a general square. You're right, that's more like a human than a Kawokee. There's an empty area at the center." The perimeter of the original image was enormous. Jasmine climbed one of the large granite rocks to its crest and looked out over the field. From her vantage point, the lines of dead and stunted grass were unmistakable. So was a square patch of dirt where nothing grew. "I've got something."

Jasmine climbed down from her position and headed to dead patch. Pulling up the sod, a thin layer of earth came away from a plate of metal underneath. Paul brought a shovel from the wagon and cleared the dirt until they had enough removed so they could pull up the rusted metal sheeting. Hidden underneath was entrance filled with rocks.

The pair removed rubble until they uncovered the ceramic peak of the roof to what she hoped was the underground bunker. They concentrated their efforts on clearing the rock from the area and together they removed a slab revealing a narrow hole under the peak that extended beyond an arm's reach into the darkness. It reminded Jasmine of the entrance to a Kawokee den.

With a little probing, Jasmine removed enough rocks for her to squeeze inside. She set her wrist-com to flashlight mode, but before she could climb inside, Paul said, "Careful."

"Whoever tried blocking the entrance wasn't too worried about anyone finding this place."

"That woman, Elder Sarah, and the settlement, they did this. They're responsible for destroying this place."

There was no denying Paul's statement. For all the years humans existed, they still had not changed. The bigotry and hatred of the elder's actions spoke volumes.

"When Corbin told me about missionaries burning Kawokee religious text, I never asked him any specifics. I've never heard of The church of enlightened whatever, but I have no problem calling them fanatics." Jasmine pointed to the hole they made. "Do you think you can squeeze through or do we need to make the area wider?"

"I think I can manage."

"I'll go first." Jasmine crawled over the rubble. Her

clothes caught and snagged on the rocks beneath her but the smooth ceiling made it easy to slide along. Unlike the wood of a Kawokee structure, this was cut stone reinforced with super-dense plastic used in spacecrafts.

"This place is made from parts of a ship." Jasmine coughed, having stirred up a cloud of fine dirt when she moved a small rock to the side. She tried not to think of all the stories she read of people getting buried alive, or tombs equipped with secret traps. The one thing she did not want to deal with was a door. Whoever blocked the entrance might have thought pulling down the structures on the surface was enough to hide the ruins, but a barred door would set them back weeks. Jasmine did not relish moving rocks from the passage with the likes of Elder Sarah close by. The structure was too big to have only this one tiny entrance but finding another might take days.

She need not have worried. Loose dirt slipped away beneath her, and the distance between the rock pile and the ceiling widened. The tight space they squirmed through kept widening until they could stand. Jasmine slid down the remaining pile to a smooth floor. Even without their lights, they could see lettering on the walls which glowed with a yellow-green hue.

Paul touched the surface. "Is there still power after hundreds of years?"

"This is Quantum Dot paint. It uses background radiation found in everyday objects. It's still used for emergency lighting on spacecraft. The lettering is Old Earth. It's the same as on the heat shield we found." Jasmine could not read the words but the painted arrow pointed to a switch. She twisted and pulled on it before she felt it move. The smooth walls of the chamber glowed and brightened.

"There's a power source somewhere."

The floor was littered with dirt and broken bits of glass and metal. Jasmine switched her wrist-com from light to camera and took pictures. She stopped at one wall where she spotted Kawokee bones and mummified bodies.

Paul followed Jasmine as she recorded everything.

"It's all smashed." His words echoed in the silent expanse.

With tears in her eyes, Jasmine forced her legs to move and continued to document the long room. Several large openings were near the back. Over the largest doorway at the back, was a curved glass panel with ornate lettering fitted into the wall. The next room was another long chamber.

All the while, Jasmine kept recording. The walls bore scorch marks but were smooth. Twisted brackets jutted from the walls with metal and wire hanging down. All the brackets bent away from the center of the scorch mark. "Explosives. Someone put a lot of effort into destroying this place."

"Look at this." Paul pointed to a metal plate at the far end of the room. The thing covered most of a wall. "Whoever made this wanted it to last a thousand years. It must have been important."

The twisted metal plate was at the center of a wall blackened by scorch marks. Despite the discoloration, the edges of some of the letters were visible. A large section of the plate was cut away.

"This was it. I'm sure of it. Someone destroyed it." Jasmine closed her eyes to hold back her tears. When she opened them, she could not stop the flow and wept as she recorded the image.

The sound of Macalister's voice coming over their radios made them both jump. His loud voice distorted through the small device. "Jasmine, Paul. Get out of there now. Four men in pursuit. Two are coming at you from the west; two from the trail."

Paul took the small device from his belt. "Then how do we avoid them?"

Jasmine rushed over to Paul. "We can't go. Everything is here. They tried to destroy everything, but maybe there's something they missed."

"Go back the way you came for two kilometers then head east until you come to a creek. Follow that down to a clearing. We'll meet you there. If you leave now, you might lose them."

"Understood." Paul pocketed the device and grabbed Jasmine's arm.

"We can't go. There might be something here."

Paul tightened his grip and almost carried her back to the entrance. "Whoever did this put a lot of effort into it and had sixty years to make sure the work was complete." Jasmine did not fight him as he pushed her back up the rock mound to the surface.

Tears filled her eyes making it difficult to drive, but she followed Paul's ATV as best she could. Part of her wanted to turn back and seal herself within the ruins while another more primal part of her wanted to rip apart the people who destroyed the temple. Jasmine held her breath when they paused at the creek. Paul looked back as if listening for something.

The sound of motors whispered through the trees. "They spotted our trail."

Both drove along the creek as fast as they dared. Mud, deep water, and steep banks kept them from driving through the water, but the undergrowth was no better. The fading daylight did not help, and using the lights on the machines would only make them easier to spot. When they reached the clearing, the shuttle was already there. A loud noise like thunder came from behind them and a nearby tree exploded. Paul's ATV swerved to the side. When it tipped over, Paul jumped clear.

Jasmine stopped long enough for him to pick himself up and climb onto the back of her vehicle. His pants were torn and blood soaked the holes.

"You're hurt?"

Through gritted teeth, he said, "Drive."

Jasmine tried not to think about Paul's bleeding leg and

focused on the shuttle. Macalister stood at the open bay doors with a rifle in hand. A bluish glow shot from the energy weapon and ripped the air leaving the taint of ozone. The sound of water on a hot skillet preceded the demise of hapless greenery as it shriveled and burned from the attackers' wild shots.

She did not dare to look back to see if Macalister hit anything but drove the ATV up the ramp and into the shuttle. Once they were inside Macalister hit the controls for the doors, sealing them inside.

"Paul's hurt."

"It's just a scratch."

Antsy swore and grabbed Paul's leg, making him cry out and pull away.

"You're hurt and Antsy agrees with me."

Paul grimaced and took a better look at his injuries. "I'll live. Hand me the med kit, and you go tell Macalister what we found."

She passed him the kit, and Antsy rummaged through the box as much as Paul. When Jasmine looked around for Macalister, she did not see him. The rumble of the engines and sudden movement of the shuttle told her he was in the pilot seat and not concerned about a smooth lift off.

Confident that Paul would be fine, Jasmine weaved her way toward the front of the shuttle. She fell into a seat when Macalister pulled at the controls making the shuttle tilt to the side. "If this is your idea of a rollercoaster ride, I'm not having fun."

"Those crackpots had some serious weaponry. Until we are out of range, they could shoot us down."

"Religion and weapons. Not an unusual mix for war." Jasmine held tight as the ship shot skyward. "Everything was there. All they had to do was send a message, and we would have had all the answers sixty years ago. None of this would have happened."

"Fantastic. We'll come back with enough firepower and run them off or at least keep them at bay. Right now, I wouldn't mind leveling the place. We'll get the key."

Antsy threw himself into a chair while Paul limped to the one next to Jasmine.

"How's your leg?" she asked.

"I'll be limping for a while, but it's fine." Paul pointed to Macalister "Did you tell him?"

"You said in your transmission the information's there. We just need to clear out the crazies. Right?" Macalister studied their faces.

"They destroyed everything." Jasmine's voice was so low, she was not sure if anyone heard her.

"What? What do you mean?"

"I mean they destroyed everything. They used explosives. I think they killed Kawokee to do it."

"Nothing's retrievable?" Macalister's jaw tightened.

Jasmine shrugged. "Maybe. But even if we didn't have the settlement to deal with, it would take time and a good team of archaeologists to do anything."

"What could archaeologists do. This is a virus we're talking about."

"Archeologist rebuild the past. I remember this one tour my family took on our visit to Earth. Something to do with a destroyed temple or castle. The priests of that time wanted to erase the name of the woman who lived there from history. An archeologist not only found the site but rebuilt the entire building and surrounding structures. The 3D hologram is gorgeous."

"So, we need an archeology team. That's good; isn't it?" asked Macalister.

She blinked away the last of her tears and shifted in her seat. "It doesn't matter. Even if we had a team, they couldn't find anything in time to save what's left of the Kawokee. It took decades to rebuild that temple on Earth. We might have that much time, but the Kawokee don't."

CHAPTER 24

"Computer. Authorize. Macalister."

The computers musical voice said, "Accepted."

"Load Nest Search. Append new data points. Recalculate."

"Calculating trade routes. Eliminating villages. Idle."

Macalister studied the display with dozens of potential locations and probabilities. "Subtract past locations of Jasmine Char". He touched the node nearest it. "Comment. Monastery One." Touching another, he spread his fingers. "Load infrared. Overlay images. Eliminate fixed points. Query table count by size. Display."

The image changed to a graph. Macalister sat a little straighter and rechecked the parameters.

"Query table count and average by size and scan ID ordered by date." He only had to see the first four graphs before he was sure. "Got you."

The computer responded, "Unrecognized."

"Log out." Macalister checked the hallway camera when the door to his cabin pinged.

"Grant." He heard the lock disengage. "Come," he sighed.

"Where have you been?" Campion slid the door closed behind him and sat as far from Macalister as possible.

Macalister leaned back. "Seeing that all options are open. I've given you a full report. The Sanders team has made excellent breakthroughs. It was unfortunate we were sixty years too late."

"You spend all your time helping the renegades. Have you forgotten about the main body of research?"

"Not at all." Macalister crossed his arms. "We wouldn't know about the nests if it weren't for their information. Nor, for that matter, of the terraforming ship. You can at least tell the worlds who's responsible for the outbreak."

"What do you mean?"

Annoyed with Campion, Macalister tried not to shout as he gripped the arms of his chair. "I've just handed you a scapegoat trussed up and tied with a bow. That cult wants the cure destroyed. Now you can either take advantage of it or piss on it, but if your research doesn't pan out, you'll need someone to blame. Those ruins held all the information we needed. It still may, but we need to get a team in there. Someone who specializes in that kind of stuff. An archaeological team."

"Why do we need a new team?" Campion looked down his nose at Macalister. "What's the matter with the people we already have?"

Macalister parroted Jasmine's explanation to him. "They don't have the equipment or the knowledge. We need experts, not technicians. Or would you like your name linked to the destruction of vital clues?"

"I'll ask for an archaeological team. If one is sent, I doubt they will show up in time for the next shift."

"Good." Macalister relaxed and settled back in his chair. He did not dare give even a hint of a smile. "We'll need to guard what's left of the site until they get here."

"Why would you need to guard a ruin?"

"The cult might try to do more damage to the place. Plus, there's the danger of thieves and trophy hunters, once word gets out. The archeological team will need every broken shard they can get their hands on once they get here."

Macalister studied Campion, disappointed with having to spoon feed the man the obvious. "The biggest problem is the cult. I don't think they're going to give up. The ruins are right outside their settlement. They'll kill anyone who steps near that place. Most of the site is underground but what was on the surface is now overgrown. If we burn the surrounding foliage, we can at least have a good line of sight."

Campion surprised Macalister by the quickness of his comment. "If they're that close, advise them to evacuate for their own safety. If they get caught in the resulting forest fire, that's their problem. We don't have enough resources to arrest and keep them for a trial. Public opinion will have them hanged, anyway."

"Then I'll assign my men to the site immediately."

"What? And leave the test facility unguarded?"

"It's not unguarded. You hired enough locals."

The petulant child that was Campion retuned and demanded answers. "Why can't the locals guard the ruins? Your soldiers should be at the test facility. At least they know what they're doing."

"Who do you think will be doing the thieving? I trust my men to follow orders, and I'm not trusting that site to a bunch of thugs who can't think past their next beer."

"But my research—"

"How is the research going?" Macalister leaned forward, folded his hands, and watched Campion squirm.

Campion cleared his throat. "Not well. We thought we had a breakthrough when we identified and prevented a protein sequence that proved fatal. It seems the virus is a soup of several fatal genes. It may take much longer than we hoped. In addition, the number of viable females is low, and they must be disposed of after a few tries. They can only get pregnant every few months even with hormone injections. The stress on their bodies makes them unable to function normally leaving doubt about any results.

Macalister stood and opened the door for Campion. "How long until you run out of subjects?"

"Two months. Maybe less."

"Finish your current tests, then dispose of them all. Stop paying for village females."

"Won't the sudden stop make the Kawokee suspicious?" Campion rose from his seat.

"It doesn't matter anymore. You will need to hire more hunters."

"I assume you are preparing to take a nest." Campion rubbed his hands together.

"I've located a nest and will train a team. We'll strike in two months."

CHAPTER 25

"Will you please slow down?" Pain shot up Jasmine's legs as she slipped on a patch of ice. She stumbled but kept her body upright. The trail up the mountain was steep, and the snow-covered rock was treacherous.

Paul's arms shot out to steady her then relaxed. "We should not be here."

Her shoulders ached as she slid off her pack. "It took weeks to get permission."

He picked up her pack. His lips were drawn into a thin line, and his eyes searched hers. "They are letting you take all your equipment. Doesn't that tell you something?"

Jasmine rolled her eyes at him. "That they trust us?"

Paul did not smile. "Fawsha says the hunters have stopped taking females. The Adwals are afraid the sky-leader is planning to attack nests. The Adwals will try to defend the nests, but they hope you and the Sanders team find the cure before that happens. If even a few nests are destroyed, the Kawokee civilization will vanish, and humans can do to their own kind what they wish."

"You make it sound like we're going to murder everyone infected."

"It sounds like the human thing to do." Paul turned

and set a slower pace.

Jasmine pushed in front of him, walking as fast as she could manage.

"Stop." A Kawokee stepped from behind a tree on the opposite side of the stream, his crossbow aimed at them.

Paul pulled back his hood. "Paul and Cow to see the priestesses."

The cold wind carried flecks of snow to bite Jasmine's cheeks as she pulled her hood back.

"You are expected." The Kawokee lowered his weapon and pulled on a rope. Jasmine watched in amazement as a bridge lowered from the trees and positioned itself at their feet.

Paul led her to the center of the bridge and pointed down into the water. "The stream bed is filled with tar to slow anyone trying to run across." He then motioned at the trees. "And up there are archers."

Jasmine had to look closely to see the ladders in the trees and the platforms in the branches. The few she saw were hard to spot. "This place is well-defended."

"I'm sure there are other things we can't see."

Once they were over the bridge, the guards pulled it back into its original position. Paul and Jasmine followed the archer down the trail to a rock wall. A stone that covered most of the wall turned inward like a door, and a figure wearing a fur coat came out from behind it.

"Hello again, Paul and Cow." The priestess lowered her hood. "Please follow me to somewhere warm."

"Priestess Ingwa." Paul bowed, and Jasmine followed suit.

When all three were inside, Ingwa turned a crank, and the stone closed behind them. "I'm sorry you didn't get pregnant. Did you have at least four males?"

Jasmine cringed at the thought. "No. Only one." Paul remained silent.

The priestess nodded. "Well, it can be hard to get commitments. Perhaps next time."

If there was a next time. The thought had Jasmine wondering if anything would ever turn out right.

They followed the priestess into a cave. The warm glow of oil lanterns mounted to the tunnel walls greeted them as they turned toward the heart of the mountain. Moist air touched their faces, and they shed their coats as the temperature rose. The trio descended a smooth and well-lit path.

The path entered a huge chamber where coal burned in clay ovens along the walls. "This is our library." The floor and walls of white sand and resin were smooth and sparkled. Carved hardwood poles held the lanterns high while metal reflectors both protected the walls and ceilings and spread the glow. Diamond shaped shelves stood in rows, filling the center of the room. Several Kawokee were sitting at tables reading scrolls.

Ingwa stopped at a table and picked up a small, ornately painted glass vase. "You want to study the salve. This may help your scientists. She placed the vase in a padded box.

Jasmine couldn't believe it when Ingwa handed it to her. She clutched it to her chest. "I know how precious this is to you. Aren't there other females who need it?"

Ingwa's shoulders sagged. "Your needs are more pressing. No Kawokee wants to give birth out of season. And there are only so many females of birthing years."

Jasmine put the precious package in her pack. "How old is it? Could it still work?"

"We don't know. It may be useless before the next ceremony. We've always burned any extra salve and made new batches when the time came. But considering the situation...this came from Isea in the steppes."

The priestess's down turned ears and averted eyes told Jasmine that something terrible must have happened in that region. Her curiosity clashed with her desire to run back with her treasure, but she also knew she would never get a second chance to see the rest of the facilities. Not wanting to upset Ingwa further, she said, "I wish to record everything to do with preparation of the salve and anything that's done at the nest."

"The only ceremony at the nest is salve making. It is a complex process." Ingwa lifted a large clay cylinder from an alcove in one of the rows of metal scroll racks. "It is all in here." She lifted a large scroll from within the cylinder and placed it on a long table. Ingwa unrolled it to a marked section. "I'm sorry I could not have it translated. None of us can write or speak Standard."

"I'll record the documents for translation later." Jasmine rummaged through her pack until she found what she wanted. "I'll take pictures of the scroll, and then I'd like you to explain how to make the salve as if you were teaching a new priestess."

"We were sure you'd want that." Ingwa smiled and watched as Jasmine photographed the entire scroll. When Jasmine finished, the priestess re-rolled the scroll, placed it back in the cylinder, and secured the container back in the alcove. Ingwa then led the pair to a room with a table covered in bowls and devices. Another scroll was unrolled across the table. "These are the instructions we use just for this part. If you are ready, I will get the priestess who teaches the process."

"Yes. Please do."

Ingwa did not leave right away but watched Jasmine set up the camera again and recorded the scroll and everything on the table.

"This device, it copies everything from the scrolls in an instant?"

"Yes. It takes images anyone else can look at later." Jasmine caught Ingwa's glance at the door. "What is it?"

"It takes days, if not months to copy a scroll without mistakes. Perhaps one day you can return and record everything in our library."

Jasmine could not help grinning at the idea. "I'd like that."

The priestess nodded and left the room. Minutes later, she returned with another who nodded at both Paul and Jasmine. "My name is Katwin."

"Hello Katwin. Thank you for this opportunity," said Jasmine. She checked that the machines were recording and listened as the priestess talked.

"The preparation of the salve begins minutes after a baby is born by putting the afterbirth in one of these." Katwin opened a box and produced a jar with a ring in the lid. The bottom of the jar tapered to a point with a valve. "Once the afterbirth is ground up, it's placed in here. The vessel is swung until the blood and flesh separate."

Jasmine guessed the device was a large centrifuge. She listened and thought she understood. It reminded her of undergraduate chemistry, a course she hated. After a while, she could not concentrate. The entire lecture took two hours.

Ingwa thanked Katwin who smiled and left.

Paul packed away the equipment. "Thank you, Ingwa. We must get back."

When they entered back into the main library, Jasmine asked, "What or who is the Awkae?" At the priestess's confused look, she added, "We met an old priest awhile back who talked about the Awkae and building a bridge? He passed away before he could explain."

Ingwa nodded and waved her hand toward the multitude of scrolls. "There are many stories and much teachings from our ancestors, some of which we do not comprehend. When humans arrived on our world, many people looked to the scrolls for answers. Most contain great knowledge, but there are some which are obscure. If I recall, the story of which you speak is one of those scrolls. It is memorable only because it is dark."

Was the priest trying to warn her of something? "How do you mean?"

"The Awkae appears after the last Kawokee dies. Though some scrolls mention the Awkae may show up before then. The bridge the Awkae builds brings back the dead. But those who cross it are only a shadow of what they were in life."

Jasmine relaxed, seeing no connection to her with an old monster story. "That is dark. Why would the old priest want to see this Awkae?"

"This priest was old?"

Jasmine nodded. "Very."

"Age and fear can do strange things to the mind." Ingwa shrugged and said, "It is cold and dark outside. Stay the night. There is much you haven't seen."

Paul looked to her. The tension around his eyes told her he preferred to be on their way. Jasmine felt the urgency, but was not looking forward to walking far in this weather at night. "Like what?"

Ingwa led them through other less ornate chambers with tables, chairs, and sleeping furs. These rooms she ignored and continued through several other chambers before she stopped at a low door. "Enter here one at a time and slowly." Ingwa stepped through the passage and Paul went in after.

When Jasmine ducked down and entered, she kept her hand on the stone above her, careful not to bang her head. The chamber the short hall led into had a cathedral ceiling, and she straightened. The air was filled with parrots. Row upon row of cages with nests inside that lined the walls and shelves. Bowls of water, seeds, or fruit dotted the area. Despite the dozens of birds, there was little odor and the floor was clean.

"This is where we keep the birds. They naturally react to other pregnant females who want to take their nests."

Jasmine jumped as a bird in a nest near her screamed and flapped her wings as she passed by. The creatures were more docile at Gehnica. Here they scared Jasmine. She stayed further away from the next cage as she passed, but not far enough. The bird inside was as loud as the first. She heard no noise when Paul or Ingwa entered. Before she could think about the puzzle, other birds became upset. They hissed and screeched at her.

"Come, let's get you out of this room." Ingwa scowled at Jasmine once they were back in the corridor. "You said you weren't pregnant."

"But I can't be." She had not been paying attention or tracking the time since her last period. There were too many distractions. It didn't take long for her to realize it had been well over two months since the ceremony.

Jasmine heard Paul's voice, but she was too absorbed in her own thoughts to understand.

Ingwa pulled her hand. "Jasmine. Answer me. Did you stay the full ten days?"

"No. We had an emergency." The fear she had leading up to the ceremony settled into hope during those first few days with Paul. Then came the heavy disappointment as the days wore on and she was not pregnant. There was the time she felt sick as they traveled from Bridgewater to meet the Sanders team, but she never made the connection. The thought of being pregnant soon turned to fear. The virus did not keep women from getting pregnant but caused miscarriages within the first trimester.

Jasmine slid down the wall and sat on the floor. Fear had her close to hyperventilating. "Will I lose it?"

"Be calm, Jasmine. Let me examine you. It will help if you don't pass out."

She felt Ingwa's hands on her stomach and tried concentrating on breathing. "Paul, I'm pregnant." Jasmine could not read the look on Paul's face, she could barely see through the tears that welled up and spilled over onto her cheeks.

He took her hand in his as he knelt beside her. "I know. We need to get you to a nest. You'll be safe there."

"I don't want to lose her." *Her?* Jasmine's logical mind screamed at her not to become attached while her emotions clung to the possibilities.

"Wipe your eyes, Jasmine. Your child is healthy."

Ingwa lifted her head from Jasmine's abdomen where she was listening to the child within. "You're past the critical period. If you take care of yourself, a healthy child will come in spring." Her ears twisted forward as she turned to Paul. "The nearest nest is many weeks by horse. The way is hard and guarded against humans." She turned back toward the library. "Go back to the library. I'll bring the others. We must decide what to do." Ingwa ran down the opposite hallway.

The thought of going to a nest had been her fondest hope when she was in Gehnica. As much as she wanted to go there now, there were other priorities. She was used to taking risks with her own life, but now she had to consider her child. The decision should not be hers alone. "We have to take the salve to the Sanders team and tell them about me." She pressed her stomach but felt nothing unusual.

Paul helped her to her feet. "I can take the salve to them while you go to the nest. The priestesses can take you there."

"Sanders will need to examine me and perhaps run tests. They have to study the salve before it is useless." She hurried toward the library with Paul close behind. "If Campion's scientists knew we found the cure, they might stop looking for nests."

"Do you trust them that much?"

Jasmine had her doubts, but she insisted, "I'll be safe with Sanders and Arluza. Macalister will see to it."

"You know what humans are capable of."

Something in what he said hit Jasmine like a physical blow. She stopped and turned, pushing him back. "Why do you refer to humans in the third person? Are either of us Kawokee?" She curled her fists at the thought of hitting him.

Paul stepped back and put up his hands. "Why are you so angry with me? Yes. I think of myself as a Kawokee. I only interact with humans when I must. The Kawokee are my family and my people. I know humans. I thought you did too." His eyes reflected his confusion and pleaded with her.

"I know what might happen if the scientists decide the cure is more important than my life and my baby's." Jasmine placed her hand over her abdomen. "I want to run and hide until the baby was born, but at what price? Arluza has already run the numbers. If one nest falls, the population of all the cities that depend on it will drop by 80 percent in seven years and will not recover for another twenty. Do you want me to hide, or do I risk my life and my baby's to save them?"

In the back of her mind, Jasmine wanted Paul to tell her to hide, to force her from what she knew was right.

Instead, he pulled her close and kissed her. "You see. You are Kawokee."

CHAPTER 26

Jasmine waved goodbye to Paul as he hurried to report to Fawsha at the nearby border village. As far as she knew, it was the only border village still occupied. Part of her wanted to go with him, or have him by her side when she told the others, but would he allow her to do what she planned?

When Paul disappeared into the trees, Jasmine took a deep breath and slowly let it out. Only then did she turn and head through the town's gate. The building Sanders and the rest were using as their home base was close to the tavern.

There was a shuttle parked on the landing pad, so she was not surprised to see Macalister when she entered the lab. He looked up from his many screens. "Welcome back."

"Thanks."

A weird feeling creeped up her spine when he rose from his chair and followed her into the main hall where new equipment piled the tables. She tried not to think about it but assumed he would want his information first hand.

Arluza ran up to her and gave her a hug. "We've made

another discovery. It turns out the Kaw virus and the Pox use the same polyDNA. That's how Kawokee survived."

The news was a minor point for Jasmine's own research, but she was curious. "Was the image of the bronze plaque of any help?"

Her question turned Arluza's smile to a frown. "No. The cult did a good job of destroying it. The only thing we learned was the name of the terraforming ship. Records give us the date it left Earth, but without a speed or where it stopped before it got here, we can't say how long it's been. If you brought back the plaque, we could test it. But even that wouldn't prove a connection with the Kawokee religion."

His frown turned to a wavering grin. "I know I shouldn't be happy, but Campion ordered the place guarded and sent for an archaeological team."

"You're joking."

"Macalister said so." Arluza pointed at Macalister. "Seems the old goat ordered him to torch the area."

Jasmine glanced at Macalister. "How and why? I didn't think Campion saw past his own nose."

Macalister nodded sideways. "True, but he covers his own ass. Archaeologists are due on site in a matter of months."

"So, if he can't deliver a cure…"

"He'll give them the persons responsible."

"Jasmine," Sanders loud voice and beaming smile kept her from thinking about the cult. "Did you get the instructions for making the salve?" Even with his cane, Sanders movements were a snail's pace, so Jasmine came to him.

She had been holding her breath, waiting for this moment and became entangled in the straps of her pack when she took it off and opened it. "Better than that." She set the box on the floor and removed the vase. "I have some of the salve."

Arluza took the container and examined the bottle.

"Good. We'll start with an electrophoresis. Once we have that, and we know how it's made, we can narrow the search. Is there a chance of getting more?"

Jasmine took the jar back. "This is the cure. There is no need to analyze it."

Arluza's eyes almost closed like they always did when he was about to say something condescending. "But we need to know how to make more. This jar may contain thousands of things, maybe millions. We have to sift through all that to find the specific antigens that will block the reproduction of the virus. We would need thousands of jars like this and months of work."

"It's made from the afterbirth of those who have children the previous year. There is no time to analyze it further. This is our only sample, and the stuff breaks down the longer it sits. Ingwa wasn't even sure how viable this stuff still is. I've got the instructions. We can make more the same way the Kawokee make it. And since we have better ways of preserving things, maybe we can extend its expiration date. All we have to do is treat a few of the town's women who want to get pregnant. When they give birth, we'll use the Kawokee methods and have more salve to work with. Not to mention a fresh batch from a human subject."

Sanders stepped closer and put a hand on hers. "It may work on Kawokee. We don't know if it works on humans."

"We know." She felt like her face was on fire. Jasmine could have contacted them with her news when she first found out but fear kept her silent. The words caught in her throat, and she had to force them out. "I'm three months pregnant." She watched Sanders' and Macalister's face. "And I have the Kaw virus."

Macalister was his typical, unreadable self. If he hadn't helped them so often, Jasmine would have feared the man.

Sanders leaned away from her. "How did you get on the ship?"

"I wasn't officially tested."

"Then you can't be sure."

Jasmine set the bottle on the table and glanced at Arluza. He was looking at his feet again. "You don't understand. Sometimes having scientists as friends has a few perks. I knew this would be a one-way trip for me. And I've been careful to hide it from those around me."

"If you want more proof, I can verify it." Arluza shuffled from foot to foot before explaining. "When she first stayed with the Kawokee, she caught the Pox and survived. We know that only those infected by the Kaw virus survive."

Sanders scowled at both Arluza and Jasmine. Several times he opened his mouth, but then closed it. "How do you know you're pregnant?"

"The birds reacted to me. They didn't when I was in Gehnica."

"Birds? Never mind. We'll need something more precise." Arluza took a few running steps to a lab table and put on gloves. "I'll run a HCG test. It will tell us how far along you are."

Sanders shook his head. "You want to ask the women of the town if they want to try a Kawokee cure? We can't allow such a test without clinical trials."

She held out her arm as Arluza drew some blood. "There is no time for clinical trials. Didn't you hear me? The priestess said this sample is old and may not be effective. The longer we wait the less chance it has. If we don't deliver a cure right now, Campion is going to destroy the Kawokee. And without the Kawokee, we're all dead. At least those of us who are infected. It'll be a witch hunt if it isn't already."

Macalister took a seat. "She's right. Campion's had hunters looking for a nest for weeks. I'm surprised he hasn't attacked one already."

Sanders took the jar. "How many can this treat?"

"I don't know how much is in there." Jasmine felt

nervous as Arluza put the blood sample into a machine.

Everyone watched as Arluza checked the output. "She's pregnant. Judging by her hormone levels she's twenty-five weeks. I also ran a test for the Kaw virus and residual Pox virus. Both are positive."

Macalister massaged his temples. "We need to prove we have a cure right now. Jasmine has to go to the other facility so Campion's scientists will be convinced. That is the only way we can stop him in time. It will also make the scientists less willing to get involved in genocide."

Jasmine was only half listening to the men. She wanted to ask Arluza about the numbers again, just in case she misheard, but Sanders and the ensuing argument derailed her question.

"No. She'll be a test subject."

Macalister waved a hand as if to pat Sanders. "Most of their scientists fear another Godiva trial. They will take every precaution to see that nothing happens to her."

Arluza jumped to his feet. "I don't buy it. They murder Kawokee females every day."

Macalister turned his head at the outburst, but fixed Jasmine in his gaze. "The laws protect humans and only humans. Non-humans have no rights."

She stepped between Macalister and the others. "He's right. They won't harm me, or my baby. Besides, if I walk in as a volunteer they're less likely to throw me in a cage."

Arluza shook his head. "What about Paul? I assume Paul is the father. Does he know what you're doing?"

"Yes. He is the father. And yes, he knows." She turned to Macalister, her hands shaking. "Can you tell them we found a cure? When can you take me to the other facility?"

Macalister nodded. She half expected him to salute. "I can have you there in an hour."

Arluza spun her around by the shoulders. "Now? You can't go now."

She hugged him, trying to calm him down. "I have to go before I lose my nerve." Jasmine pulled away.

"Everything is in my pack. Plus, I downloaded a copy to the ship with your name on it. Talk to the town's women, or even some of the other settlements. Get volunteers. Give anyone who's ovulating .25ccs subcutaneous and tell them to spend the next two weeks enjoying themselves."

Jasmine lifted her pack and set it on the table before she nodded to Macalister. He led the way out of the facility. Behind her, Sanders called, "Take care, Jasmine." She didn't want to turn and see Arluza's stricken face. In her mind's eye, she saw Paul there too. He stood there, shoulders slumped, like when they said goodbye not an hour ago.

Macalister waited until they were alone in the shuttle. "Are you prepared for what goes on there?"

Jasmine wanted to be with a friend as she faced the other group. No matter how much Macalister had helped her cause, he did not fill that bill. "I know all about what they're doing; not that knowing will help me. But they aren't prepared for me, either."

He set the shuttle's course. "I'm still having trouble believing it. How could a primitive race have a cure for a man-made virus? Why would the terraformers make the virus and give the cure to the natives? What happened to the terraformers?"

"I'm still looking for those answers, but they can wait." She was pleased he took an active interest in her research. "Do you think the terraformers were trying to help the Kawokee?"

"It may surprise you, Ms. Char, but military science studies such things in detail. It would be the first time in history two cultures collided without violence. The Pilgrims and the Indians, the Conquistadors and the Aztecs, in every case, the stronger culture destroyed the weaker one. We are all just animals competing for food and territory."

It was nice to not hear, We've evolved past that, but Jasmine wasn't sure she agreed that all humans were like animals. "Surely you agree some individuals are civilized."

"Like?"

"Like me. I'm taking a chance going to this other group, hoping to stop the killing."

"You're taking a risk, but you believe the odds are in your favor. If you knew your actions would save the Kawokee and harm humans, could you make such a sacrifice?"

Jasmine had no retort. "Are you civilized?"

"I wish I were. If I thought it was possible, I'd try. I've seen more of humanity than you ever wish to see. When you study them closely, some are smarter than others, but no one is civilized."

Jasmine almost thought it was someone else's voice. Normally, Macalister was clinical and distant. He was the stereotypical soldier.

Macalister squared his shoulders. "We're here." His voice was cold again. Jasmine felt the shuttle settle and the pitch of the engines change. When Macalister rose from his seat, Jasmine followed. Jasmine felt less sure of what she was doing and had to force herself to move. The building loomed out of the darkness like an evil fortress. A rough-looking man with a rifle crossed their path as she followed Macalister to the facility's entrance.

She was even more frightened when she saw the lab filled with cages. Only a few held Kawokee. The ones in the cages did not look up as she passed. Jasmine kept her head rigid and looked only at Macalister's back.

He explained the situation to a man sitting at a desk, feeding test tubes into a machine and reading the display. She recognized the scientist Macalister spoke to but could not remember his name. As Macalister recounted everything Jasmine told the Sanders team, the man's eyes narrowed. "This better not be a hoax."

The man rushed off but came back with others. Jasmine did not dare speak for fear of screaming at everyone. Just looking around told her they were no better than the cult. She was glad when Macalister spoke for her. It meant she did not have to risk looking like a hysteric.

"If this salve works, we will need a lot more," said the first scientist.

The half dozen men and women all asked her questions at once until one woman silenced them by sticking her fingers in her mouth and letting out a shrill whistle. Once everyone was quiet, she smiled and asked Jasmine, "Do you mind if we run tests?"

"Not at all."

The scientists' excitement grew as they repeated the tests Arluza performed. "How is this possible?"

With the feeling that she was getting somewhere and the growing hope of stopping Campion's insanity, Jasmine told a rapt audience about the salve. They argued among themselves about what must be in it and asked when she could get more. As she explained how she came by her treatment, Jasmine had to repeat several points to answer their questions. She explained there was no more salve, but they could make some from her afterbirth.

While they listened to her story and the thesis that brought her here, one said, "Let's do an ultrasound."

Jasmine followed the woman to an examining table with the others in tow.

The one in charge took the device and touched the three probes to her stomach. An image appeared, and the crowd looked up. Jasmine very much wanted to see it too, but the screen pointed away from her.

When they gasped, she knew something was amiss. "What's wrong? Is the baby okay?"

The woman crossed her arms and squared off in front of Macalister. "You wasted our time."

"What's wrong with my baby?"

Several of the scientists scowled and walked away. "I thought you were a scientist. This is an abomination. What do you think it proves?" The head researcher gave her a disgusted look.

"What?" Jasmine hands hammered on the table.

"You are carrying a Kawokee."

Jasmine had been expecting her to say it was deformed or dead. News that she was carrying a Kawokee made no sense. "No. That's impossible."

The woman turned the monitor around. A three-dimensional shape floated above the surface of the screen. The fetus was small, but the shape was unmistakable. As Jasmine stared, it moved.

"No. I never slept with a Kawokee. It's human. It has to be human." Even as she said it, her eyes told her otherwise. "It isn't possible."

"I'll ask the others if they want to run any tests. We might learn something from the fetus."

The meaning of the woman's words broke through Jasmine's shock. "No. You can't."

"It isn't human." The woman sneered. "Why would you want to keep it? But don't worry. No one wants to study your half-breed thing." she nodded to Macalister and barked a laugh.

He said nothing to the woman. Macalister's jaw was set when he raised his head from the wrist-com he had been typing on. He took Jasmine's hand and helped her up from the table. Jasmine was angry at the woman's sick joke, but also frightened. Once off the table, she wrapped her arms around her body and willed herself not to cry. She hated this place and couldn't wait to leave.

Macalister kept a hand on her shoulder as he walked her out of the exam room. The woman's nasty comment about Jasmine's child not being human echoed in her ears. She didn't want it cut out of her. Even if this was not the baby of her dreams.

A strange and somewhat scary thought occurred to Jasmine as Macalister led the way through the room with cages toward the front door.

"What if she's lying?"

"Why would she lie?"

"I never slept with a Kawokee, only one man. And Paul's human. Maybe she said that hoping I would abort so they could study my baby?"

Instead of answering, Macalister grabbed her hand and twisted it behind her back. "That was a feeble attempt to delay us. You and your group have been useful, but I have all I need, Ms. Char. It would have taken me months to find a nest without your help."

Pain laced up Jasmine's arm, and no amount of squirming could break her free of his grip. She trusted the man and was shocked at the callousness of his betrayal. "I never went near a nest."

He pushed her along an isle between the cages. "Exactly."

The way was blocked by ten men wearing leather armor and bristling with guns, knives and ammo. "You sent for us?"

"Load fifty cages into the shuttle. We leave in ten." Macalister pushed Jasmine through an open doorway into a room no larger than a walk-in closet. Jasmine stumbled. Caught off balance, she landed on the floor as the door locked behind her.

CHAPTER 27

Macalister shouted over the intercom at the laughter and jokes of the hunters as he neared the target. Part of him wished he had not sent all his men to guard the old ruins.

"You all have a headset with an ID on it and three fully charged cells. You'll have three more when this is over. We'll land in the middle of a nest to avoid border defenses. I'll coordinate your movements, so listen for my commands. Failure to obey orders will get you killed. We take fifty females. No more. Avoid killing children if possible."

He checked the thermal maps again. The ship was programmed to land on a spot away from each of the vent holes. There was no sense landing on the nest only to have it collapse beneath the shuttle. He kept his hands on the controls in case he miscalculated. Red dots moved and disappeared on the intel screen. He had no idea how many Kawokee were in the nest or how many were pregnant females, but he hoped there would be enough to fill the cages. The Kawokee knew enough about humans to hide their heat signatures, and Macalister had to applaud their efforts. He watched the screen as the last of the Kawokee dived into their holes before the shuttle touched down.

From the control room, he could hear the hunters' curses as he opened the hatch.

There were three main entrances into the main burrow. The orientation of the entrances made each one an ideal bunker to defend the other two. He held his tongue as the eager hunters poured out the shuttle bay doors, firing uselessly while getting into position. The squad split into three teams and attacked their assigned entrance. Their leather armor would stop most bolts, but he still expected to lose two or three hunters.

"Keep low. Circle left." Macalister found it depressing that he had to tell the hunters what was obvious. They were slow to obey and fired blind every time a bolt hit their protective leather gear. Through the cameras in their headsets, he saw the Kawokee positions. The first shots into the entrance killed three. The fighters were pregnant females. Macalister cursed his misfortune. How many females could he possibly take if they also fought? He expected them to panic and abandon the entrance at their first loss. Instead, new defenders stood by the bodies of the fallen and fired at their assigned targets, ignoring the flanking force that threatened them.

Macalister did not expect such discipline. Their persistence was rewarded as one of his own men was fatally hit. The image from the man's headset pointed at the sky and his vitals registered an abnormal heart rate before it flat-lined. Poisoned arrows. A squad member bent over his comrade giving Macalister a good view of the wound.

"Leave him Alpah2. He's dead." The moments Alpah2 spent examining his teammate and not firing put the other two members of the group at risk. The loss of any one team meant the Kawokee could put both the other teams in a crossfire.

"Alpha2. Leave him," Macalister snarled.

Macalister watched through the monitor as Alpha2 rifled the dead man's pockets and removed two power cells.

The hurried shots of the hunters infuriated Macalister. It should have taken minutes to take all three entrances. They had yet to take one. The Kawokee aimed carefully, retreating as the one behind advanced. They formed three rows and worked cooperatively to move the wounded and dead. Their methodical actions mirrored that of hardened soldiers.

Mesmerized by the synchronized dance of the Kawokee, he ignored his own men until another went down. Alpha team was down to two men, and again Alpha2 endangered his remaining teammate by scavenging the fallen member.

"Bravo4. Join Alpha team."

With a series of lucky shots, the front line of defenders at Entrance Bravo fell in quick succession. Bodies filled the ramp down to the entrance. Three members of Bravo team charged into the burrow wading through the dead.

Macalister watched as the first one entered. Stones inset the walls of a long corridor. When he saw the stones at the end of the corridor turn, he barked, "Out. Out. Out." The words still rang in the shuttle when Bravo1's headset went offline. The blue-white flash from Bravo2's monitor took a moment for Macalister to comprehend. How did the Kawokee get energy weapons? How did they know to construct such a clever trap? How did they know where he would attack? He suspected the answer to all these questions was the same; Fawsha. There was something about that one; something he could sense but not define. He had seen it in all the most dangerous enemies he had faced.

Bravo3's camera caught the image of the pins in the ceiling supports being pulled out by a wire. A second later the roof fell on him.

Macalister smiled as Bravo3 went offline. His admiration of the Kawokee's military skill rose several levels. They deserved to win. Sadly, he could not oblige them. He started the shuttle's engines and manually lifted the craft, touching down near the first vent. The ground fell below the craft, and he lifted again. He landed the craft giving cover to his remaining troops. "Execute plan B."

Macalister was sorry a limited engagement was no longer possible. Bolt holes built into the construction of a den occurred to him, but the exits had not concerned him. He would be better prepared next time.

The hunters poured through the hole into the burrow. Macalister watched each on the monitors. His men shot anything that moved as pregnant females swarmed them with knives and pikes.

"Do not shoot the young," he repeated over and over. The hunters' laughter was their only response.

When the females were dead, the older children took up the weapons. He lost four more hunters as they shot unarmed children huddled in corners or escaping down passages.

Against orders, Alpha2 scavenged cells off the dead Bravo team while the rest of his men pulled surviving Kawokee from the burrows. It was back breaking work, and the progress was slow. The few pregnant females still breathing were put into cages and loaded into the shuttle. Macalister left the control room to administer first aid, trying to save as many as possible. He arrived in time to see Alpha2 crawl out of the hole with power cells bulging his pockets. Macalister drew his own pistol and shot Alpha2.

"Everyone go outside. Divide those cells between you."

As the men swarmed Alpha2's body, Macalister switched his weapon to full auto and sprayed them with gunfire. He walked over to the bodies. One hunter was still alive. Macalister used the heel of his boot to crush the hunter's windpipe.

He looked over the carnage and found one more Kawokee. She was barely breathing. Macalister dragged her into the shuttle when the familiar scent of blood warned him something was wrong. At first, he thought it was his imagination until he saw the pooled blood under the cages at the back of the hold. The two Kawokee in the end cages had their throats cut. The one in the center sat with a small knife buried in its chest. Her unblinking eyes mocked him.

Angry at not finding the concealed knife, Macalister rechecked the remaining captives.

He dragged the dead ones to the bay doors and dumped them down the ramp. Less than a dozen pregnant females were all he had. Macalister kicked an empty cage, breaking the door from its hinges. At a rough estimate, there were at least three hundred females in the nest and five times as many children. It should have been an easy operation with every cage filled.

He could find another nest, but what good would that do if the men he sent in slaughtered everything in sight?

CHAPTER 28

Fawsha looked over Miwi's shoulder at the machine. Alooza's eyes were red. The fat one, the one they called Sandawz, never looked healthy, but was more hunched today. Jasmine was not with them. Alooza spoke her name.

The hair on the back of Miwi's neck stood on end and her ears flattened as she gave Fawsha the news. "The other group took Jasmine prisoner two days ago."

On the screen, the fat one spoke Paul's name.

"Sandawz wants to tell Paul in person." Miwi looked at Fawsha for permission.

Fawsha nodded, and Miwi ran out of the burrow. Did the humans expected him to save Jasmine? He was glad they could not read his body language any more than they could understand his words. Jasmine was the least of his worries.

Fawsha studied the faces of the two humans on the screen. What did they see when they looked at him; a leader, a savior? What would they see in a few days? An animal or perhaps a traitor.

If he had done something two weeks ago, he could have saved the nest. If he had acted months ago, he could have saved all the humans and Kawokee who died at

STACY BENDER & REID MINNICH

Bridgewater. The choice had always been before him; act, or let others die in his place. There was no changing the past. The Adwals would stop him if they knew what he planned. Fawsha knew it would cost him his soul, but his soul was already lost.

LutPaul entered the burrow and sat in front of the screen beside Fawsha. His hands trembled as he asked, "Is it true? They took Cow?"

Miwi had not waited for Alooza to inform LutPaul of Cow's situation. Fawsha nodded at the box. "Tell them about the nest."

There was nothing secret in the news, and he did not need to hear a translation. A small nest was destroyed the same day Jasmine went to the other facility. Over a thousand died. Most were children. Only a handful survived.

He waited for LutPaul to finish talking to those on the screen. "Tell them I will go to the place where Jasmine is held. I will negotiate with the sky-leader for her release."

He ignored the confused frown on LutPaul's face as Miwi translated his words to the humans.

Sandawz and Alooza spoke at once. Miwi translated a few questions before Fawsha reached over and turned off the machine. He ignored the looks LutPaul and Miwi gave him saying, "LutPaul. You will see Miwi safely to Alooza. I'll travel to the prison. If Jasmine is not able to interpret, I'll send for Miwi."

LutPaul stood and clenched his fists. "I will gather the troops."

Fawsha shook his head. "No. There will be no troops and no attack at this time. I will walk into the town alone. You will stay with Miwi. If I fail, you must report to the Adwals what happened."

Miwi's fur bristled in agitation as she squared her shoulders. "I am not afraid of the humans. You have always used me as your interpreter. Jasmine's Kawokee is weak. She might not understand you."

Fawsha shook his head. "I have little to say to them." He put on his coat.

LutPaul caught his arm. "It's safer if we travel with you."

"You have your orders." Fawsha lifted the saddlebags he left near the door. No one said a word as he left the burrow. Fawsha hurried through the snow toward the pens. He selected a sturdy horse and rode it to the trail north of the village. Once out of sight, Fawsha doubled back to the cave at the far end of the village. He tried not to think of what someone would do if they followed his trail and guessed what he was up to. He found the marked spot on the ground, pulled back the tarp, and dug the clay pot from the sandy soil.

The temptation to open the container and infect himself before his courage waned was great, but doing so would defeat the outcome. Delirium would overtake him well before he reached the prison. He had to take his time and pray his convictions held firm.

CHAPTER 29

In the days spent locked in the room, no one threatened her baby or came in except to leave a few pieces of fruit and bread. It was not the food the scientists ate. It was what they fed the Kawokee captives. She, at least, had a supply of water and a toilet.

The solitude gave her no distraction from thinking about her baby. It was not some alien thing living inside her. She loved it as it was, perhaps even more for being a Kawokee. If it was Kawokee. Every time she thought of the image on the screen, the same questions circled in her mind. Her isolation may have given her time to think, but the answers still eluded her.

The sound of the door unlocking made Jasmine jump. It was not time for a meal. When Macalister stepped into the room, she balled her fist. There was no chance of killing the man or getting out of the town, but she would settle for leaving a mark. She lunged and tried to dig her nails into his face. Instead, she ended up pinned against the wall.

"Calm down. You have a visitor."

The thought of Paul coming to her rescue and what could happen to him flashed through her mind.

"Paul? Is he all right?"

The corner of Macalister's mouth twitched. "See for yourself." He released his hold, and Jasmine moved around him to the door.

The sight of Fawsha standing outside in the hall surprised and confused her. He stood clutching a covered clay crock as if his life depended on it. The bright colors and intricate design signified it was made for storing grain. Something in his posture and his face told her he was not himself. His eyes were half closed, and he kept looking at the floor.

"What's going on? Have they captured you?" she asked in Kawokee.

"I am here to negotiate." Fawsha's voice was flat and weak.

Macalister nudged her through the door and into the hallway. "I'm sure our guest would prefer to talk outside. He refused to talk with me unless you were present."

Jasmine wanted to tell Fawsha to run away, but she knew he would not. "Scar betrayed us," she said in Kawokee.

"I know. It's not your fault." Fawsha's voice grated as he talked through his teeth. *Did they beat him?*

They followed Macalister to the outer office where several doctors waited. When she heard breaking pottery, Jasmine turned to see Fawsha on his knees. He had stumbled, losing hold on the large lid of the crock, shattering it on the floor. Rages filled the inside. The wax sealed top of another bottle peeked out from within the packing.

"Is that the salve you said was in such short supply?" The scorn in the scientist's voice cemented the fact Jasmine had lost all credibility among them.

A few others had the nerve to act as if Fawsha was bringing them a present. One scientist tried to snatch the jar from Fawsha, but pulled back when the Kawokee bared his teeth.

"We need to analyze the contents. Tell that thing to hand it over."

Jasmine wanted the strangle the man. "Free the females."

"Are you insane?" The man looked down his nose at her. "No matter. We'll get the contents now or later."

All this time Jasmine had been trying to save humanity, she rarely thought about the individuals. If these scientists were a representative sample, she preferred to leave humanity to its fate.

Macalister pulled Fawsha to his feet and herded Jasmine and him out the door. Several men with weapons patrolled the area. Others watched the gate.

"I'm surprised your men didn't shoot Fawsha on sight," said Jasmine.

"They're not my men. They're Campion's hired guns."

"You still tell them what to do."

"Rabid dogs have more discipline." Before Jasmine could make another comment, Macalister asked, "What does he want?"

Jasmine translated his question, and Fawsha responded, "I will only speak with the Adwal of the sky-canoe."

"And if he does not want to speak with you?"

"Then this town will be destroyed." There was no emotion in Fawsha's voice. It could have been fatigue from carrying the large container he refused to put down, but Jasmine was not so sure.

When Jasmine told Macalister Fawsha's demands, his smile disturbed her more than the scowl she expected.

"He's expecting you. Shall we go?"

Jasmine stayed close to Fawsha as Macalister ushered them into the nearby shuttle. Fawsha had to be terrified. The risk to his own life by just stepping within its research facility's gate was madness. She hoped to spare him some panic by describing what his first shuttle ride would be like. "Before we get to the big canoe, you will feel like you're falling for a few minutes. Don't be afraid. I'll be with you."

Fawsha's eyes grew round at seeing the interior of the shuttle, but only for a minute. Jasmine helped him to his seat and strapped him in before taking the chair next to him. As the shuttle lifted off, he watched out the clear shielding until the world below was swallowed by a cloud. After that, his attention returned to the crock in his lap. His hand protecting the jar shook.

Jasmine did not expect him to be so upset. He turned his head and looked at her through half-lidded eyes. "They knew you were pregnant. They have the cure. Why did they attack the nest?"

"They say I carry a Kawokee. That it's not a human."

His eyes closed, and his face turned skyward. "You took a Kawokee?"

"No. I took only Paul. I don't know why they won't believe me. At first, I thought they were lying, trying to trick me. But I couldn't figure out why."

Fawsha's head lowered and tilted. His eyes closed. "Everything we tried failed." He wheezed as he talked. "We wronged you greatly. We tricked you into taking the ceremony, hoping you would take the cure to the humans." His head hung low, and he shivered.

Macalister did not turn around when Jasmine unbuckled her seatbelt, but she knew he was watching. She moved slowly in the heavy gravity as the shuttle accelerated upward and knelt before Fawsha. "I couldn't be happier. You gave me a wonderful gift."

Fawsha didn't look up.

"I love my baby. I don't care if it's Kawokee or human." She reached to give him a hug. Even before her hand touched him, she felt the heat coming off his body. The back of Fawsha's neck was wet. "Are you sick?"

When he did not answer, Jasmine looked at the container in his lap. The small jar nestled in the large crock was surrounded by a cloth. She could not imagine how he acquired the precious salve. The jar at the ceremony and the jar she took to Sanders looked identical and had the same red wax sealed lid. The pale seal on the one in the crock looked more like the jars in the kitchen of the border village. When she pulled at the rags, she recognized what they were. "Are those my clothes?"

"What is going on, Ms. Char?" Macalister rumbled.

Fawsha lifted his head, and his hand shook as he fumbled for the ring in his ear. "I'm sorry, Cow."

Several thoughts pounded at Jasmine for attention. First, was the realization that Fawsha was desperate enough to use germ warfare to save his people. Second, was the fear for her unborn child and what affect her being exposed to the Pox during pregnancy would have on it.

The questions that had tormented her since the day she stepped foot on the planet, clashed with what she found and clamored for her attention. What happened to the Terraformers? What did they do to the Kawokee? Why did they create the Kaw virus, and why did so many diseases affect both species? How could she be having a Kawokee baby. There was one possible explanation, but she had no proof.

"Macalister, do you know the name of the Terraforming ship? Arluza never got around to telling me the name."

"It was the Cherokee. Why?"

The hysterical laughter that bubbled up within Jasmine could not be contained. Even Macalister's stern gaze could not make her stop.

"What's so funny?"

Jasmine sat on the floor, leaned against Fawsha's seat, and stopped laughing. "You don't get it, do you? You still don't get it."

"Get what?" Macalister unbuckled his seatbelt and turned toward the pair.

"Fawsha, say Cherokee for me please."

She watched as Fawsha frowned before complying to her request. "Kawokee."

The frown on Macalister's face sent Jasmine into another bout of laughter. "Now do you understand? The reason there was no war between the Terraformers and the Kawokee is because the Kawokee are the Terraformers. They turned dead planets into living worlds. How hard would it be to change their own DNA to escape a disease that was killing them? With a crippled ship and no way to leave, what do you do? You put the survivors on a viable world, and the information you want them to keep, the very thing that will guarantee their survival, you turn into a religion."

Jasmine giggled at Macalister's sour expression. "We've been had. They're human. Every single one of them are human. Genetically altered."

She shifted to her knees and gave Macalister an evil grin. "And in the eyes of Multi-World Common law, genetically altered humans are still humans." Jasmine watched hoping to spot some minute hint of regret on Macalister's face, but he saw no reaction.

"I strongly advise you to get back in your seat, Ms. Char. Thirty seconds." Macalister shifted back into his seat and placed his hands on the controls.

Fawsha lay still but was breathing. Disappointed at not receiving a reaction from the man, Jasmine returned to her seat and buckled in. "Macalister, there is something I should tell you."

"What is it, now?"

The larger ship caught the shuttle in its locking field. She struggled to speak as her stomach jumped into her throat. Fawsha's body jerked against his restraints, but he barely opened his eyes.

Jasmine's conscience pricked at the back of her mind. She could not wait for long. The shuttle was contaminated. Part of her mind screamed at her to keep quiet, to allow every person who followed a maniac into murdering an entire culture to die. Another part told her she would be a murderer; no better than the ones she killed.

"What will the scientists do when they find out they killed humans?"

"They won't know. Campion will bury you and the truth. What is it you wanted to tell me?"

Jasmine glanced at Fawsha, then back at Macalister before lowering her gaze. "I don't want to repeat myself. I'll wait until I can talk to both you and Campion."

The shuttle settled into the dock, and Macalister rose from his seat.

As the ship's bay doors closed, Jasmine felt her pulse pound. In the span of minutes, so much had changed. Part of her was appalled that Fawsha would commit mass murder, and that she was willing to help him do it, but the logical part of her brain understood the desperation which now drove them both. Macalister showed no sign of regret or shock at the revelation of Kawokee being human. Jasmine choked back the scream of warning as Macalister snatched the crock from Fawsha's lap. The movement jolted the Kawokee awake, but the seatbelt prevented him from lunging for the clay container. The warning glare Macalister gave Jasmine when she released her seatbelt and jumped to her feet chilled her blood and froze her in place.

Macalister paused at the hatch with his hand on the button. "I need to talk with Campion. Your access has been restricted. Stay in the common areas until I come for you." The shuttle door opened with a hiss. Jasmine watched as Macalister dug his hand into the cloth strips to remove the small bottle. He descended the ramp and dropped the crock on the bay floor.

Released from his cold hard gaze, Jasmine helped Fawsha out of the restraints and pulled him to his feet. "How long have you been sick?"

"Two days." Fawsha grunted, and his whole body shook. "I itch."

Her own memory of having the Pox was a blur of pain, and she wondered how Fawsha stayed coherent let alone stand. Even with the healer's numbing salve, Jasmine would have torn her skin to shreds if she had been able. The jerking of Fawsha's arms showed he was barely able to control himself.

Jasmine doubted any of the doctors would be willing to help Fawsha. The red med kit mounted on the shuttle wall was all they had. Jasmine swore in frustration when she opened it and found half the contents missing. Either someone had used it and not recorded the incident or a thief managed to slip onto the shuttle and raid the box.

"Think, think, think." Jasmine's frustration level rose as she pulled at her hair, trying to control her chaotic thoughts. "I'll be right back. Stay here."

Jasmine scurried out of the shuttle, tripping over the crock, scattering half its contents into the shuttle bay. She swore and took several slow steps before the pain in her shin subsided. When she spotted the bright red med kit she hurried forward and pulled the thing from the wall. Jasmine limped back to the shuttle to find Fawsha sitting on the floor. His teeth showed through curled lips, and his fingers raked the fur of his chest, leaving streaks of wet sticky ooze.

"No. Stop." Jasmine dropped to her knees beside him and tore open the med kit. A prayer of thanks slipped off her tongue at the sight of the fully stocked kit. Jasmine dug through the meds for flight sickness and the bandages for cuts and found the package of pain gels. "Yes." In her haste, she ripped open the container, and the safety sealed green pearls scattered on the floor.

Try as she might, Jasmine could not get the gel out of its foil covering. "I hate these things." Searching the med kit, she found a pair of scissors and cut the seal. She handed Fawsha the pill. "Swallow this. It should take away some of the pain."

Jasmine watched as Fawsha gagged and coughed. "Sorry. We don't have any water."

"I must touch the leader." Fawsha gritted his teeth and pushed his hands under his thighs. "Tie my hands."

Jasmine looked around. The only thing handy were the strips of her clothes spread across the bay floor. She hurried down the ramp and grabbed several long pieces before returning and helped Fawsha back into the padded chair. His arms were slippery with sweat as she tied his wrists to the armrests. It would not hold him long when the itching became intense, but she tied him as best she could. If the pain meds did not take the edge off, Fawsha would gouge his flesh.

"We have to get your fever down."

"Must—"

"I know. But if Macalister suspects anything, we'll never make it. He'll kill us both. I'll get you some water. Maybe I can find you some nice hot broth."

The thought of Fawsha dying twisted her stomach in knots as she exited the shuttle and hurried down corridors toward the dining hall. Worry mixed with the anger that sparked every time she thought of either Campion or Macalister. Jasmine wished she could shove their faces in the contaminated bowl and watch them suffer. What if she couldn't get to Campion? Could she infect the entire ship and kill everyone? They were all guilty to one degree or another. Even she was guilty by helping Macalister find a nest. The Kawokee lives where just as precious as any human. They were human. If only she could convince everyone on the ship.

Jasmine knew Macalister was right. Campion would bury the evidence. She did not want to think of what would happen to Fawsha or herself if they could not get to him. Safety precautions were built into every ship. The filters and ultraviolet scrubbers would kill any airborne pathogens. She could not run around the ship like a mad woman, throwing cloth strips in people's faces. As Jasmine passed people in the hallway, she thought about deliberately touching them. She even attempted to bump into someone and realized she could not do it. How much harder would it be if she tried to infect them?

Tears filled her eyes and spilled down her cheeks as she reached her destination. There were few people in the dining hall. No one spoke to her as she wiped the tears from her face and pushed buttons on the food dispenser. Jasmine took a tray and collected two bowls of soup, two salads and several water bottles. Her first attempt at carrying the heavy tray ended with spilt soup all over the counter. Her effort to clean up the mess turned fruitless when the napkin dispenser jammed, leaving her with only a single cloth square to soak up the mess.

"Stupid, stupid, stupid. I should have used a lid."

CHAPTER 30

Macalister stepped out of the lift into the dimly lit administrative wing and knocked on the door to Campion's office. After a minute without a response, he tucked the jar of salve under his arm and pressed a button on his wrist-com. "Computer. Locate Campion"

"Campion, location. Section S, room 1." The computer's pleasant voice had Macalister grinding his teeth. It was not the first time Campion had him running in circles. The man's childish plays for power usually amused Macalister, but he was in no mood for games today. Macalister returned to the lift and hit the button for the correct level. As he waited for the door to open, he typed a message on his wrist-com. "You wanted to meet?" There was no response when the lift doors opened, nor when Macalister arrived at Campion's private suite. "I'm here, Campion." When the door did not open, Macalister pounded his fist on the panel. "Computer, Macalister. Authorize, Security S1 Unlock." The door slid open and Macalister stepped into the foyer of a large suite.

Campion scampered out of his bedroom pulling the ties of his silk robe closed. "This better be good."

Macalister held the jar of salve tight and used a finger

to bring up the text on his wrist-com. He shoved the message into Campion's face. "You said you wanted to meet with the Kawokee leader immediately."

Campion swatted Macalister's hand from his face. He turned his head as the bedroom door at the other end of the large room clicked closed. "I said nothing of the kind. Who would want to talk to those things? I was responding to your message about test subjects, telling you I needed more of them immediately. Come back later. I'm busy." Campion turned his back on Macalister.

Many possibilities flashed through Macalister's brain. He lingered on where a few well-placed strikes would best make his point. Instead, he set the jar on a table before rushing at Campion's back and shoving him into the bedroom door.

The door sprang open, sending Campion to the bedroom floor. A woman in the bed screamed, pulled the silk sheets over her breasts, and bolted for her clothes.

Campion stumbled to his feet. "I'll see you court martialed for that."

The satisfaction of hitting Campion was short lived and did not curb the growing frustration within Macalister. He stepped past Campion to one side of the bed away from the door and said softly, "Get out."

The woman hugged her clothes to her chest and ran out the door.

"I need you to complete this mission." Macalister felt so wired he swore he was shaking, but his voice remained calm. "What you do after that is of no concern to me. I came to warn you that your little project is in peril. The Sanders team believes the Kawokee are genetically altered humans descended from the terraformers."

"So what?" Campion sat on the edge of the bed.

Macalister gritted his teeth and punched the door, cracking the decorative plastic panel. The sting in his hand and the whites of Campion's eyes helped him regain his composure. "You are supposed to be a scientist. At least try to sound like one. Think before you speak. Now, answer your own question."

Campion's lips twisted to a grin. "You're afraid of the public outcry if they find out we've been experimenting on modified humans. Well, don't worry. The only people who know are Sanders and his team. They're all infected and won't be leaving this planet. I'm quite sure you can make certain they don't communicate with anyone."

The muscles in Macalister's neck tightened and the temptation to destroy everything in the room pounded at his being. "You're an ass. This is not about your career. This is about finding a cure. While you screw every tech and write your memoirs, I'm risking my life to ensure every possible option is left open."

"And a poor job you've done." Campion crossed the room to the dresser and put on his clothes. "The females you brought were so badly damaged it will be months before they're useful. One has already died and two miscarried. You haven't found another nest yet. At this rate, we'll be here for years. I need you to take every nest the Kawokee have as soon as possible, and bring me some live subjects this time."

"You'll get more soon, but the Sanders team may be closer to finding a cure than we thought. Jasmine Char is infected but is several months pregnant. She carries a Kawokee."

Campion stopped what he was doing and looked at Macalister before bursting out laughing. He plopped on the bed with one foot in his pants. "Your previous report already said Kawokee and humans are close enough to crossbreed. So what if she got knocked up by a Kawokee?" Campion chuckled and finished dressing.

"She claims she only slept with a human." Macalister waited, hoping Campion would stop snickering. He continued, uncertain if the man was listening. "She says it was only possible because of a special Kawokee salve. There is a Kawokee leader with me here on the ship. He brought a jar of it, but we'll need more."

Campion walked out of the bedroom, leaving Macalister to follow. "You didn't need to interrupt me for that. Take the salve if you want it, and space the native. Space the salve as well for all I care."

Macalister grabbed the jar off the table and considered smashing Campion's head with it. He trailed Campion to his private dining room. "I will see that all options are left open, and all theories tested. We also have Jasmine and her fetus. They must be studied."

"You should let real scientists decide what's real and what's fantasy. I will not have my project delayed by a lot of useless theories." Campion removed a slab of meat from the deep freeze and placed it in the processor. "Well done. Lightly salted." As the processor hummed, he said, "Let the Sanders team have the salve." He opened the door and the smell of real beef filled the room.

Macalister slapped his hand over the meat and shoved the plate off the table onto the floor. Before Campion could object, Macalister punched him in the face, splitting his lip and sending him to the floor. Macalister pressed his knee into Campion's chest, grabbed his throat, and shoved the bottle in his face. "Your team has found nothing. I've seen the Kawokee infants and brought you live, pregnant Kawokee. This theory has some convincing evidence. Have your team start testing the females with the salve. The Sanders team will not test on Kawokee. They won't endanger Jasmine or her fetus. There are still several Kaw subjects still available. By the time I get dirtside, you will assign one of your scientists to try the salve on them and analyze the rest. Do not make me come back up and type the command myself from the wrist-com on your severed arm."

Campion struggled beneath him and clawed at Macalister's arms. Only went the scent of ammonia tainted the air did Macalister release the man and head for the door.

He barely caught Campion's gasping words. "When this is over, your dead, Macalister."

Macalister chuckled and glanced back at the fool crumbled on the floor, face bloodied and pants soiled. "We're both dead. You just haven't figured it out yet. The fact that we've murdered humans won't stay buried long. Even finding a cure won't save us." He exited the suite, crossed the hall, pushed the button for the lift, and cradled the jar in his hands. "But we will complete our mission."

CHAPTER 31

The racket from birds trying to nest just outside his window annoyed Macalister. He scratched the back of his hand before tapping the wrist-com to silence the buzzing. His head pounded as he rolled out of the bed.

One look at the screen on his wrist-com told him that Campion was furious. His face was a red blob on the tiny screen. "You wasted two days having my techs study a jar of fruit preserves. They say there's nothing in it but food ingredients and common bacteria. They've run every test they have and there's nothing in it that can penetrate a cell wall. You panicked over a hoax." The sound of drawers opening and being slammed shut along with Campion's curses came over the speakers.

The morning sun seemed impossibly bright. Macalister crawled out of bed and drew the shades.

"Well? What have you got to say now?" Campion shouted. "Are you even listening to me?"

Unable to focus on the wrist-com with a headache, Macalister transferred the image to his tablet. Campion was scratching and slathering ointment liberally along his neck. The hairs on the back of Macalister's arms rose as he expanded the image as large as it would go. He spoke quietly as his mind sifted the possibilities. "Your neck and the side of your face are red."

Campion pointed his finger at the red blotchy mass. "Of course, it is. You choked me. I've recorded it as evidence against you. There won't be any denying you attacked me."

Macalister looked at the back of his hand and examined his wrist. A line of small pus-filled blisters traveled up to his elbow. Campion's tirade remained little more than background noise as Macalister's mind tried to work around the pain in his head.

In his fury over Campion's continuous stupidity, Macalister paid little attention to Fawsha or Jasmine when he had returned to the shuttle. Nor had he questioned why they remained on board. He could have easily forgotten them aboard the ship. Once dirtside, he left the pair in the makeshift prison cell and had not bothered with them since.

Why would Fawsha insist on seeing Campion using a bottle of jam as bait? Did Fawsha think he could reason with the man if they were face to face? Campion's voice was like a hammer on his ears, and Macalister was tempted to cut the connection until what the man was saying registered in Macalister's conscious.

"Several techs claim to be sick If you're encouraging them to slack off, I swear I'll have your stripes."

"Sick? Who's sick?"

"Just about everyone. You spread a rumor about the Kawokee being genetically engineered and now no one wants to work."

Macalister cut the connection, ending any further comment. Fawsha hadn't been flight-sick. This was deliberate. Macalister returned to his tablet and researched the Pox. Each picture told the story of a victim's pain. Boil covered bodies, bloated abdomens, and blackened limbs from hemorrhaging blood vessels were common. Likewise, were the pictures of blood seeping from every orifice in a person's body. In one image it looked as if the person's eyeballs had burst from the pressure of blood within the orbs.

Multiple videos accompanied the images. Macalister clicked on one. Two people dressed in biohazard gear stood on either end of a corpse. When they tried to lift the body by the shoulders and legs, the flesh slipped off the bone sending the corpse to the floor. The abdomen ruptured, spewing its unrecognizable contents across the cement.

"That's going to be you, Campion." Macalister leaned back in his chair. "And me."

He rubbed his head, but Macalister knew the throbbing would not go away. When he stepped out into the hallway, the artificial light seared his eyes and the facility noises hurt his ears. The utility room in which Jasmine and Fawsha were held was down the hall and around a corner. In his present state they could have been across the continent. Macalister half closed his eyes and ran his hand along the wall to guide him. Once at the door, he pressed his thumb to the locking mechanism and disengaged it. He opened the door to find Jasmine sitting on the floor with her back against the wall. Fawsha lay beside her sleeping, his head in her lap. A pile of empty medical foil safety seals sat next to a jug of water.

"You knew, didn't you?" asked Macalister.

Jasmine looked up at him but did not move. "Knew what?"

Macalister lifted his arm so that she could see the boils. "About this. About what Fawsha was doing. It's the Pox, isn't it?"

She shrugged and looked away.

"You'll be happy to know your plan worked."

"It wasn't my plan. Fawsha was desperate. He threw away everything he believed in to save his people. I didn't even know he was sick until we docked."

"You didn't say anything."

"No." Jasmine shook her head slowly and brushed her hand along Fawsha's side. "You convinced me not to."

"Silly me. I should never have told you what Campion would do." Macalister leaned against the door jamb and debated his next move. "Come with me. Both of you."

Jasmine hesitated before waking Fawsha. Macalister listened to the foreign words Jasmine spoke and watched as she helped Fawsha to his feet. He led them down the corridor and exited the building. The sun beat down on the scorched ground both within and outside the gated perimeter.

She asked, "What's going to happen to us?"

Macalister ignored her question and motioned the guards on post to stand down and open the gate. He did not look at her as he spoke. "My job is to make sure every path to find a cure is unhindered. I've already made an in depth report, detailing your cure and that all other research has failed. I've also included the information about the Kawokee being modified humans. All I need to do now is send it."

As he scanned the tree line, Macalister spotted Paul. The man had stepped from the cover of the underbrush but moved no further. "Your ride's here."

"What?" Jasmine looked up into his face and followed his gaze.

Macalister nodded toward Paul. "Go on. Get out of here."

"You're letting us go? I don't understand."

"That's because you're a civilian." Macalister glanced down at Fawsha. The Kawokee held tight to Jasmine's hand but stared back at him. "Well played, comrade. It's an honor to die by your hand."

"Are you crazy?" said Jasmine. "You've got the Pox. You're dying."

Macalister focused his attention back on Jasmine. "Perhaps we're all insane. But considering all the things I've done in my life, I'm getting off easy. Too bad I'll be in no condition to enjoy Campion's pain. Now get out of here."

Jasmine hesitated before moving past the gate. Both her and Fawsha's pace quickened the closer they got to the tree line. Paul bolted out of the shadows, putting himself between her and the camp.

Macalister recognized the man's protective maneuver, even if it was unwarranted. Macalister had no intention of opening fire on the trio. They had won the battle and possibly the war.

CHAPTER 32

Paul tried to quiet Samanka. She reached for Jasmine and grunted insistently. Jasmine took her daughter in her arms. Samanka touched the corners of her wrist-com and played with the symbols floating in the air. Had it only been one month? All the fear of giving birth and the worry over the accelerated gestation proved needless. Samanka was perfect. All five of the women who took the Kawokee salve smiled, bellies swollen, from the front of the small crowd of well-wishers. Soon, they would be standing in their own ceremony with their babies. Behind them were a dozen smiling couples and their Kawokee guides that made the journey from a nearby town despite the spring storms. Each had a place in line, waiting for more salve.

Fawsha took the baby from her. In a few short months, his fur had turned gray. A permanent sadness had wrinkled the sides of his face around his eyes. "What is the name of this child?"

Samanka gripped his ear where the earrings used to hang and pulled it toward her mouth.

Paul nodded to Jasmine to take the lead. "Samanka."

Antsy growled his disapproval of the name.

Fawsha quickly wrapped the long string of beads

around Samanka waist before, she grabbed the end and stuffed it into her mouth. "You are bound to this name. It will follow you. Your deeds—" His voice shook as he choked out, "Both good and evil, will be remembered through it. Keep it unblemished."

Jasmine put her hand on Fawsha's arm.

Fawsha's voice grew strong again. "You are this day, Kawokee."

The small crowd cheered, and Jasmine took Samanka into her arms.

Sanders and many others from the camp came to congratulate her. Combined with those who traveled from other settlements, she only had time to say thank you as they moved past her toward a tent set up in the edge of the field. The smell of food wafted on the breeze making her mouth water. Arluza brought up the end of the line.

"I'm so happy for you. Enjoy yourself today, but you better get your rest before the ships get here." Arluza turned his head away like he always did when hiding a wicked smile.

Jasmine took his shirtsleeve and pulled him around. "Ships? I know another science ship is being sent, but I thought there was only one."

"We just got another update from the inner systems." Arluza turned his wrist-com so Jasmine could see the list of articles. "There is one science ship, but it's in a race with ships from every habitable planet. The news that infected women can have children has started an avalanche."

"Do they know the children will all be Kawokee?"

"Of course. Macalister's last transmission was very clear. Granted, there are still those who want a cure that will give them a human child, but it's amazing how many people don't care." Arluza touched article after article giving Jasmine only enough time to read the headlines.

"Do you think this science ship will be a threat to the Kawokee?" Jasmine kissed her daughter's fingers.

Arluza tried to pet Samanka's ears, but Samanka latched onto his wrist-com. "Not a chance. Macalister transmitted the unaltered research data. That line of research has failed. This ship is interested in understanding the salve. He also leaked footage of the how the Kawokee were treated. Everyone on every world knows what happened here." Arluza produced a memory chip from his pocket. "Except what Campion did to me and the others. Macalister left that for us to decide." He rubbed the chip in his fingers and put it back into his pocket. "The public outcry forced many high-ranking members of the central government into hiding. A coalition of politicians are calling for new laws to prevent this type of thing from ever happening again." He brought up an article and turned it toward her. "And guess who they all point to as a hero who should draft the new legislation."

Jasmine saw her face plastered in the center of the article. "I won't be part of that. They can't. It's impossible." Samanka buried her face in Jasmine's neck as her small hands clutched at Jasmine's collar. A few people in the tent turned to look her way. Jasmine smoothed her daughter's bristled fur.

Arluza's grin melted, and his face paled. "Don't worry. This is still a quarantined world. They won't come here and you can't leave."

Paul hurried out of the tent to her side. "Is everything okay?"

Jasmine closed her eyes and nodded. "Everything is fine. I'll be there in a minute."

Paul gave her hand a squeeze and walked back toward the tent as Jasmine and Arluza followed.

"Maybe they'll never find a cure," said Jasmine, kissing the top of Samanka's head.

Arluza sighed. "We will someday, but it won't be soon. The scientists of the Cherokee were masters of their craft. Without a hint of what they did, it's impossible to even know where to start."

"I should have seen all this from the beginning. The clues were all there. Kawokee culture is the same as a generation ship's culture."

"How so?"

"The terraformers lived generation after generation in closed spaces. To live on a world with no roof over their heads would have been uncomfortable to them. Hence the underground constructions. Then there is the attitude toward community and their strict laws. On a spaceship, mistakes can hurt more than just one person, they can destroy the entire ship. Remember how long ago those things were made? By our standards they were little more than death traps."

Arluza's smile returned to his face. "Hindsight made everything easier to understand. At least everything except for how to reverse what they did. Too bad the only record was destroyed by the religious order."

Jasmine scowled. "That's the only thing that bothers me. Why only make one copy. If it was that important, why not make more plaques?"

"I suppose there could be other plaques hidden somewhere on the planet no one knows about. I don't think they expected a group of crazy people to destroy something they thought would last the lifetime of the planet."

"You really like G; don't you? You greedy little thing. What's the matter with T, A, and C? They'll get lonely." Jasmine pulled the string of beads out of her daughter's mouth. Samanka grabbed for the string and refused to let go.

"What did you say?" Arluza's jumped in front of her, stopping her in her tracks. His hard eyes demanded an explanation.

She touched each bead. "A, C, G, T. I hated making this bead thing, but I had to do it to get the salve. The priestess demanded you get it right or you get ousted."

"Those are nucleotides. Cytosine, thymine, adenine,

and guanine. The beads are a DNA sequence." Arluza's brow furrowed. "This could be the viral vector they've been searching for. We have to tell someone."

When he turned and stepped in the direction of the tent, Jasmine grabbed his arm. "No. Wait."

"But we have to tell someone."

Jasmine bit her lip and looked down at her daughter. "Do we?"

BOOK TWO OF THE KAWOKEE SERIES

The Right to Belong

ABOUT THE AUTHORS

Stacy Bender and Reid Minnich are authors who live in
Cincinnati.

They love to hear from readers. Contact them at
stacycbender@gmail.com
reidminnich@ymail.com

Sign up for news
Members are the first to know about upcoming releases,
events and deals.
stacybender.net
reidminnich.com

Printed in Great Britain
by Amazon